Publish and be damned
www.pabd.com

Testing Zoe

Abby

Publish and be damned
www.pabd.com

First published in Great Britain 2005 by Abby. The moral right of Abby to be identified as the author of this work has been asserted.

ABBY'S BOOKS
www.abbysbooks.com
info@abbysbooks.com

Designed in London, Great Britain, by Adlibbed Limited.
Printed and bound in the UK by 4Edge.

ISBN: 1-905290-33-0

Warning

The content of this book is sexually explicit. Please read no further if you are likely to be offended by explicit description and language.

Sadomasochism is explored in the context of mutual sexual experimentation between consenting adults.

This book is pure fantasy fiction: the characters and situations created within it exist only in the mind.

CONTENTS

Author's position on condoms:
Definitely YES in real life, definitely NO in fantasy fiction!

Prologue

A TASTE OF THINGS TO COME

"Do you want to be my slave?"

The young woman knelt before the man - completely naked, her eyes down.

"Yes, Master," she whispered.

"Really be my slave - not just play at it. Serve me and suffer for me, for as long as I want you to - maybe for the rest of your life?"

She bit her lip. "Yes, Master."

The man, whose name was Philip, began to pace up and down in front of her.

"I shall expect you to prove it, you know. I shall test you like you've never been tested before. For the next year at least, you will be intensively trained. Punished mercilessly, and used - used more than any woman has ever been used before!"

He could see his slave trembling, and suddenly stopped to lift her chin and look into her moist, hesitant eyes.

"Zoe," he said. "Of all the women I have ever seen, ever touched - you are the most beautiful."

He stroked her flowing blonde hair, and reflected on how true this was. He had been entranced from the moment he'd first set eyes on her.

"But I want more than your beauty," he continued slowly. "More than your body, more even than your subservience and obedience - though I shall certainly demand these. I want your soul! I want you to be mine with every fibre of your being!"

The kneeling girl quivered, her huge naked breasts stupendous to behold.

"Don't fail me, Zoe!"

Master Philip's new slave shook her head - and sealed her fate!

How had it begun, this penchant for submissiveness in an otherwise confident and modern young woman? A mystery. Something in the genes, maybe; something passed down through ancient generations from a primeval past ruled by strict social hierarchies and life-preserving subordination. Or perhaps just a chosen personal preference - a hunger for excitement, and for living on the edge, and not wanting life to be mundane and ordinary, as it so easily could have been.

Zoe would have said she had always known where she belonged - that is, on the floor at the feet of a strong, dominant man. She learnt it slowly, from her own early fantasies and arousals, and from how she had felt as she explored sexual situations in her youth, and from which of those situations had become so much more enjoyable and mind-blowing and yearned-after than others.

She was adamant in her insistence that her voluntarily adopted life position did not and should not apply to all women; it just so happened that it applied to some, and to her.

Ah, the joys of discovering submission! It had begun with the feel of a man's rough beard on her newly grown breasts; with a kiss that was more violent that she had expected; with a rumble of instruction from a deep, insistent voice that had sent shivers through her; with a loss of virginity so purposeful and perfect that it had swept her up onto an emotional high from which she had never really descended.

And Master Philip? He had been even more direct and demanding than the others. He had known so exactly what to do. He had touched her in that particular way that called to such a deep and inescapable instinct, that there had been no question about compliance. He had, basically, understood her.

Zoe would have said, if she had ever been asked, that submissiveness was in her blood.

But she wasn't asked. She was merely accepted and absorbed into the fold of men who knew and loved, from their own innate tendencies, what it was she needed and represented and had to offer.

"Your training - your testing - is to begin now," said Master Philip. "Stand up!"

Wordlessly, Zoe got to her feet.

"Assume position number three."

This - one of several taught to her on the night of their first meeting - involved spreading her legs as wide as possible, crossing her arms behind her, and throwing her head back - and her tits forward. She took up the correct posture rapidly - she wasn't a complete beginner, after all!

"Now walk through that door - don't say a word unless you're spoken to, and make sure you obey my every instruction."

Quaking, entirely unsure of what she had let herself in for, the blonde beauty made her somewhat ungainly entrance into the room beyond.

It was full of men.

They whistled and leered at her - not that she could see them very well, since her eyes were fixed dutifully on the ceiling.

"Feel free to have a play with her if you want to, gentlemen," said Master Philip. "I like to see my slave mauled."

Several of the men stepped forward and invaded Zoe's personal space with probing hands. Her tits were squeezed, her nipples pinched, her buttocks kneaded, her sex explored, and even the entrance to her back passage roughly sought out.

"What, are we really all going to get her?" asked one particularly excited little character.

"Yes."

"And watch her get a good thrashing?" said another man, blowing smoke into Zoe's face. Zoe flinched at this, and broke position to glance over at her Master.

"Of course," was his reply.

"Looks like she's not as keen on that bit," said the smoker, continuing his lewd caresses.

"It doesn't matter what she likes or doesn't like. She'll do as she's told."

Zoe quaked and quivered with a controlled sort of fear. The thought of being at the mercy of so many men - she counted fourteen of them, including her Master - who wanted to see her being submissive was mindblowing. But when she saw him - Master Philip - standing there, so much in charge, so much wanting and expecting her to succeed in this first test of his, she knew she would do anything for him.

She loved him - with a slave's love, which demanded more suffering than most.

"Now you all get yourselves comfortable and help yourselves to drinks," Master Philip was saying to the men he had assembled, "and I'll start showing you what Zoe will do."

And so, for the next half hour at least, Zoe demonstrated to the men - many of whom really had never seen such a thing before - what it was to be a slave.

She responded immediately and completely to the string of instructions her Master threw at her, and in so doing found herself in a state of contentment approaching bliss. She didn't have to think - just react. Her Master was in complete control of her existence. However difficult and humiliating his demands, she felt she had nothing to worry about, so long as she met them.

They fell from his lips in rapid succession.

"Get down on all fours, Zoe, and crawl around the room so we can all look down on you. Split your legs wide, and shake your bum around - more! Open your mouth and lick your lips, like a proper slut. Kiss that gentleman's feet - passionately! Grind your tits into the floor while you're doing it. Move onto the next one. Lick his boots. Roll onto your back and put your face under the sole of his foot - kiss it! Crawl along the line of men, on your back. Knead your tits with your hands while they each lift a foot up for you to kiss the underside of. Keep your legs wide open and thrust your hips up, like you can't wait for the fucking to start. Make sure you've kissed everyone's feet - including mine, please. You can lick mine. And keep your tits moving all the time, so they look pretty for us.

"Now, crawl round to my guests again, one by one, and say hello to what's in their trousers. Hurry up! Thirteen cocks in your mouth, quickly, one after the other. I consider it to be your job to keep them all erect. Like a juggler with plates spinning on poles - I want to see you rushing from one to the other, keeping them all going! Right. Now some more of those nice positions I've taught you. Number seven, please. Roll back onto your shoulders, then drop your legs out wide to the floor. Isn't that something, gentlemen? Move yourself round so we can all see your pussy. Three hundred and sixty degrees - and quickly! Now position nine - bend over and touch the floor, and push your tits through your legs. Good girl. Isn't that a lovely smooth bottom? Shake it around for us, Zoe. Take a good look, guys - it won't be staying that smooth for long. Back to position two. Kneeling, tits held forward, head back - right back, properly - and your mouth open. What a lovely sight! Now who wants to step forward and lower their balls into that soft, warm mouth, and let them rest there while Zoe sucks on them and licks them gently? All of you? Well, be my guests! Only you'd better form a queue!"

So Zoe struggled to keep her mouth wide open while a succession of hairy balls were dropped into it, and she wondered with considerable amazement at her own debauchery.

But all this was just a warm up - though a couple of the men had got into such a state already that they begged Master Philip to be allowed to come in his slave's gaping mouth. They were given permission.

"Time for some whipping, I think," said Master Philip. "I shall start, and then let some of you have a go. Drape your delightful self over the back of that armchair, Zoe. Perhaps two or three of you men would care to hold the lady's arms so they don't get in the way. That's it. Pull tight - she's likely to struggle."

Zoe was trying to get a look at what implement Master Philip had in his hand. He appeared to have extracted something from a little case. "Now it's been some days since I've whipped you, my dear, so I expect you to accept this bravely and gratefully. Okay?"

"Yes, Master," she attempted, but her voice caught - such was her agitation.

Then the first stroke fell, and Zoe recognised it as being from a rubber cat-o-nine-tails. She felt a flood of relief. Rubber whips were relatively easy to take - much less painful than their leather counterparts. Perhaps her Master intended to go easy on her. Make it look worse than it was, for the benefit of unknowledgeable voyeurs.

This hope was soon dispelled, however, by her Master's next words. "I'm starting with one of the mildest implements, but I've got a whole suitcase of things here and I intend to work my way through them, so you can see the different effects they all have."

The whip was falling regularly, mainly on her bum, but sometimes on her back or on her thighs.

The strokes got gradually heavier, and Zoe began to panic a little. This was the mildest thing he was going to use, and already it was so painful! How on earth was she going to get through what was to follow?

"Keep still, Zoe," her Master told her. "We've got a long way to go yet."

After a number of strokes with the rubber whip, Master Philip changed to a rubber paddle.

"This can be very painful, but won't leave any particular marks - just an all-over redness."

He began to sound like he was giving a lecture. His audience was certainly appreciating it. The level of attention and intensity in the room grew with every stroke which fell on Zoe's ever-yielding flesh.

Master Philip was theatrically drawing his arm right back each time he aimed his blows at the waiting, upturned bottom, which made them look a lot heavier than they really were. They made a loud, rather amusing noise as they landed.

"Paddling is a step up from a spanking, really - nice sound, and doesn't hurt your hand!"

Zoe was automatically trying to flinch away from each stroke of the paddle. With her legs unsecured, the bottom half of her could wriggle and dodge, and generally entertain its viewers, without restraint.

Only when she got a little too lively did more hands pull her arms down further over the chair, and push on her back and waist to keep her in place.

"Perhaps we should move on to a tawse next," said Master Philip. "From now on we should be seeing a variety of marks appear on that lovely arse."

The tawse stung badly. It seemed her Master was not in a mood to spare her. He was enjoying his central role of expert demonstrator, and there was no room for indulgence - not tonight. Though she tried to keep still, tried to go with the pain, as he had taught her previously, it was getting more and more difficult not to be vocal.

She began to whimper, and then beg, in a little stream of pathetic pleas. "Oh, please, Master – have mercy! It's getting quite painful - not so hard - ah - please, Master - ouch!"

To her chagrin she heard him describing her behaviour as a predictable phenomenon.

"Slaves usually go through this begging stage. She'll soon move on to crying, and then to yelling. Especially when I start using this."

She didn't see it, but felt it - a long, thin cane, applied with skill just across the tops of her thighs. Five times in rapid succession! It was a small consolation that, unintentionally, she proved her Master wrong on this occasion. First she yelled with the shock of the awful, sudden pain, then she cried - sobbing uncontrollably as the strokes continued to fall all over her burning bottom.

Luckily, however, her hide had been thickened by experience, and the fact that she was getting very, very aroused, despite herself, also helped to make the pain more tolerable.

Master Philip was getting tired, and, after a few more minutes of teasing, threw the cane onto a table, and sat down in a chair with a drink.

"There's so much more to show you - especially the best way to punish her breasts and crotch. But I'm sure you'd enjoy having an experiment yourselves. There are the whips, gentlemen, and there's the woman. See what you can do."

This could have been a scary situation, but Master Philip's wink reassured her. It was a game that he would make sure was kept under control.

The men didn't need telling twice. Zoe was pushed and pulled and dragged and chased about the room, with the men inexpertly landing a few strokes on her whenever they could. This was a long way from being an orderly, stylized punishment like those she usually received - tied up tightly and with nothing to think about but obedience. This was a chase, a game, a scramble. This was all male sweat, and fruitless struggles, and demanding mouths seeking to kiss her, and rough hands bruising her wrists as they pinned her down, and occasional blows falling randomly, amateurishly all over her body, and - for nothing could have restrained this pack of men now - stiff cocks, forced into her mouth, and up her fanny, and somewhere else too.

It was a wild, mad group fucking like she had never known before. While it was happening, she had been a bit anxious, despite her Master's reassurances. But when it was over! When it was over, and a safe memory of something she had survived… well, put it this way, it would be years before Zoe stopped wanking over the thought of it!

Don't suppose that this first group onslaught was the end of that evening's action, though. It wasn't at all. When most of the men had exhausted and spent themselves for the first time, Master Philip dragged a disheveled Zoe onto her feet, and pulled on her tits in a way he knew she responded to.

"I hope you guys aren't in a hurry to go," he said to the by now largely naked bunch. "I've got lots of ideas for testing Zoe all night. After I've fucked her myself - I don't think I can hold out much longer - I suggest we have a little lesson in suspension; I'll string her up in that corner. Then I'll show you what can be done with some clothes pegs and some candle wax. And we absolutely must have a spunk show - get a few of you to finish off all over her tits together - after I've paid them a bit more attention with my little switch. Oh yes, Zoe's going to learn what it means to be my slave, tonight!"

Through a veil of tears brought on by passion and pain, Zoe felt the men reach for her again - her Master's words had inflamed them to continue to make the most of his most adorable plaything.

She could have resisted, but she had no desire to.

She was lost!

Chapter One

PUBLIC PLACES

One bright morning, after a typically sex-filled and obedience-orientated night before, Master Philip informed Zoe that she was to undergo a special test, which would involve going out with him in public as his 'slave', and behaving exactly as he instructed.

"It is a question of trust," he explained, as she looked at him tentatively. "You must abandon control to me totally - obey me without question, and trust that I won't let any harm befall you."

Zoe couldn't help wondering what exactly he had in mind, and what she was letting herself in for, but she was ready to be tested, and the thought of going out with her Master was exciting, so she nodded her agreement.

"Let's have a look at what's in your special wardrobe, shall we, and choose something appropriate?"

He took his slave by the hand and led her into one of the spare rooms (his house had several) where a built-in wardrobe and an extra rail held a variety of different garments, all of which he had purchased - or had made - for her.

Ignoring for the moment the more extreme rubber and leather creations, he browsed through a selection of mini skirts, and picked out an exceptionally short, shiny black satin one.

"Put this on - now," he told her.

The skirt was very tight, but had been adjusted to allow for Zoe's relatively small waist and relatively full hips, and so fitted perfectly.

It was much shorter than the currently acceptable day wear fashion of mid-thigh. It came down to only just below the swell of her buttocks at the back, and seemed to barely cover the bush of her pubes at the front. It was prostitute length.

She tugged it downwards, self-consciously. "Surely it's too short to go out in, Master?" she couldn't help saying.

The response was predictable. "I'll be the judge of that!"

"But look," she whispered. "You can see the marks on my thighs!"

It was true, the previous day's activities had left tell-tale stripes on the smooth white skin of her legs.

"They'll be hidden by your stockings," said Master Philip dismissively. He rummaged in a drawer, and pulled out some black hold-ups. "Here, try these."

He sat on a chair and watched as Zoe pulled them on. The elasticated tops came to just about the same level as her skirt. If she stood completely still, she was decent, but as soon as she took a step, little flashes of pale flesh could be seen between the two blacks.

Zoe wondered where on earth her Master intended to take her dressed like this, and hoped at least it would be some sort of adult club, and not until after dark!

"Now these." She was handed some painfully high heels - four inches at least, and black and shiny to go with the skirt.

"Now you're ready from the waist down," Master Philip said.

Zoe might have guessed that she wouldn't be allowed to wear knickers, though with a skirt this short, it seemed exceptionally risky and blatant. She would have to be really careful about stairs!

"Walk up and down a little, so I can watch you."

Her Master's voice was always so calm and authoritative, like he couldn't conceive of being crossed. She responded to it automatically.

"Swing your hips a little more! Mm, that's nice. Yes, the careful observer might spot the signs of punishment as you walk, but most people wouldn't even recognise what they were looking at. Now let me see what it looks like when you bend forward. Turn right round. Good. And try sitting down. Very nice!"

Zoe looked down with horror at the amount of thigh exposed when her skirt rode up on sitting. She started to tug the stockings up, but he stopped her.

"Leave them. And part your legs a little." He got up and crouched down right opposite her, dipping his head to look up her skirt. "Oh, yes, you can see everything."

Zoe began to worry a little more about where they were going. She didn't want to get arrested!

"Well," her Master was saying, as he stepped back to the wardrobe, "much as I like to see those fat tits of yours bouncing around like that, I suppose we'd better cover you up just a little. How about this?"

He held up a very small, very low cut, sequined tee-shirt.

She didn't dare comment. She couldn't tell if he was serious.

"Or this one looks nice." It was leopard skin, and slashed almost to the waist. The back was virtually non-existent.

"Where are you taking me?" She absolutely had to ask.

"Never you mind! Out and about. I think this one might do. Let's see what it looks like on you."

His third choice was a flimsy red summer top, with the narrowest of straps over the shoulders, and a top edge that sat more than half way down her unsupported tits. The material just about reached her waist at the back, but at the front – since the whole garment was deliberately too small and too short – her tits pushed it forwards so that it hung down away from her body, exposing a good few inches of stomach, and creating that fascinating cave effect; the feeling that you could just slip your hand under the front of it and touch naked, jutting out tits exposed from beneath to the air, as was exactly the case.

"Stand up on this chair," he instructed her, and she climbed up on to the indicated piece of furniture precariously in her high heels. "Now reach upwards, as if you were getting a book from a high shelf. Lovely!"

Master Philip was standing just beneath her, looking up into the aforementioned cave, to check what sort of effect the garment gave. Zoe was dreadfully aware of the picture she must present in her sluttish clothing, her top and skirt both riding up to expose her charms. At least it was only her Master having a look, and not some disapproving stranger.

"Now stay like that, on the chair, with your arms up, until you hear me come out of the shower. Understood?"

"Yes, Master."

"Then I want you to get yourself made up - very made up. Nice and plastered with flashy eye-shadow and blusher, and bright red lipstick - the brightest you can find, and with lip gloss on top. Make sure your hair is as bushy as you can make it, and put lots of jewelry on, do you hear? The gold chains I bought you round your neck, round your wrists and round one ankle. And those big heavy earrings, and lots of rings! God, you are going to look a tart! I may end up having to tell people that you're going to a fancy dress party, or something."

Before he left Zoe straining upwards on her chair, he inserted a finger up her somewhat exposed pussy, and stirred it round a little. Then he withdrew it, and raised it to his nose, savouring the bouquet.

"Your juices give you away, my girl," he said. "I'll swear you're more excited about this little excursion than I am!"

Within the hour, they were both ready to go out. Zoe had taken great care to get her make-up looking very spectacular, as instructed, but though being so blatantly decorated turned her on, she remained concerned about going out like that in the middle of the day. What on earth would people think, she wondered - then realised the answer was clear. They would think she was a slut and a tart, who dressed in an outrageously wanton way for the benefit of a man or men, and probably got up to the sorts of sordid activities that respectable women hadn't even heard of. And of course they would be right!

She was just sorting out her handbag when Master Philip appeared, all in black and pulling on a leather jacket.

"You won't be needing that," he said, taking the handbag away from her.

What, no money? No credit cards? No tissues? No mirror? This certainly was an exercise in complete dependency.

"Can't I just take a comb, Master?" she pleaded.

He ruffled her hair. "You look lovely as you are. It doesn't matter if you get a bit unruly - it adds to the image."

"What about lipstick?"

He considered. "Let me see, I could make sure you didn't smudge it eating or drinking by keeping you deprived of those pleasures for a while. But something tells me it might just get smudged in some other way, and since we may be out a long time - yes, I suppose you'd better take it."

Zoe extracted her stick of brightest red, gloss lipstick from the discarded bag, and held it out to her Master. "You'll have to take it, Master. I've got no-where to put it."

Master Philip raised his eyebrows. "I'm not carrying your things around! You can do that yourself."

"But where?" Zoe was confused. "It won't stay down my cleavage. It would have to be in my stocking tops - but then people will see it!"

Master Philip took the lipstick from Zoe and turned it round between his fingers, taking a long look. Suddenly, she thought she knew what he was thinking, and drew in a sharp breath.

"Open your legs," he told her. "You can carry it in your pussy."

"No, Master," she begged. "It won't stay in! It'll slip out!"

"Not if you keep a tight grip! It'll be good practice!"

Wide-eyed, Zoe felt her Master push the little tube into her private hole.

"There we are," he said. "Out of sight, but not too deep."

It felt hard and uncomfortable, like a too-big, too-low tampon. She grimaced, and her Master shook a finger at her.

"Now just you make sure it stays in there! Think how embarrassing it would be if it dropped out when someone was looking! To be honest, your arsehole would be a better place for it, but I suppose we can't risk not being able to get the thing out again. I like the whole idea, though. Perhaps I'll have a little pussy-handbag designed specially for you. Quite a novel way to carry things around and keep your hands free!"

So, when Zoe tottered out from the house to the car, not only was she ultra-aware of how incredibly shocking she must look, but she was having to concentrate like mad on squeezing tight down below, so her secret little piece of personal luggage didn't escape!

They drove into the centre of town, parked in a car park, and went into a burger bar.

"Just fancy a quick spot of lunch," said Master Philip, claiming a table. "Get me a quarter-pounder with chips, and a cola. Nothing for you!"

Zoe stood in the queue wishing the ground would swallow her up. Teenage boys leered at her, and giggled amongst themselves. Women frowned and muttered. Children pointed.

She brazened it out, giving her order with a confident smile, but the poor young girl at the till couldn't keep her eyes from Zoe's cleavage.

It was only now she realised that there were faint marks from yesterday's whipping all over those exposed mounds as well!

She sat down next to her Master again with a glum expression.

"Don't worry, my dear," he said. "Anything goes in today's world. No-one will give it another thought."

However, by the time he had finished his meal, the manager of the place was standing looking at them - trying to decide whether he had grounds to ask them to leave or not. Zoe tolerated yet more stares when at last Master Philip announced that it was time to move on.

Clicking out onto the street in her stilettos, she found her reception there something similar. Far more black looks than interested ones, but some expressions of curiosity, as if people thought she must be involved in some sort of promotion or event, and that a camera crew would presently appear in her wake.

She gripped her Master's arm and moved close to him, trying to hide, but her short skirt, her rude cleavage, and her painted face all gave off signals she could do nothing to counter. Never had she felt so out of place and embarrassed and worried as on that afternoon, forced to go shopping with her confident and unconcerned tormentor, through streets that seemed far, far too busy.

He led her deliberately across some cobbles, which made walking in her high heels extremely difficult.

He made her sit and wait for him alone on a bench, humiliated by the cutting taunts of a bunch of young girls.

He had her run across the road to fetch him something, so her tits bounced up and down provocatively and her skirt rode up even further.

She had to suffer several direct comments from older women along the lines of, "How dare you!" and "No respect!" They hurt her, but what could she do? She was under her Master's control, and that was what mattered most.

Next they got on a double decker bus and Master Philip made sure that Zoe went up the stairs in front of a couple of young lads whose jaws had dropped at the sight of her. There was no doubt that they got more than a glimpse of her naked crotch as she climbed the steep steps. She wondered what they'd think if they knew about the lipstick - she couldn't imagine that such a possibility would ever have occurred to them.

She sat down in the back seat, next to the window, and the two young men squeezed in beside her. Master Philip took the seat just in front and pretended to be unaware of how the boys fidgeted and sniggered, pressing Zoe further and further into the corner and drooling openly over her tits, which bounced about as the bus bumped along. It did occur to him to ask her to take the lipstick out and touch her face up, but perhaps a crowded bus wasn't the best place for such games!

When eventually they reached a certain street, Master Philip got up. "Come on, we're here."

Zoe was forced to squeeze out past the two lads, who made no move to make her task easier and in fact made sure their hands brushed 'accidentally' against her stockings. She noticed that they also got off the bus at that stop, but lost sight of them as her Master pulled her along the street with him at a deliberately fast pace.

"In here," said Master Philip, as they came up to a building fronted with black boards. It was clearly a sex shop.

Inside, the lighting was low, mainly to disguise the tackiness of the products. A lone customer inspected vibrators in one corner.

A wiry character sat at the desk, leafing through a tabloid paper. He recognised Master Philip.

"Hello, guv!" Then he took in the spectacle which was Zoe. "Cor! Very nice!"

"Hello, Lew. I've brought her for you, like I promised."

The shopkeeper swallowed. "What, you mean - ?"

"Yes. I told you I was pleased with that equipment you got for me, and I'd show you what I was going to use it on."

"The stocks and things, yeah. Well, thanks!"

"You're welcome."

Master Philip turned to Zoe. "I've brought you here so this gentleman can fuck you. Make sure you do your best."

"Yes, Master," Zoe replied meekly. She had come to expect this sort of thing.

The customer had been eavesdropping this amazing exchange, and now stepped forward to try his luck. "Um, any chance of me, er, having a go too?"

Master Philip looked him up and down. Suit, glasses, hungry expression. He turned to Lew. "It's up to you," he shrugged.

"Yeah, he's alright," said Lew. "I don't mind. I guess I'd better close up."

But just as he stepped towards the door, the two lads, who had obviously followed them from the bus stop, came in.

"Sorry, got to shut for a bit," Lew said, trying to usher them out, but Master Philip interrupted.

"Perhaps they'd like to join in. How do you feel about it?"

"Well, I'm all for a good gang-bang, but can she handle it?"

"Of course! No problem."

"Okay then." Lew dropped the latch and switched a sign to 'closed'. He turned round and pulled his cock out in one movement. "Let's get down to it!"

The young lads could hardly believe their luck, but though a little flustered, weren't about to miss an opportunity. Virtually jumping about with youthful enthusiasm, they stepped up to Zoe and began to feel her up roughly - one going for her tits, the other for her bum.

The gobsmacked customer was already wanking furiously.

Master Philip leaned against the counter and watched as four randy men, three of them complete strangers to him, descended on his sex slave, in a sleazy back-street sex shop. Just the sort of scene he enjoyed!

Zoe was shaking a little but none the less, not too concerned. It was true - she knew from experience - that she could handle four quite easily, and with her Master there with her, she felt secure. This was what being a slave was all about, and she wasn't going to let him down.

She lifted up her top theatrically, showing her tits to the men.

"I think you'd better take the lipstick out now," Master Philip said to her, once the action had got started, and to the surprise and amusement of the four men who were about to fuck her, she extracted the sticky stick slowly from between her legs and placed it on a shelf.

Several fingers took its place immediately, and she found herself being dragged down onto the grubby floor, with her skirt yanked up, and cocks being pushed into her face.

"I want to be last," said Lew, watching with interest as the first of the youngsters poked Zoe with frantic thrusts.

Master Philip was about to say, "That pleasure's mine!" automatically, but decided to save himself. This was only a warm up, after all.

For twenty minutes or so Zoe all but disappeared beneath the heap of hormone-charged masculinity, but since all concerned were so excited - for the four men, at least, this wasn't the sort of thing that happened every day - they were soon spent, and leaning back against the shelves with spaced-out looks.

They had all chosen to fuck her properly and had come up her pussy, so there was no spunk on her face or tits, as there often was in such situations. But still, she looked very fucked! Her clothes hanging off, her lipstick smudged from sucking cock - as her Master had anticipated - and smears of dirt on her cheeks and tits from the carpetless floor.

The shop owner, Lew, took absolutely ages fucking her, and orgasmed with the strangest roar, for which he immediately apologised. Soon after this, the customer and the two lads left, offering slightly embarrassed thank yous - to Master Philip, not to Zoe, of course!

Lew went and sat in his chair behind the desk again, and lit a cigarette. "I hope you'll bring her round again sometime. I could easily get a few more guys, if that's what you wanted."

"Thanks," said Master Philip. "I'll think about it."

He stepped over Zoe, sprawled beneath him, and wandered round, browsing through the produce.

"How much is this?" he asked, picking up a grotesquely huge dildo.

"Hey, free to you, guv."

Master Philip showed the monster to Zoe, who was pushing herself up off the floor.

"What do you think?"

She shook her head. "It's too big, Master."

Master Philip grunted. His slave's young pussy was nice and tight, and he certainly didn't want to stretch it too much, but he suddenly had an urge to see the thing up her. He removed the packaging.

"What about your mouth? I'm sure that's big enough," he said, and held the huge dildo dangling downwards just above Zoe's face.

"Open wide."

Zoe stretched her jaw open and took the pink rubber knob into her mouth. Master Philip pushed it a little deeper then let go, leaving it standing upright like a little pillar embedded in her face.

Zoe didn't dare move her head from its tilted-back position, in case the thing fell out. Master Philip grabbed the end of it again, and began to fuck her mouth a little.

"Lick it - that's right. Make it nice and wet so it'll go up you. Mind you – " he glanced down at the spunk cascading down Zoe's legs, " - you're pretty wet down there already."

Next he had Zoe stand with her legs open and bending forwards to touch her toes. He placed the end of the dildo at the entrance to her recently used hole and began to push.

Zoe tried to relax, but was sure the dildo was too huge.

"Master," she whispered. "I don't think it'll go!"

Lew came out from behind his desk and stood against Zoe's bent back, pulling her skirt up and parting her buttocks with his bony hands, so he could get a good view.

"Push harder," he said to Master Philip, bracing himself as Zoe's doubled up form was pressed against him, as a result of the pressure with which Master Philip pushed the giant phallus slowly but surely up poor Zoe's slit.

Unlubricated, it wouldn't have gone, but with the host pussy dripping with four men's spunk, the enterprise was a success. It hurt, but then what was a little more pain to Zoe? She concentrated on keeping still while the men walked around her, admiring the spectacle she made with her bum in the air, her skirt not serving much purpose, and the hugely thick dildo protruding rudely from her snatch.

Her Master wiggled it around for a bit, in a way that started to make Zoe feel quite aroused, then pulled it out sharply, leaving her with that empty feeling.

He handed Lew the wet dildo. "Can you put this in the post to me? You've got my address."

He contemplated his slave's inviting vagina, but again decided against availing himself of it at that moment. He was rather enjoying his present state of semi-arousal and anticipation.

"Right, then," he said to Zoe. "Stand up, and get your face in order. What a mess you look!"

Lew gave her some tissues and, as well as she could without a mirror, she tidied up her make up, added some lipstick, and mopped some of the spunk up from between her legs.

"Now put your lipstick away again."

"But Master! It'll never stay in now - it's too slippery!"

"Rubbish! You'll just have to squeeze harder! Now, come on. I want a drink."

So Zoe pushed the lipstick inside her again - such a tiny thing compared to the recent dildo - and accompanied her Master out of the sex shop and into a nearby pub.

She didn't dare tell him, however, that just as she'd stepped onto the street, and he'd been saying his goodbyes to - and it sounded like making plans for a return visit with - Lew, the lipstick had, as she'd predicted, slipped out onto the pavement, despite her best efforts to keep it in.

A passing shopper saw this happen, but turned away without comment, and Zoe was so embarrassed she just kicked the thing into a gutter and carried on walking.

The pub turned out to be the first of many they would visit that afternoon and early evening. Master Philip announced that they were going on a pub crawl of some of the city's most downmarket alehouses, purely for the purpose of creating a stir, and forcing Zoe to behave blatantly and wantonly in public.

He would send her for drinks, insisting she pushed her way through the busiest parts of the bar, so that lots of men would get a chance to rub up against her and fondle her surreptitiously.

He would insist she sat with her legs open, in a position where lots of men could get a good look up her skirt.

Or he would sit on a stool by the bar and have her stand beside him in her high heels, and, as he put an arm round her waist, gradually work her skirt up at the back or the side, so the shocked customers could discover that she wasn't wearing any underwear.

Once, as he made conversation at the bar with a group of three or four builders, he quite clearly pinched Zoe on her exposed midriff - squeezed her flesh hard between two fingers, all the time staring into her eyes to remind her not to make a sound.

The builders soon cottoned on and joined in the game, and Zoe found herself surrounded by men discretely pinching her bottom, thighs and tummy, while she tried not to squirm or cry out, so as to avoid attracting the attention of the barmaid and the innocent-looking couple sitting nearby.

Master Philip got a real buzz out of seeing how other men looked at his slave, and knowing that he had the power to give her to those men if he so chose.

Once or twice, strangers were bold enough to actually ask him if anything was 'on', and he rewarded their courage by sending Zoe off with them in the hope of finding a quiet place where she could suck them off.

Once, she got pushed into the back of a van in order to see to a couple of beefy labourers with her mouth, and in the very next pub, was actually secreted into the men's outdoor toilet, where she found herself kneeling and sucking off five or six either expectant or surprised visitors, before her Master finally came and rescued her.

"Lipstick!" he instructed, as she got up from the concrete floor, and so Zoe was forced to admit that she'd lost it some time ago.

Master Philip was not pleased. "I'm sure you did it deliberately! Even if it'd been slipping out, you could've pushed it back in with your hand!"

This would have been extremely difficult in public, but nevertheless, Zoe accepted that she had disappointed her Master.

"I'm very sorry for losing it, Master," she said meekly.

"And look at your knees!"

Zoe looked, and saw that her stockings were torn from where she had been kneeling on the rough floor.

"What a give-away! You should have been more careful." His face took on a familiar expression. "I think maybe you should be spanked for your transgressions, don't you?"

"Yes, Master," came Zoe's resigned reply. "Please spank me. I shouldn't have lost the lipstick, and I shouldn't have laddered my stockings. I deserve to be spanked, Master."

Thus a grotty pub toilet saw more than its fair share of action that day, as Master Philip bent Zoe over the pan and gave her twenty or so hard, heartless spanks on her bare bottom.

They left just as the landlord came to investigate why half of his customers were gathered around a largely uninteresting toilet door!

As they neared yet another pub - poor Zoe's feet were really aching by now - her Master took a different tack.

"I want you to go in there on your own, and wait for me by the bar. I'll be with you in fifteen minutes or so."

Zoe looked at him with horror. She had become very aware of the holes in her stockings, and was sure that her lipstick must be seriously smudged. Her hair had got a little caked in spunk, as a result of some of the afternoon's activities, and she felt like she could only bear to be out on the streets because she was under the protection of an imposing man like her Master.

To go into a pub alone at any time was difficult, but dressed as she was - surely she would be thrown out, or someone would call the Police!

Master Philip read the reluctance in her eyes and delighted in it. He pushed her away from him. "Go on. I'd give you some money, but I'm sure somebody'll buy you a drink!"

And he was gone!

Shaking, Zoe turned towards the pub. Taking a deep breath, she pushed the door open and found herself in a particularly busy, particularly smoky lounge bar, which was almost full of people - mostly men, and many of them 'suits' on their way home from a day at the office.

Attracting more than a few glances immediately, she made a bee line for the toilets, intending to hide in them for as long as possible.

There was only one small toilet however, which was occupied, with another woman waiting, and when she tried to use the mirror to straighten her skimpy clothes and wild hair, she got such a disapproving frown that the busy, anonymous room outside suddenly became the preferable option.

Trying - unsuccessfully - to look inconspicuous, she made her way to the bar, and found a lone stool in a corner. She made no move to attract the barman's attention, but when he had served everyone else who was waiting, he came over to her, and gave her a suspicious look.

"Yes?" he said.

Of course, Zoe had no money! "I'm sorry - I'm just waiting for a friend," she tried with a smile, but it was clear that the barman thought she was soliciting, an impression he confirmed by what he said to her next.

"I'll give the friend five minutes."

Zoe was actually quite taken aback by this unhesitatingly voiced assessment. A lot of women wore short skirts and had bushy blonde hair. There were a couple of girls in this very bar in quite sexy clothes, and more lipstick than Zoe had on, after her orally active pub crawl. So why couldn't she be just a girl waiting for her boyfriend? Did she really look so extreme?

She looked up at her reflection in a mirror behind the bar. For a long time.

It must be the tits, she concluded. They were obscenely full, and the nipples stood out very prominently through the thin red top. Or else it was the amount of silvery make up around her eyes. A bit much for early evening, perhaps.

"It's the look in your eyes, sweet," said a voice right next to her, making her jump like never before.

She saw him first in the mirror - tall, blond, attractive - then swung round.

"I heard the barman," the stranger explained. "He's probably quite good at spotting knowing women, in this part of town."

"But," Zoe protested, "I'm not – "

"Not a knowing woman?"

She hesitated. "Not what he thought."

The stranger pulled up a recently vacated stool. "You surprise me. Can I buy you a drink anyway?"

"Yes, please."

At least having a drink and sitting with a man helped her to blend into the scenery. She drank gratefully, and accepted some peanuts.

"I'm Adam, by the way."

"Zoe."

He had a good long look at her, head to toe. "How about it, then?"

"What?"

"Oh, come on. If you're not selling, it must be free. I can't believe you're just a tease."

Zoe sighed. "Look, really, I'm waiting for someone."

Adam insisted. "Can't you just pop out with me for a minute? Or give me your number at least."

Zoe shook her head. "I can't do that." How could she explain that she was somebody's sex slave, and could only screw around with her Master's permission?

"Okay, just tell me then. In principle - if things were different - would you let me screw you? For free?"

"You're very frank!"

"Would you? In principle?" He was stroking her thigh with his fingertips.

"Probably."

At this point Zoe saw from across the room that Master Philip was just coming into the pub. He caught sight of her, and strode purposefully in her direction.

Zoe tensed. She hoped her Master wouldn't object to her having been talking to someone. He must have been expecting something like that to happen, surely?

When he registered that she wasn't alone, he put a hand on the blond stranger's shoulder.

"You chatting up my woman, mate?"

Zoe went cold, but to her complete amazement, Adam responded with a huge laugh, and stood up.

"Phil, my lad! Long time no see. How are you?"

There was a lot of back-slapping and hand-shaking.

"You found her then."

"Well, she's a bit obvious."

They moved to a table away from the bar.

"I hope you haven't been throwing yourself at my old chum Adam," said Master Philip to Zoe, who was still blushing with embarrassment and mild anger at having been duped.

"Well, she said she'd fuck me in principle," Adam spoke up, "but then she did seem to be staying loyal to you. I don't know, though. If you'd given me another five minutes, I might have got somewhere."

Master Philip laughed. "Don't worry. You can have her. As for you, Zoe, I shall see that you are punished for even considering giving yourself away without my permission. Perhaps Adam would like to do it?"

"I see, like that is it? Well, yes please, I wouldn't mind. If she doesn't."

Both men looked at her, and Zoe was struck by what a handsome duo they were. She pictured herself lying between them, and crawling at their feet, and having them both spank her at the same time.

She pictured Adam fucking her - sitting on him, maybe, while Master Philip whipped her back, insisting that she ride his friend faster, faster!

Her mind ran through a catalogue of images, and she found them all very pleasing.

When Master Philip prompted her to say whether she'd mind Adam punishing her, she could only shake her head, afraid that anything she might say would betray too much enthusiasm - too much passion, even - for Master Philip's liking.

"See, she's a slut through and through," said her Master, and then started on an account of the previous night's activities and what Zoe had been up to already that day.

Zoe sat and fidgeted, afraid that the men at nearby tables might overhear, but Master Philip didn't make much effort to lower his voice.

"Anyway," he concluded. "I'm glad you could make it. Hopefully it should be an interesting evening."

"What did you have in mind?" Adam asked. "I've got a hotel room nearby, incidentally."

"Well, of course we could use that if you wanted. But if you don't mind performing in public, I was thinking of this porn cinema."

Adam raised his eyebrows. "Sounds interesting."

"Only I've had a word, so they expect us. To make sure it's nice and busy."

Adam's expression spoke volumes. He downed the last of his drink. "Let's get going!"

The porn cinema was along a little backstreet. Through a nondescript door marked 'members only', down some stairs, and you were in another world! A dark, hot, smoky world, packed full of men - mostly wanking.

The man at the desk waved the three of them through without charge, and as they pushed their way into the overcrowded cinema, several dozen faces turned towards them, eyes locked onto Zoe.

The films were hard, straight porn, and of reasonable quality, but most of the men in the room saw them as secondary. They really came here for the atmosphere - for the other people. Either for other men, if they were that way inclined, or to wait for the occasional couple who might come in and have a little play around. This sort of behaviour was well-established in this and many similar places, and the regulars always had a tale or two to tell the newcomer of what they had seen, or more rarely, what they had done.

Tonight the atmosphere was expectant. Word had spread quickly. Master Philip had brought Zoe in here before, and they went further than most couples - much further.

Master Philip and Adam held Zoe between them, and battled their way to three seats which had quickly been vacated in the front row. They sat down rather slowly and deliberately, just to make sure that no-one could miss the fact they were there.

At this point, it has to be said, Zoe felt wonderful. Scared, but wonderful. Here she was in her slut's costume, in a room full of randy, expectant men, and her two companions slowly but surely easing her legs wider open and lifting her tits from her top.

Anything could happen in a situation like this - and she thought she had an idea what!

Hands - strangers' hands - began to creep over her shoulders from the rows behind, and slink down to her breasts. When it became clear that the two men with whom the slut had arrived weren't going to object to groping, the strangers became much more bold, and suddenly the threesome were surrounded by men three deep and falling over each other to get a feel of Zoe's exposed flesh, or at least a good look!

Master Philip and Adam hoisted one each of Zoe's legs over their own laps, stretching them apart painfully, so her pussy was visible to all. What felt like at least six different men's fingers began to probe at her crotch, and at the same time, cocks appeared over her shoulders, begging to be sucked, and spunking - already! - over her quivering tits.

"Rub that spunk in and get some cock in your mouth," said Master Philip, his voice deliberately intrusive in the otherwise silent atmosphere (silent except for the soft music and soft groans emanating from the film). The men could hardly contain themselves - in many cases they couldn't, and there were some mumbled apologies as people inadvertently spunked over other people's clothes!

After she'd sucked about ten cocks - some all the way - and at least six more had come on her tits (not to mention some in her hair, and at least one in her ear!), Zoe got hoisted round so she was kneeling on the seat, her bum in the air and her mouth still occupied.

She noticed that Master Philip and Adam both had their own cocks out and were wanking gently, and she reached out spontaneously to give them both a hand.

"I told you," said Master Philip to Adam, across Zoe's tits. "I've never known such an utter slut as this one!"

He looked around at the men, who were mostly just silhouettes against the cinema screen.

"Who wants to fuck this slut? She's all yours."

"I will!" said a few voices. And a moment later the first of several anonymous cocks was up Zoe's pussy.

It was very hot in the cinema, especially with loads of bodies pressing up against you, and Zoe's skin glistened with sweat, amongst other things!

It was also incredibly escapist. Zoe couldn't have said how much time had passed since they'd come in, or how many men she had pleased. She was in her element, surrounded by men, and perfectly happy in the knowledge that she was fulfilling her Master's wishes.

When the action died down a little, Master Philip took control again, standing up and slipping his belt off.

"I think sluts like you should be publicly whipped, don't you?"

"Yes, Master." Zoe quailed, but stuck her bum in the air without prompting.

Their audience got excited again at this added element of debauchery. Most of the films that got shown in the place stopped short of proper punishment scenes - yet here they were getting to watch it in real life, and for free!

"Care to join me?" Master Philip asked Adam, and so it was that Zoe got a severe and prolonged belting from two very dominant men, with an astounded audience of at least fifty, including the indulgent management, looking on.

With Zoe moaning and men still spilling their spunk over her front end, Adam got himself in quite a frenzy, and with the greatest pleasure, eventually threw his belt aside and grabbed Zoe by the hips, pulling her back onto his cock.

He fucked her hard - very hard - her drooping tits slapping forward against strangers' legs, her eyes closed as her wonderful Master thought to reach under her and rub her clit with expert fingers, as his friend fucked her so nicely.

Adam came with a huge groan, and pulled out shaking his head.

"Bloody brilliant! Best fuck I've had in years. Lovely tight pussy - I recommend it!"

Master Philip now decided he had waited long enough and slowly inserted himself up Zoe's absolutely dripping hole.

Again, he helped her with his hand while he fucked - something he didn't always bother to do, but certainly knew how to when he felt like it. He also knew what to say to turn Zoe on - and bring her off. She needed crude instructions.

"Why is your mouth empty?" he growled. "There's still some hard ones around. There, suck that big one! Keep it in your mouth and work on it while I fuck you. That's it, you bitch, you should always be kept working at both ends. One at a time isn't enough for you, you tramp. Just look at you, caked in spunk, and getting whipped in a porn cinema! I've never known anything like it. Since you seem to enjoy it so much, I think I should leave you here for a while on your own. Yes, there's new guys coming in all the time - look here's a few you haven't sucked off yet.

I think we'll piss off for a couple of hours and have a nice meal, while you stay in here and keep working away to satisfy all these strangers. What do you say, Adam? A nice steak or something, while our slave gets left in this dark smoky room on her own, with dozens of men fucking her and whipping her - oh, yes, they've seen it's allowed now, and they've all got belts, you know!"

He was gratified to feel Zoe tense and shudder beneath him as she came, and at last let himself go entirely, and fucked her quite as harshly and lecherously as most of the strangers had done.

Drained, Zoe slipped down onto the floor, and leant on some guy's legs as she looked up at Master Philip and Adam putting their belts back on and zipping themselves up.

"You weren't serious about leaving me?" she said, clutching at her Master's trousers.

He stood and looked down on her, feeling a huge rush of pleasure - a deep, emotional pleasure - at the knowledge that he had such complete control over such a beautiful, compliant woman.

"Of course I was! Don't worry, I'll have a word with the blokes upstairs and make sure they keep an eye on you. And make sure that you don't get out of here!"

"Master," she whimpered, leaning forward to kiss his thigh, and at the same time accepting a stroking on her head from Adam. "You're so cruel!"

"That's the idea, isn't it? See you in two hours or so, and remember - behave yourself!"

It was three hours before the men came back, full of food, drink, good humour and excited comradeship. It's a good feeling, sitting in a restaurant with your mate, knowing you share this amazing secret - that there's a stunning, ultra-submissive plaything getting gang-banged just down the road, and waiting for the two of you to go and get her and take her to wherever you want and do whatever you want with her.

That was a pretty special meal!

God, was Zoe in a state! Her skirt was ripped up the side and she had completely lost her skimpy top. It had been torn from her, and the pieces lay trampled underfoot. Her stockings had also got taken off her, and were no-where to be seen. No doubt they had been slipped into someone's pocket for later use!

What make-up remained on her face had been smeared around, and diluted by all the sticky liquid that had passed over it. Her hair looked - well, like the hair of a slut who's spent about four hours solid surrounded by dozens and dozens of over-excited men!

She was grubby - her knees and bum particularly, from when she got pushed down onto the floor - and her big tits were noticeably red as a result of these two burly biker type characters having just recently spent the better part of half an hour holding her down and spanking them just about as hard as they could.

It really wasn't an exaggeration on these occasions to say that word spread around the whole city that a slut was available for fucking and spanking in such and such cinema. The cinemagoers formed a community, and many of those who left, moved on to other establishments to boast about what they'd seen. Phone calls were made, and friends told friends, and, in short, there was no let up for Zoe over those three hours. If anything there was an increasing number of men trying to get to her as time wore on.

A couple of times the management had to intervene a little (of course in general they didn't object, as it was great for business), when so many men crowded round that the seats threatened to collapse, but in general Zoe was left to cope on her own.

When Master Philip and Adam got back, they couldn't get anywhere near her. They had to pull dozens of men back out of the way before eventually finding Zoe on the floor in a corner, with a huge muscular guy just shooting his load over her caked, dripping, much-pummeled snatch.

"That's all, folks," said Master Philip, picking a shattered, quiet Zoe up in his arms, and accepting her ecstatic hug of welcome. "Back soon."

They covered her in a jacket, and took her to Adam's car, which was parked in a hotel car park nearby. They placed her on the back seat, and sat in the front, looking back at her.

"Are you okay?" Adam asked, a little worried, looking at the state of her, that things had gone a bit too far.

She nodded. They had brought her a bottle of lemonade, and watched as she drunk it very thirstily.

"Didn't get hurt?" Adam queried, then realised how stupid a question this was. He had hurt her himself, earlier, with his belt, hadn't he? "Seriously hurt, I mean."

But Zoe was shaking her head. "Of course not. It wasn't too bad - mostly just spanking. Nothing I couldn't handle."

Master Philip took the empty bottle from her. "Adam's concerned for you. He doesn't realise quite how used you are to this sort of thing."

Zoe reached out a hand to Adam. "Don't worry, I really do know what I'm doing, I promise."

"She enjoys it. She begs for that sort of thing. Don't you, dear?"

"Yes, Master," said a resigned Zoe.

"How many times did you come, after we'd left you?"

She blushed. "A couple of times, Master."

"Did you think of us," Adam said, "out there in our restaurant, as much as we thought of you, I wonder?"

"Oh, yes!" There was no doubting the sincerity of Zoe's replies. "I'm so glad you - I mean, you both - came back."

Master Philip laughed. "Greedy sow! Always wants more than one. Aren't I enough for you?"

Then his expression changed, and suddenly everybody was kissing and groping again.

"Let's go up to the room," Adam suggested, more than ready for another fuck, but Master Philip still hadn't had enough of showing all Zoe's capabilities off to his friend.

"One more test, Zoe. Just a little longer. Will you do it?"

"What?" she asked.

"A quick drive round the parks?"

There was a bit of a silence.

"What do you mean?" asked Adam.

Master Philip explained. "Haven't you heard of dogging? It happens wherever there's a car park near some bushes, basically. Usually out in the country, in picnic places by main roads, but also in several of the parks in town. The same sort of thing as in the cinema, you know - lots of hopeful guys hanging round, looking for a 'show'. It depends where you go, and when, and who's there, but it can be useful for the kind of games me and Zoe like to play."

He turned round and reached for the seat belt, forgetting that Zoe hadn't actually answered his question. "Come on, I'll show you. We'll try the Common first."

It was late by this time, and well after dark. Not the sort of time one would imagine people going for a walk in the park. Yet, when they pulled into the little parking area in the middle of the Common, there were at least ten other cars there, positioned neatly round the edges, facing outwards.

"Drive round slowly, then park up in that corner. Face out."

"It matters, does it?" Adam asked.

"Yes."

Master Philip was peering out of the window at the cars already there. "I recognise some of these," he said. "A few of the lads I know are here. Now, kill the engine, and lights off."

They sat for a while in the dark and the quiet. Traffic passed on the main road in the distance. There was some movement over on the other side of the car park - you could just see the glowing ends of cigarettes.

"What happens?" Adam queried, looking back at Zoe, who was peering out of a side window anxiously.

"Well," said Master Philip, "usually people do things in the car, and after a while - if they recognise your number plate or get the right signals

- the doggers come over for a look. Maybe they get a feel of tit through the window, or get their dick sucked."

"Is that it?"

"No, you can get out and go into the bushes. Lie the lady down on the grass, or something, and invite the guys to have a go. Sometimes it's disappointing - they're a bunch of voyeurs, really. But once you get known, and the right guys hear about it – "

"Then you can get your slave fucked?"

"Oh, yes." It was Master Philip's turn to peer at Zoe over his shoulder. "I brought her here every Friday night over the summer. We got up to - what was it, Zoe, forty five?"

"Forty eight, I think, Master."

"Forty eight what?" asked Adam.

"Men, of course. In one night, that is."

"Christ!" Adam exclaimed. "Forty eight men fucked her in one night? I'm not sure I believe that!"

"Believe it! You saw what it was like in the cinema - and there they have to pay six quid to get in! Out here it's free. Which means, incidentally, that you get even scruffier guys - don't you, dear?"

Zoe knew all about the car parks. She didn't have much regard for the kind of men who hung out in them, but since she had only ever been to such places with Master Philip, the doggers, like the bushes, were really just scenery - a background to what was really going on, which was the interplay and rapport between her and her Master.

"There's another car coming in," said Adam in a worried tone, and they watched the headlights swing round and then die as the newcomer parked quite near them.

"I know that one, too," said Master Philip. "That's the guy that likes to use your arsehole, Zoe. Remember?"

"I sure would like to fuck her again tonight," said Adam, getting excited by the sexual tension of the situation.

"Well look, take her back to your hotel for the night if you want. I don't mind. We'll just let her see a bit more action here first, shall we?"

Adam's response was a horny groan - undoubtedly affirmative.

"Have you got any rope or anything in the car?" Master Philip asked. "There's a big log just over there we could tie her over."

"Rope and handcuffs," said Adam, smugly. "I like to be prepared - in case the opportunity arises."

"Good man. Let's get out then."

The night was still and quite warm, which was a good thing, considering the state of Zoe's undress.

"Can't I keep the jacket, Master?" she begged, as she got dragged out of the car.

"No way. Go and stand out there so the guys can see you."

Zoe picked her way over the rough ground in her high heels, pulling at her torn, short satin skirt - her only piece of clothing. She watched as several men got out of their cars and converged on her.

Very soon after, they were grabbing at her tits and probing for her pussy. No words of greeting were uttered, never mind requests for permission - they weren't deemed necessary.

When Master Philip and Adam stepped round from where they'd been rummaging in the boot, the men broke their silence. "Haven't seen you down here for a while," said one, in a conspiratorial undertone.

"We've been busy."

"I bet!"

"Well, there's lots of places to go," said Master Philip. "When you've got a slut like this one, you have to share her round fairly!"

Adam joined in the groping. He was quite taken with Zoe by now, and working up to asking Master Philip if he could borrow her regularly. Unfortunately, he didn't have a permanent sex slave of his own - women like Zoe were rare.

"Come on," said Master Philip, and headed into the undergrowth, making no effort to hide the rope and handcuffs.

Zoe remembered the log. Remembered the feel of the rough bark against her tits and stomach and thighs. Remembered the huge size and weight of it - utterly inescapable - when Master Philip had tied her down over it at full stretch. Bum up in the air, completely available to anybody - absolutely anybody - who should appear from behind the bushes at the right moment. And here she was, with the same thing happening again - deja vu!

Admit it though, she said to herself, as Master Philip and Adam worked together to tie her down, and ran their demanding, dominating hands over her half naked, very vulnerable body.

Admit it - you're sick with excitement that there's two of them! You're thrilled to be the slave of two Masters!

Master Philip was taking his belt off again. "A little whipping show first, I suggest, then maybe we leave you here for a while, so the guys can have their fun, eh?"

More men had appeared from somewhere, and a huge group now stood around, waiting with bated breath and stiff cocks for the action to begin.

"This is my slut and sex slave," said Master Philip to the crowd of 'bush wankers', as they were sometimes known. "I've brought her here for your entertainment. And I'm going to punish her for your entertainment."

He swung back with the belt, then landed a heavy blow across Zoe's quivering, upthrust buttocks.

"And then," he said, whipping regularly now as he spoke, "I'm going to leave her here on her own all night! All night, tied to a fallen tree in the park, so anyone can use her. Tied up and naked and with a sore bum - getting fucked til dawn!"

Adam had crouched down near Zoe's head and was trying to judge her reaction as Master Philip spoke and whipped.

"All night, he's saying now, can you hear? I wonder if he's going to ask you first, or just leave you anyway. Not that it matters - I'm sure you'd say yes if he did ask you."

He moved even closer to her. "Zoe," he said. "Why are you here?"

But the blows were making her gasp and cry out, and she couldn't - or wouldn't - speak.

"Why are you here, Zoe?" Adam pressed her. "Is it because you love Master Philip?"

Still concentrating mainly on handling her pain, Zoe only nodded.

"But you'd still be here if it was me, wouldn't you? If it was just me, instead of him. I know you'd still be here."

Master Philip was getting a bit carried away now. He liked the way the strap falling on Zoe's bottom caused such a loud noise. He enjoyed the element of risk-taking - whipping arse in a public place! Using the sounds it made as a herald, announcing to whoever might be lingering around that something kinky was going on. An open invitation to fuck.

"You're here," said Adam to Zoe, "because you're a submissive slut who loves getting her arse whipped. Aren't you?"

"Yes," Zoe groaned. She knew what she was, better than any man ever would.

"Say it," Adam demanded.

"I am a submissive slut who loves getting her arse whipped," Zoe whispered.

A few of the men had joined Adam at Zoe's front end, and someone pulled her head up by the hair, so they could see her face better - and prepare the access route to her mouth.

"Louder," said Adam.

"I am a submissive slut who loves getting her arse whipped!"

"Keep saying it."

"I am a submissive slut who loves getting her arse whipped. I am a submissive slut who loves getting her arse whipped. I am a submissive slut who – "

But she couldn't continue.

Adam, shortly followed by a couple of the other guys, drenched her obedient mouth with huge quantities of warm, bubbling spunk!

Chapter Two

SAUNA SLAVE

"Where are we going, Master?" Zoe asked one morning, as Master Philip bundled her into the back of his car.

It was several months after she'd first agreed to be his slave. Months during which she had indeed suffered, but also grown to adore her Master and revel in her new, harsh existence as his plaything.

"Did I ask you to speak?"

"No - I'm sorry, Master."

"You forget yourself. However, I shall tell you that I am taking you somewhere and leaving you there for two weeks."

Zoe longed to ask where, but knew better than to press.

"I am going on holiday for a fortnight, to the South of France," her Master continued, after they'd driven a few more blocks. "I shall relax on the beach and visit a certain lady friend of mine who works in Monte Carlo. You, meanwhile, will spend two weeks as a Sauna Slave."

Zoe sat silently as the large, plush car swept on through the city. A sauna? She didn't think she'd ever been in one. The word conjured up two conflicting images in her mind - one of an expensive, top notch health spa where rich women went to refine their figures, the other of seediness and squalor, a cockroach-ridden basement where creepy men went to do creepy things. She wondered which of the two the sauna to which they were destined would be.

In fact, when Master Philip eventually stopped the car outside a smart building tucked away in the corner of an industrial estate, she was optimistic. The door was labelled 'Private Health Clinic' and the reception area, when she was ushered into it, looked comfortable and clean. Appearances could be deceptive, however, as she would shortly discover.

A large man sat at a desk, and waved them through with a blank expression. Obviously Master Philip was known and expected.

Just around a corner, her Master pulled her up outside a door marked 'office', and twisted her arm roughly.

"Are you ready for your holiday?" he said. "I expect you shall spend the whole two weeks in this building."

Zoe thought briefly about things like clothes, and toiletries, and her handbag. It seemed, however, that the idea of having her own possessions with her was now a thing of the past. Presumably she wouldn't need anything, though it was very strange to be deposited somewhere for two weeks without even a toothbrush.

She decided to go with the flow. "I think I'm ready, Master."

"Good," he said. "If I hear favourable things about you when I get back, I'll consider taking you away with me next time. You might come in useful to carry my cases or something."

He knocked on the door, and to Zoe's surprise and secret horror, a female voice called out, "Come in."

The woman within was well on the way to being mature, and somewhere between plump and fat in build. She was laden with jewellery, her hair was piled up in a tall bun, and her brightly painted red lips were set into the caricature of a cruel smile. The other thing Zoe noticed immediately was the impossibly huge size of her breasts, which were half exposed by a flimsy, low cut top.

"Philip, dearest," the creature gushed, getting up from her chair to kiss him maternally on the cheek. "I've been so looking forward to seeing this little slut of yours. Since your phone call, I have made plans."

"Zoe," Master Philip pushed the said slut forward. "This lady I have known for some years. She runs this sauna, and will be looking after you while I am away. You will call her Madame, and do whatever she tells you. Now take your clothes off."

Zoe deliberately hesitated and squirmed beneath the woman's amused and curious gaze. Men she had got used to, since beginning to explore her submissive nature - but the idea of undressing in front of another woman! It seemed impossible; she rebelled against it, innately.

"This is poor," Master Philip acknowledged. "She is only just beginning her training, but I expected better. Zoe, do I really have to tell you twice? Take your clothes off now, so that Madame can look at you. I'm sure you possess nothing that she hasn't seen before."

Reluctantly then, Zoe slipped out of her skirt and top. She had nothing on beneath, and stood hunched, trying to hide her crotch with her hands.

"Get your hands behind your back, girl, and split your legs!" Master Philip snapped. "You must obey without question! I may display you to whoever I like! And take your shoes off as well. Being barefoot should add to your humiliation."

Zoe complied. Madame stepped forward and took one of Zoe's firm young breasts in an ageing hand.

"I see how it is," she said, inspecting Zoe's blushing face. "She hates women. She wants only to submit to men. That is something which you can work to overcome in her. Her stay here should help a little."

Master Philip nodded. "She has a long way to go, I know. I hope you'll still have a lot of men make use of her, though? I admit I like that idea best."

"Of course! This is a brothel, after all!" Madame continued her inspection of Zoe, running a hand over belly, buttocks and thighs. "Any restrictions?"

"Not really," was Master Philip's ominous response. "Do what you think best - but remember she's a relative novice. Save me something to build up to!"

"But she can be fucked?"

"Oh, yes!"

"And whipped?"

"Certainly."

"How hard?"

"Hard!"

"It would be nice if I could mark her early on - so the customers can see what she's here for."

"Do that. I wish I could stay to see it, but unfortunately I have a plane to catch. Oh, and don't let her get too much pleasure. I want her to learn her place."

"Don't worry," said Madame as Master Philip made to leave. "I will keep her nice and lowly for you, and she may even learn a thing or two. Now go and have yourself a nice trip."

Master Philip addressed Zoe once more. "This is just one of many tests - as I've told you. I want you to be ready to be my slave again when I return - whatever happens here."

Filled with trepidation as she was, Zoe nevertheless had no doubt that she would want to be with her Master again - on whatever terms he wanted. Just the thought of him walking away now and leaving her seemed horrendous.

"Master, I'll do anything," she blurted out passionately. "Anything to be yours, still."

He scowled at her. "We shall see," he said, and left her alone with Madame.

Struggling not to cry, Zoe turned away from the door and summoned her resolve - even tried to smile at the strange woman who was to be her mentor.

"I understand what you are feeling, my dear," Madame said with a sigh. "I have seen all this before - it has been my life. Believe me when I tell you that the difference between him and me telling you what to do will soon not seem to be so great. You think you love him, but you only love to obey. He plays his part well, but so do I - as you will see." She patted Zoe on a naked buttock. "Shortly, I shall give you that whipping, but first, I'm sure you'd like to have a look around your temporary home. Come, take my hand, and I'll give you the tour."

Zoe, confused now by this apparent kindness, hesitated again, terribly flustered.

"But, Madame! My clothes!"

"You won't be needing them. In fact I should have given them to your Master to take home. I have no intention of letting you out of here for a moment - you are my prisoner!" At this she grabbed Zoe's hand and dragged the timid girl back out into the reception area.

The hunk at the desk turned and looked the naked apparition up and down very deliberately.

"Is this the slave?" he asked, in a thick accent.

"Yes, Carl. Isn't she pretty? Carl is one of our five doormen. He knows all the regular customers and will ensure that only those people we welcome will be allowed in here. I'm sure you will get to know little Zoe better quite soon, Carl."

The man smiled broadly. "Looking forward to it."

He pressed a button and a door was released that let the two ladies into - to Zoe's surprise - what looked like another reception area, a more comfortable one, with another bulky man presiding over it.

"This is the real reception," Madame explained. "Carl takes care of any casual callers, while Eric - this is Eric - keeps the customer records and deals with payments. We work mainly on account, you know. If you were to be here longer, I might get you to help with the paperwork - it's such a chore - but I'm sure we can think of some more interesting things to do with you over two short weeks!"

There was one major difference between Carl and Eric - the latter was completely naked. As he stood up from his desk to greet Zoe, his ten inch penis did the same.

"Charming," he said, his eyes busy. "Is she starting right away?"

"Yes," Madame replied. "I don't see why not. Only I've agreed to mark her first; I may need your help in a little while, Eric darling."

"Of course. How many will it be?"

But at this point they were interrupted by an inner door opening and another naked man stepping out of it. This one was considerably less impressive than the hunky receptionist, though he made no move to cover his bony frame in front of the women.

"Ah, hello," said Madame. "This is Mr Williams, one of our regular customers."

Mr Williams took a good long look at Zoe's charms. "Very nice," he said. "Shame I have to go now - perhaps I'll pop in again later in the week."

"Zoe's with us for a fortnight - more as a slave than as a regular girl," Madame told him. "Though of course you can have her if you wish."

"A slave, eh? How interesting." Williams handed the towel he'd been carrying to Eric. "Any chance of a quick fondle of those tits?" he asked conspiratorially.

"Of course," Madame replied. "Zoe - chest forward!"

Obediently Zoe arched her back and suffered several long seconds of Williams' crude ministrations. Eventually, he sighed. "Must dash, though. See you soon."

Madame ushered Zoe towards the back of the second reception area.

"Through there – " she indicated a thick red curtain hanging across one wall of the room " - is the lounge, where the girls wait. We'll come back to that. First I'll show you the rest of the territory."

Behind the door through which Williams had come was a changing area, with several rows of lockers. Leading away from this was, to one side, a descending staircase, and on the other a long corridor with wooden doors at regular intervals along it.

"We have twelve private cubicles," Madame explained. "They are used by the girls and their 'guests' of course, but also as genuine rest rooms. We get more than the occasional lorry driver coming in for a wash and a nap in the daytime."

As they traversed the corridor, Zoe caught sight of several naked men sitting or lying on the couches within the rooms. They looked out through the open doors with interest, and Madame voiced a subtle greeting to one or two.

"The customers do tend to congregate round the rooms where the action's happening," said Madame in an undertone. She shrugged. "I don't discourage it."

As they passed one closed door, Zoe thought she could hear a regular grunting sound coming from behind it. It was clear that this was indeed where the real business of the sauna was taking place.

"At this end we have some toilets, the solarium and massage room, and a small gym. There are stairs at both ends of the building down to the main facilities. After you."

They passed a number of men - all naked or with towels wrapped round them - and most looked at Zoe with some degree of guarded curiosity. At the bottom of the stairs, a door opened onto a rather nice swimming pool. Situated beside it were a steam room and sauna - both quite large - and beyond it, a series of three hot tubs - of various temperatures, Madame informed Zoe.

Finally, back at the end below the changing room, there were some showers and more toilets. All this was to become very well known to Zoe over the next few days.

Her first impression was that the atmosphere was quite pleasant. No sign of windows or daylight anywhere, but pretty lighting, enticing warmth, and a not unpleasant smell of - well, of sauna.

The atmosphere was also very masculine. At least twenty men lounged around, many in silence, but some chatting heartily. Lots just popped in for a quick swim, or a relaxing stint in the steam room, she was told.

Not all called into the upstairs lounge to make their choice of intimate companion - but all knew they could, if they wanted to.

It was to this lounge that they now returned, and there sat four young women, sipping drinks and reading magazines. They were clothed, rather to Zoe's surprise; either in dresses - short ones, admittedly - or robes. It seemed they didn't share the men's habit of wandering around naked.

"Girls," said Madame. "I think I told you about Zoe."

All four glowered unwelcomingly, and Zoe became more aware than ever of her complete nakedness.

"Now don't worry," Madame assured her team. "I'll make sure she doesn't take any business away from you. If anything, she should create more, since we can use her in more extreme ways to get them going. And," she added with a touch of humour, "I'll get her to take the ones you don't like."

One of the girls sniggered. "Like Mad Melvin?"

"And Huge Harry?" another added with a smirk.

"Exactly. Now why don't you nip along to the sunbeds, or something – I intend to use this room to get our slave looking more the part. Unless you want to watch, that is."

"No thanks!" was the consensus of opinion, and the girls filed out past Zoe, throwing her looks of disgust. Women who did it for money didn't like women who did it for free. This was something Zoe had already discovered in life.

"Actually, one of you can sit in the outer office," Madame called after them. "And send Carl and Eric in here."

The men arrived, the curtains were drawn, and a silence descended.

Madame reached up to the top of a cupboard and brought down a three foot long, half inch wide cane. She handed it to Carl. Then she reached up again and produced a short riding crop, which Eric held his hand out for.

Zoe backed away, wide eyed. Surely both these ultra-fit looking young studs weren't to punish her at once? She felt lost and vulnerable with these strangers, and wished her Master had stayed with her at least a little longer.

"Doubtless I shall give you a caning myself, very soon. But today I feel a little weak - and this task requires strength. I want you well marked - so it looks impressive and lasts at least a week. Now, how shall we do it?"

They did it with Zoe draped over the back of a couch, with both men laying their implements over both of Zoe's buttocks, but alternately and from opposite sides. They also did it with their target standing up against a cupboard, her legs wide and her arms at full stretch as she held onto the top of it as instructed. This time they moved on to her back and legs as well, bearing in mind Madame's objective of marking the slave all over.

Next they did it with Zoe lying face up over a giant cushion on the floor. This way her belly and tits got some attention, not forgetting the fronts of her thighs. Then she was dragged to her feet again and bent forward over a table, and the men swapped tools and made their strokes a little harder, as they got well and truly into the swing of things.

Again, she had to bend over the sofa, this time backwards, with her tits facing the ceiling and in fact falling a little towards her face. Their undersides were treated to a furious onslaught with the tip of the crop, while at the same time the cane added one or two particularly broad marks to her stomach and legs.

With her body all afire, she even had to stand with her arms out in front of her, specially so that the implements could be applied to them - all the way up and down, and including her palms.

During this prolonged punishment, Madame paced around the action, shouting encouragement to the men and haranguing Zoe to keep still, or spread her legs wider, or hold her tits out for attention, or to keep quiet. Occasionally she added a slap of her own to some neglected piece of flesh, and seemed to enjoy pulling on Zoe's hair, and clasping a hand over the girl's mouth when her vocalisations rose to a crescendo.

Finally, with the men panting from their exertions, and Zoe's legs collapsing under her, Madame called a halt.

"Well done, boys," she said. "That was a very good job. Don't worry, I'll make sure you're rewarded well for your extra duties. Your pick of the girls, perhaps, as well as free rein with this one - but a little later, I think."

Carl and Eric looked at each other and grinned. They both knew the meaning of job satisfaction!

As Zoe lay panting on the floor, Madame drew back the heavy curtain - to reveal an audience of naked men, who had crept up to the reception area next door, and gathered surreptitiously around to listen to Zoe's introductory punishment.

"Now, now, gentlemen, the show's over, run along," she said to the guilty-looking crowd. "Eric and Carl - thank you, you can get back to your desks. And you," she looked down heartlessly at Zoe. "I think it's about time you got to work. Follow me!"

Shocked but stoical, Zoe got to her feet and followed her Mistress out of the lounge, through the gaggle of gawping men, and downstairs, back into the area of the main facilities. Here, she was pushed roughly into the showers.

"You will stay in there for the rest of the day. You will help the men to wash themselves - whether it be before or after they have been with one of the girls. You will not speak one word to them - you are not here to be conversed with. And you are certainly not to let them fuck you! Send them upstairs."

And so Zoe was left alone in a little tiled room with six showers in it, and when she was sure Madame had gone, she turned one of them on, set it to cold, and stood beneath it - at last getting some respite from the burning pain of her freshly applied weals.

She looked down at her body. She was marked with red stripes everywhere. Her breasts were prominently covered with crop marks. Her bottom must look a mess, she thought, as she ran her hands over multiple ridges.

How strange that all this should arouse her so! The idea of being marked all over, in order that those who saw her subsequently would understand that she wasn't just a prostitute, like the other girls - she was a slave.

Her hand crept to her sex. She was eager to console herself after her punishment with a nice orgasm, but at that moment she heard voices approaching, and she turned her cold shower off and retreated to a corner, suddenly afraid of what reactions the sight of her body might provoke in the men who would soon come upon her.

They were young, and sweating, and talking about the number of weights they had just been lifting in the gym.

Obviously they had missed out on her caning upstairs, as they were speechless when they saw her. They came forward for a closer look.

"Bloody hell!" said one. "Look at these marks!"

"Look at these tits!" said the other, and they both began to fondle her.

"I heard someone talking about a Sauna Slave, but I thought they were joking!" The second man addressed her. "Is that you, then?"

She nodded.

"What are you doing in here?"

Remembering her instruction not to speak, Zoe reached past the men for a bar of soap and made rubbing motions. They got the message, and laughed.

"Go on, then."

She started the showers, and began to soap the men, on their backs and chests. They fondled her as she did it, not considering that their rough hands on her fresh weals caused her pain - as did the soap, which stung where it came into contact with her marked skin.

All of a sudden, however, Zoe found herself enjoying this unexpectedly calming experience. The men were very attractive, and their fingers were doing nice things to her already pouting pussy.

One of them pushed her hand down to his bottom, and she began to soap his pert, juicy bum, her slippery fingers venturing into the crack, almost of their own accord.

"Mm," the man groaned. "I wish I could take you home with me - you'd be bloody useful in the shower every morning."

His friend was now rubbing a stiff prick against her soapy behind, and Zoe was getting carried away. This wasn't so bad a situation to be in, she was thinking. If only the cuts didn't sting so much. If only she could take these guys all the way. With this she was reminded, however, that that was precisely what she wasn't allowed to do, so, reluctantly, she pushed the insistent groins away a little, shrugging and shaking her head.

"Don't say we can't fuck you!" said the one whose bum she had so much enjoyed exploring.

She pursed her lips and pointed upwards.

"I reckon she's just the warm up," his mate said. "Well, come on then - I'm warmed up! I guess I'll settle for that redhead, or maybe the little dark one."

And so to Zoe's regret, both men rinsed themselves off quickly and left her with only cursory goodbyes.

Feeling bereft, but resigned, she put the soap back on the ledge - only to find that another man - an old, rather stooped character - had slipped into the showers behind her.

"My turn, Miss," he said, implying that he had been watching, and with, she had to admit, considerably less pleasure, she set about soaping his wrinkled skin diligently.

Zoe was busy in those showers, all afternoon. She lost count when she'd helped wash twenty or so men - but still they kept stepping into her little wet world.

As Madame had said, some were taking a shower before going upstairs for a fuck, and these were randy, and hard, and demanding.

Others were obviously spent, and stood calmly while she soaped their limp willies, and rinsed the sweat of their recent exertions from them.

Most of those men who had listened to her punishment earlier came down to see her, eager to take their turn at having a closer look at what the cane and crop had done to her voluptuous body. Quite a few made the most of her evidently subservient role by insisting, for example, that she get down on her knees to wash their feet, or use her tits to soap around their balls and bum.

She found this particularly difficult and humiliating, but the worst thing of all was when one rather tall, chubby man kept deliberately tripping her up and pushing her over - laughing as she struggled to get to her feet again, and making the most of poking her slippery body with his feet as she lay floundering on the wet floor.

At last, at last, after a seemingly endless time, Eric came to fetch her from the showers and allowed her to dry herself and sit in the inner reception area while he made her a cup of tea and a toasted sandwich - the first food and drink she had had since breakfast.

Madame came in in a coat - obviously just about to leave.

"What happens now?" Zoe asked her, forgetting that she wasn't supposed to speak.

Madame ignored the lapse. "Well, Eric and Carl have been complaining about not having been able to fuck you immediately after your punishment earlier. I was just going to look after the outer office for a while before I left, so they can have a little fun with you together. I'm sure you prefer two at a time, don't you, my little slut?"

It depends what they're doing, Zoe thought. Not when they're both caning me! But she kept quiet.

"Why don't you use the gym?" Madame suggested to Eric, before leaving them. "Perhaps you could make use of some of the equipment."

Without further ado, Zoe got dragged by Eric to the little gym, which had two or three pieces of apparatus in it, including a running platform - a treadmill - and a weights machine.

By the time a now naked Carl came into the room a few minutes later, Eric had already indulged some of his own dominant tendencies by having Zoe do some enforced exercise. He grabbed the crop Carl had brought in with him, and immediately began to lay into Zoe's bum as she jogged along the speeding conveyor, her hands on top of her head.

They teased and tormented her, keeping her at the increasingly strenuous exercises for at least half an hour, and taking turns with the crop - using it especially on her tits, which looked so spectacular as they bounced wildly up and down with her various exertions.

Then, when Zoe was really panting and sweating hard, they pushed her forwards over a bench and employed their raging erections at each end of her.

First Carl fucked her hard from behind while Eric forced his cock into her gasping mouth, then Eric took Carl's place behind her while Carl gave her a few final strokes of the crop on her back.

Zoe was so exhausted that she didn't need to be tied down. She lay collapsed across the bench, sack-like, her body yielding to the violent thrusting of the men. She had never felt so shattered, or so used - or so strangely contented.

She was glad, however, when at last it seemed to be over. Perhaps this long, demanding day had finally come to an end.

She looked up at the two doormen, and saw that they were also covered in sweat.

"Time for a shower," said Eric, hoisting Zoe to her feet.

"A long one for you!" Carl laughed. "Madame says to get you back onto shower duty for the rest of the evening."

Zoe felt crushed. Not more men to wash! She would dream about soapy willies!

"Only three more hours or so," the men taunted her. "You'll be the cleanest dirty slut in town!"

It felt like much longer than three hours before Zoe again caught sight of Eric, standing by the entrance to the showers watching her trying to avoid getting kissed by this long-haired skinny guy, whose armpits she was diligently soaping.

"Bedtime," said Eric eventually, and, quite exhausted, Zoe followed him gratefully upstairs and along the corridor, anxious to collapse into the privacy of a bed.

She found herself, however, ushered into one of the same little cubicles she had seen on her tour earlier - the ones which were used for 'business'.

"This is it," said Eric. "We've got no bedrooms here."

Zoe gazed miserably at the bare, only slightly padded couch. "Can't I get a sheet, or a pillow?"

Eric shrugged. "Haven't got any. You'll survive."

He made to leave.

"But these doors don't lock!"

"That's right. Can't risk a client trying to lock himself in with a girl."

"But the place is closing soon, right?"

"Oh no, love. We're open all night. The girls go home late evening, but there's always a few punters in even later. God knows what they get up to at four in the morning in these little rooms - I never look!"

Zoe was close to crying again. "Will you - can you tell people not to come in here?"

Eric shook his head. "It's up to the night boys. I should imagine they'll be pleased by the diversion, though."

He left, and Zoe climbed onto the plastic-covered bench and lay down. It was very uncomfortable. She tried using her arms as a pillow, but couldn't find a bearable position. She didn't see how she could ever fall asleep - especially with the light on. Though at first the cubicle seemed dark compared to the light in the corridor, once your eyes had got used to it, even the dim glow from the ceiling bulb was disturbing.

She must have slept in the end, though, for she very clearly remembered the abrupt awakening she received when someone suddenly climbed on top of her!

She jerked and screamed with shock. It was a young black man, and he wasn't alone. His slightly paler-skinned colleague stood by the side of her bench, and placed a heavy hand over her mouth.

"Hey, don't struggle, my beauty," this one said. "We're staff! We're allowed to fuck you!"

So this was the night shift.

"I'm Dave and this is Liam. We couldn't wait to try you!" Liam was already trying her! An obviously huge cock that she hadn't even seen was pushing its way deep inside her pussy. His onslaught was quite rough and his language very crude. There was no doubt he was enjoying himself, though, and when at last he had pounded his way to a climax, he grinned and giggled like a child who's had a treat, and kissed Zoe hard on the lips and on the tits, with exclamations of appreciation and gratitude.

"Me next," said Dave, pulling Liam out of the way, and sinking his own thick member into Zoe's spunk-sodden hole - so slowly, that Zoe couldn't help gasping and starting to enjoy herself.

Dave fucked her rather more gently, and her hand crept between his dark, lithe body and her own, working away quite urgently to ensure she achieved some pleasure herself.

The conversation between the two men helped her. "Oh, man! Why have we never had a Sauna Slave before?"

"Yeah, this is something else! And every night for two weeks, we've got her!"

"I was going to take a couple of days off, but I've changed my mind now."

"Look how these tits move! She's got better boobs than any of the pros, don't you think?"

"Definitely. And they're free!"

"God, are we going to have ourselves some fun."

"Hey, we could do a few guys some favours, couldn't we?"

"What, let them in here nights, you mean?"

"That's right. My mate Johnny would love this! And I know a few more, I can tell you."

"As long as Madame didn't find out."

"Well, if they paid to get in, there'd be no problem. They'd just be customers, right?"

"Right. I'll put the word out. Geez, you're going to get it, young lady! What's your name, by the way?"

She liked Dave and Liam - especially when Dave waited patiently for her to work herself up to orgasm, and Liam kissed her, all warm and wet and deep, just as she reached the magic moment. They were full of an aggressive energy, and certainly meant every word they said about bringing their friends in without thought for Zoe's opinion on the matter - but they were also good-natured, and easygoing, and fun, and when they eventually left her alone to get back to their jobs, it was after much fooling around and teasing and laughter.

But this wasn't to be the last time Zoe was woken from her sleep by male attention that night. She jerked awake a second time - she had no way of telling how much later, as nothing in the environment of the cubicle or the corridor outside had changed - with the realisation that the door was open and somebody was standing in the entrance, looking at her and wanking.

He stepped closer, and she saw that it was a non-descript, middle aged man. Without a word he came and ran his hands over her exposed, weal-covered body. He grabbed her head roughly, and forced his small cock into her mouth. She sucked on it automatically - what else could she do? - until he abruptly withdrew and deposited several spurts of thick semen all over her neck and breasts. She had hardly realised what had happened, when she saw that he'd gone already, without even having paused to acknowledge the part she had played in his pleasure.

This sort of thing was to occur every night during the time that Zoe was at the sauna. She didn't know if Madame was aware of it, but didn't dare object, guessing that her complaint would not be treated sympathetically.

She was mauled and spunked on and sometimes fucked for half the night - often what felt like all of it.

The men seldom spoke to her, just used what they found in that darkened, unlocked little cave of a room, then went on their way. It was unlikely that she would even recognise most of them again.

Sometimes the night staff came and watched or joined in, but since they usually both had her at the beginning of their shift, they tended not to bother too much about what was going on later in the night.

In the end, woken up so often to be used as she was, Zoe managed somehow to switch off from what was being done to her body and remain half asleep.

Amazing as it might seem, she would sometimes wake up with spunk dribbling out of her snatch, but no memory of who had put it there. Once she woke up on a bench downstairs in the sauna - she must have been carried there. Another time, Dave found her slumped in the corner of one of the toilets, with spunk all over her face. He shouted at her and gave her a spanking for having left her room - who could believe that she must have been too exhausted even to notice that she'd been dragged from her couch into the loos and given someone a blow job in a state of semi-consciousness?!

Zoe guessed that in future years, her sleep would often be troubled, as she dreamt that she was back in the sauna, and that hordes of shady men were groping at her sex while she slept!

After that first night, she was woken from a fitful doze by the aches and pains the pillowless bench had induced in her body. It felt like morning, though there was no way to tell in the windowless, constantly lit cubicle. She ventured out to the toilets and looked in on the pool and showers, but there was no-one about.

So she went back to the cubicle and sat herself down, wondering what the day would bring, until some time later Madame herself turned up and took her up to the lounge for a supervised breakfast of cereal and orange juice.

"We're closed from 6 am to 10 am," Madame informed her. "During this time, you will do the cleaning. Derek – " Madame indicated another muscle-ridden lad Zoe hadn't seen before sitting reading a paper in a corner " - will show you where everything is. The floors downstairs are to be mopped, the toilets cleaned, and the dustbins emptied. Make sure I don't find any used condoms lying about! Every corner needs checking! Then upstairs you need to vacuum, empty the ashtrays, and sort out the laundry. You are late today, so Derek will help you, but usually, you will do it all yourself. After all, that's what slaves are for, and the boys will appreciate a break."

Enjoying Zoe's dismal expression, the sadistic Madame carried on describing the content of Zoe's first full day at the sauna.

"After a sandwich at lunchtime - we don't do much in the way of food here, so you'll have to make do with what we can find - you will resume duties within the facilities. You will circulate around the pool, the tubs, the sauna, the steam room, the showers and the toilets. Your function will be to interest and arouse our customers so that they are inclined to come upstairs for a girl. You will let yourself get played with. You will play with the men - discretely of course, in the warm tubs, for example but, as I told you yesterday, you will not - I repeat absolutely not - allow them to penetrate you, or to come." Madame gave Zoe a savage glower. "This is imperative - do you understand? You must only take them so far, but you must not suck them or finish them off. They have to pay extra for that!"

Zoe thought about what had happened to her during the night - she was sure she'd been fucked by several customers already but she kept quiet. Maybe there were to be different rules for night time - or, more likely, none at all.

"You will continue with these general duties from lunchtime, right until late evening, unless we come and get you for some more specific duty. I certainly intend to get you fucked extensively, when the time is right, but for the time being I just want you being seen, with the objective of your presence supplementing our income by keeping the girls busy. Now hurry along with Derek and get mopping! And don't let me hear a word against you from anyone. From now on, you're the perfect Sauna Slave - or I'll have you caned and cropped again, every day!"

Madame picked up some files she'd left on the desk, and left.

Derek seemed a bit older than the other sauna employees she had come into contact with, and didn't offer her even the inkling of a smile. Fetching some keys, he showed her the contents of the cleaning cupboard next to the lockers, and, equipping her with a bucket, a sponge, a bottle of disinfectant, and some gloves, suggested she start in the toilets.

Depressed by the nature of the chore, Zoe nevertheless resolved to do her duties well, and set to work scrubbing toilet seats and floors with as much energy as she could muster. It was when she had nearly finished the downstairs toilets, and was down on all fours with her bum in the air, trying to reach the far corner of a cubicle, that she became aware of someone standing behind her.

Derek stood leaning on a floor mop, looking at her with a stony expression. He had abandoned the shorts he'd been wearing earlier, and a rock hard cock was jutting out from his hairy crotch.

Zoe felt a need to try to befriend him. "Am I doing this okay?" she asked, but he didn't reply. Instead, he slowly fed the mop handle through his hands and advanced towards her with the rounded end of it pointed straight at her upturned fanny.

She froze, scared, and watched it approach. When it touched her thigh, she tried to swivel away, but was trapped by the cubicle walls.

"Derek!" she cried, but now, at last, he had begun to smile, and she understood what amused him.

"Keep still," he said, "while I push this up your pussy."

She didn't dare do otherwise, and gasped as the hard, thick piece of wood crept past her sex lips and disappeared inside her. He kept pushing, and then started to fuck her a little with the thing. More than anything, Zoe felt extremely silly, impaled on the end of a floor mop! She found herself moving forwards in an attempt to escape the pressure, and ended up with her head right above the toilet bowl.

A little more twisting, and Derek pulled the mop handle out again, letting it drop to the floor.

Then all of a sudden, he had replaced it, crossing the tiled floor silently, yanking Zoe's posterior into position, and thrusting his own stiff rod urgently into her.

Zoe gasped, and grabbed the toilet seat for support, as Derek absolutely rammed into her, just about as hard as anyone ever had.

"This is me saying hello!" he growled. "And I'm going to say hello every morning before I start you off doing my job! Yeah - as a cleaner, I've never had a chance to delegate my work before! It's going to be fun following you round and watching you sweat, and getting you to suck me in between all the washing and cleaning you'll be doing! Wowee! You're what I call one good idea!"

Derek was as good as his word, and wouldn't leave Zoe alone for a minute while she laboured and sweated with the chores. Whenever he could he spanked or prodded her to work harder, and constantly pestered her sexually. His stamina was amazing - he never seemed to go limp. He made her suck him immediately after he'd come, and invariably sprung straight up stiff again. That first morning, and quite often afterwards, he fucked her no less than three times in as many hours.

Poor Zoe had thought yesterday was bad, but today seemed to be even worse! And it had only just started!

After, eventually, finishing her cleaning and seeing the last - for now - of the ever-randy, ever-pitiless Derek, Zoe endured a dismal lunch and then, feeling extremely nervous and alone, started her long afternoon of 'circulating' in the downstairs area of the sauna. At least she was able to move around the place today - unlike yesterday when she had spent so many hours just in the showers. No-one seemed to be supervising her, though no doubt if she had shown her face upstairs she would've got a telling off, so she wandered around naked, somewhat soothed by the warm, steamy air, and occasionally allowing herself a refreshing dip in the swimming pool - she hadn't been told not to.

For a while she was virtually alone, but it soon got busier as businessmen popped in during their lunch hour. She attracted lots of attention. The men followed her around wherever she went, so it soon became difficult to find a spot where there weren't several pairs of eyes on her, or thighs and hands sidling and roving in her direction. Some tried to engage her in conversation, and, while she hadn't specifically been told not to speak today, she answered very reluctantly, sure that she wasn't supposed to be responding like a normal human being - like a normal woman.

One guy persisted in questioning her, as she sat in the midst of several, inside the actual sauna itself.

"Go on, love, tell us how you got them scars? Got a caning did you? Bet it hurt."

But another young customer, who had just joined the group, admonished the first.

"Didn't you see the sign upstairs?"

"No. What sign?"

"The one that says 'Please do not talk to the Sauna Slave'."

"Oh."

"It also says," said another of the men, "'Please do not fuck the Sauna Slave'."

"Shame."

The men all stared at her, very blatantly.

"What do you reckon we can do with her, then?"

The first guy asserted his pushy nature once more, by grabbing one of Zoe's big tits.

"Fondle, I guess."

"And have a good look at." The younger guy pushed her legs apart and prised open her sex lips.

"And spank, perhaps," said someone else, twisting Zoe round and walloping her tender bum with a heavy hand.

And so the hours passed, with Zoe getting constantly felt up and teased and inspected, the men getting more and more carried away, as they saw how submissive and compliant she was. Several times, when they forced her hands around their swelling cocks, or made to push her head down to their nether regions, she was forced to speak up, and remind them that she wasn't supposed to be doing these things.

"I'm sorry, sir - I shouldn't," she would attempt, but more often than not, her pleas would be ignored and her mouth forced, for example, round somebody's cock - leaving her scared that Madame or one of the staff would walk in on her at any moment and be furious. There was little she could do, though. She was very much outnumbered, and the men were strong.

As the day wore on, these problems became worse and worse. Everywhere she was allowed to go was busy - even if she tried to hide in a toilet for a while, there would be men waiting to pounce on her when she came out. In the sauna and steam room she was spanked endlessly - the men looking out for each other by posting a guard outside, to warn of any staff on the prowl.

But worst of all were the plunge pools, into which she was regularly dragged by several men at a time to be fondled roughly beneath the murky water.

And of course the inevitable happened. She was soon being forced onto one cock after another, and silently shafted under the water.

Again she tried to tell the men, "Please, I don't think you're allowed to do this." But she was simply silenced with a hand over her mouth, or a cock or two inside it.

"I'm sure they don't mind really," the men would say. "Why else are you here, love?"

A couple of times Eric came downstairs to look in on her, but the men immediately assumed expressions of innocence and started chatting about the merits of one or other of the prostitutes upstairs - and in any case, Zoe wouldn't have dared complain. Perhaps they really were allowed to use her like this. Despite Madame's firm instructions earlier, she genuinely wasn't sure. The men were very good at soothing and reassuring her, and telling her that of course they could fuck her - but then they would be, wouldn't they!

The men came and went, but Zoe's day stretched on.

Once, a couple of the girls - ones she hadn't seen before - came down for a quick shower, but they didn't seem very friendly, even to the men, and had soon wrapped towels round themselves and disappeared again, with just a giggle and a smirk at Zoe, who at that moment was being squeezed up against a wall by a huge, rather overexcited guy.

Zoe longed for a break, and the chance to sit alone for a while with a cold drink, but still the men kept coming to gawp and play with her. And still she was forced to acquiesce to their furtive demands.

It was while she was in the hottest of the hot tubs, with some faceless character's cock working away inside her from behind, and her flushed, sweat-covered face being rubbed against no less than three naked pricks at the same time, that the dreaded thing happened.

Suddenly, Madame appeared round the corner, her dress sticking to her lumps and bulges in the heat.

"Zoe!" she snapped, making the poor girl jump up off the cock inside her with a huge splash. "Your Master warned me you were a slut, but this is ridiculous! Your first full day here, and already you are disobeying my most important instruction!"

"Madame," Zoe begged, disentangling herself from the crowd of men that had gathered around her. "I tried to stop them! I couldn't help it!"

The men now began to move away, doing their best to look innocent and disinterested, but Madame had focused all her wrath on Zoe.

"Well, I'm hardly going to blame the customers, am I?" she said. "You obviously enticed them too much! Get out of there, you little trollop. I'll teach you to steal business from my girls!"

Zoe climbed out of the hot water, emotionally drained by this obvious unfairness. She knew there was little point uttering another word in her own defense.

Madame ushered her into the sauna.

"Wait here til I return!" she instructed.

It was all Zoe could do not to get fucked again by the men who followed her into the little room to see what was going on. They smirked and sniggered like school boys, knowing that they had got her into trouble.

Madame returned with - horror of horrors - Derek, who was carrying a small barrel full of water, from which protruded the handles of what looked like three collections of birch twigs. He stood this beside the brazier, then straightened up and crossed his arms slowly.

"These are the birch twigs we provide for the use of our guests," said Madame, taking one of the bundles from the water. "No sauna would be complete without them. A well known method of massage - stimulating circulation beneath the skin."

Madame tapped the twigs gently against her lower arm. "Very pleasant, I'm sure."

Zoe couldn't take her eyes from the bundle of irregular twigs. She knew very well what they felt like on naked skin. It wasn't something you easily forgot. The sensation depended, of course, on the force with which they were applied!

Madame replaced the birch in the barrel, and turned to Derek. "What else have you got for me?"

Derek reached behind him and produced what had been hooked onto his belt - three pairs of metal handcuffs.

"Now, Zoe. Why don't you kneel down on the lower bench and place your arms up on the higher one. I'm sure you've worked out what I intend to do."

More concerned about the oppressive heat than anything else at that moment, Zoe looked about her in the hope that someone would speak up for her innocence and spare her his ordeal. But the sauna was crammed with men who were obviously keen to watch her plight, and were clearly not going to make a move to stop it. She even noticed a mass of faces at the window, as more spectators gathered around to see what the commotion was about.

Derek took it upon himself to help her get into position. He turned her towards the benches and pushed her in the back til she was forced to climb onto the lower one. The wooden slats dug into her calves immediately.

Clearly kneeling on them wasn't going to be a comfortable experience.

Derek took her wrists and dragged them up in front of her, to the back of the wide upper bench. Here he secured her simply and effectively by placing one wrist in one cuff, and passing the chain behind one of the planks of wood before securing the other. She was handcuffed to a sauna bench - the air around her head hot and dry, her big tits pushed against the scorching wood!

Next Derek saw to her ankles, fixing each to slats in the lower bench, just about as far away from each other as they would go. Her buttocks were dragged apart and everything - her gaping pussy and her tight little arsehole - was on view.

Zoe began to whimper. The position, the discomfort, the heat - the injustice of her treatment - all were beginning to get to her. Also, she suspected what was coming, and, remembering the severity of yesterday's punishment, was afraid of the pain that would soon be inflicted on her.

Madame withdrew a birch from the barrel again.

"I think, gentlemen," she said to the men sitting round in the sauna, "that you should perhaps leave me alone with this young lady - so none of you get hurt while I swing this, you understand. She will be left here for the rest of the day, so you will have your opportunity to give her a - er, massage yourselves."

The men departed reluctantly, and once outside, organised themselves into a queue - taking turns to peer through the window at what was going on within.

They saw Madame speak to Zoe again in a stern voice. They saw the birch twigs rise up into the air repeatedly, and descend on Zoe's back, bottom and legs with tremendous force. They saw Madame's huge tits wobble with her exertions and slip free from their flimsy restraints. They saw Derek sit down on the bench beside Zoe, and clamp a hand over her mouth so she didn't make too much noise.

It was a long, long time before Madame came out, looking very hot and exhausted. She walked wordlessly to the toilets, where she dabbed at her sweating brow with a dampened paper towel, then withdrew upstairs to her office, from whence, it was noticed, she didn't emerge for some considerable period.

Downstairs the men flocked back into the sauna to inspect the new patterns on Zoe's skin - little traceries of red lines between the healing, larger marks from yesterday.

Immediately, all three sets of birch twigs were lifted out from the barrel, as the health centre customers squabbled to follow Madame's example.

Zoe was in her own little world - almost fainting, her mouth still held in Derek's strong grasp. Admittedly the men didn't dare use the birches on her as hard as Madame had done, but to make up for this they found parts of her which hadn't yet had the benefit of the birch 'massage'. The sides of her breasts were now targetted, as were her outstretched arms, the soles of her feet, and - worst of all - her exposed sex.

She struggled and struggled, and tried to cry out, but was so surrounded by men intent on chastising her and mauling her, that she had no chance of escape or sympathy.

Derek, unable to control his arousal any longer, now freed her mouth with a harsh warning and, holding back the arm of the man at that moment birching Zoe's bum, slipped round behind her, and slipped his rock hard dick straight up her - for the fourth time that day!

Zoe, feeling his thickness inside her, was suddenly overcome by a strange feeling. It was despair, yes. It was extreme wretchedness and exhaustion. And yet, the extremity of these feelings was suddenly transposed into a phenomenal abandonment and arousal.

Suddenly, the now relatively gentle feel of the birch twigs on her back and arms seemed tolerable - almost pleasant.

Suddenly, the feel of countless hands exploring her naked, sweat-drenched flesh seemed wonderful.

And the cock - cruel Derek's plunging cock - was just exactly what she needed. Her pussy quivered with arousal. Her jaw dropped with the shock of how strangely and suddenly pain and discomfort had turned into excitement and pleasure.

She fought against her bonds, still, but now found herself enjoying the sensation of being restrained. And when someone pinched her nipples, the pain was delicious.

She just needed one thing now, and that was someone's fingers rubbing her clit! She was incredibly close to orgasm. She threw her head back, looking round at the men, trying to communicate her need without actually having to verbally beg. More than one caught her eye knowingly, and to her immense relief, she felt the soft, firm touch of fingertips rubbing the right place.

As Derek pounded away to orgasm, Zoe got there herself - thrusting her sore bottom back at him, wanking herself frantically against the well-placed fingers.

When she came - gasping and panting - at least six men came with her, much of their spunk falling on some part of her pleasure-racked body.

Oh dear, Zoe thought. She'd just been punished for letting men come when they shouldn't, and she'd immediately gone and done it again! But if punishment aroused them it would go on and on in an endless circle! She could never win!

Derek pulled out of her and headed for the door. Surely he couldn't mean to leave her here at the mercy of all these birch-wielding, highly aroused strangers? Another man was already lining up behind her to thrust himself into the wet hole Derek had just vacated.

"Derek, please! Don't leave me tied up in here!" she dared to call after him.

Derek paused and grinned. "Sorry, love. I can't remember where I put the keys to those handcuffs. Have to wait til Carl comes in in the morning with the spare set."

"No!" Zoe cried. "You can't leave me here all night! No - please!"

It seemed, however, that that was exactly what Derek planned to do.

"Don't worry - I'll get someone to bring you a drink later. Have fun."

"No!" gasped Zoe again, but he had gone.

The man standing behind her had now found his way into her hole.

"I thought you liked it, duck?"

What could Zoe say? She had liked it - she had come. But all night?

Simultaneously, Zoe felt the pain from birch twigs being drawn once more across her punished flesh, and - amazingly soon after her orgasm - another twinge of arousal in her pussy in response to her predicament.

Utterly confused, she dropped her head, and groaned.

Derek, though in general a plodding, unimaginative character, had now been given an opportunity to be creative, and actually spent much of his spare time mulling over the various ways Zoe could be put to use in the cleaning department.

He was responsible for one particularly humiliating idea that Zoe was rather disgruntled about, but to which Madame had given her blessing.

Customers had a tendency to leave wet towels lying around the place, and one of Derek's jobs had always been to collect them up and deposit them in the laundry baskets kept near the changing rooms. Why not get Zoe to collect them while he took a sauna and a swim himself? Why not get Zoe to collect them in her teeth?

He gave her a lesson in how to do it one morning, with Carl leaning against a wall nearby, watching.

"Why don't you tie her hands up behind her?"

"I was going to. That's what this little towel is for."

Zoe let herself get tied up and frowned down at the dirty wet towel lying on the floor nearby. She wondered what part of a man's anatomy it had been used to wipe clean.

"Down girl," said Derek, as if she were his pet dog, and she dropped to her knees and leaned forward to grasp the offensive piece of laundry in her teeth.

"It's a nice spunky one, with some suspicious brown stains! Could be mud off his feet, of course. Come on, get up now and carry it upstairs."

The men laughed at Zoe's expression of distaste, and followed her up the stairs, spanking her bum and prodding her when she tripped on the long towel she was dragging and had to try holding it at a more sideways angle.

Twice she dropped it, and twice she struggled to get an edge of it in her teeth again. At last she got to the top of the stairs, and Derek told her to start a pile in one corner.

She dropped the towel with relief, but was soon being shouted at to go downstairs again and carry on with her chore. "There's plenty of them round the place for you to collect." Derek knew this because he'd thrown a few extra ones into some corners a little earlier. "And don't let us catch you trying to do it with your hands. Here." He adjusted the towel wrapped around her wrists so it covered her hands completely. No chance of cheating, the way she'd just been thinking of doing!

So Zoe padded naked around the largely deserted sauna, periodically getting down on her knees to grasp a used towel in her teeth and dragging it back to a central point at the bottom of the stairs, before starting the boring task of getting them all up to the changing room.

She wouldn't have minded so much if she knew she'd be alone, but there was always someone popping down to watch her at work. It infuriated her when a couple of the men would come and sit by the pool, chatting and watching her work, because she knew that her exertions were contrived and unnecessary. With their help the chore would have been done in a fraction of the time! But that wasn't the way things were.

Sometimes, Madame would come down, showing a new customer or two around the facilities. She would point to the pool and the tubs, and then casually explain, "Oh, and that's the Sauna Slave cleaning up yesterday's laundry. Don't get in the gentleman's way, you clumsy fool!"

At last Zoe had found every stray towel in the place, and struggled up the stairs to transfer them from the pile to one of the laundry bins. But approaching the end of her task, the inevitable happened. Derek walked in and decided to be difficult.

"Who told you to use that one? It should be the right hand one today - come on, move them all over."

Of course the two laundry bins were just the same and it didn't matter in the slightest which was used, but this didn't stop Zoe having to bend over and struggle to transfer the towels again, still using only her teeth.

Watch her straining to reach the last one, her feet kicking in the air! Watch Carl come and push her into the bottom of the basket and cover her up with the water and spunk-sodden laundry! Oh, what fun those guys had with the sex slave!

Zoe, who during her time with Master Philip, and even before it, had already come to understand the degree of escapism brought about by SM activities, was nevertheless learning that lesson all over again - and how!

When you never saw daylight, you never wore clothes, you never watched telly, you never read a paper, you never used a telephone, you never went to a shop, you never chatted to a friend - it was as if those things ceased to exist. Within a few days, Zoe had become totally absorbed in her life as Sauna Slave. Water, and steam, and towels, and naked men, and birch twigs, were all that existed in her environment.

She felt like she was living on another planet. The only thing that helped her keep some sense of reality was that her stay here was only for two weeks. She kept count of the days, consoling herself all the time with the thought that her stay was nearly a quarter, then a quarter, then just over a quarter, then a third, over.

Early each morning she got a drink and some sort of breakfast, then spent three or four hours labouring over cleaning chores, watched over by Derek, or sometimes Carl. Then a supervised shower and tooth brushing, followed by a dreaded lunch in the lounge, with the girls just arriving, and delighting in mocking and pestering her.

Then Madame would often call her into the office for a lecture accompanied by a little caning or paddling, following which she would be dismissed into the bowels of the building to suffer hour upon hour of sexual torment from the flocks of men who were frequenting the sauna.

Apparently, it had never been so busy!

Since the men couldn't all get to Zoe, and some preferred privacy in any case, the girls upstairs - of which there seemed to be at least eight in total - were kept in employment. In fact, two or three additional ones were called in - housewives retained on standby in their suburban homes.

The men seemed happy to obey the first instruction on the sign in the inner reception area - 'Please do not talk to the Sauna Slave' - but largely ignored the second! There was little Zoe could do - she was constantly outnumbered, and constantly being shafted in some corner or other. The other men served to provide a screen, so even when Madame or one of the staff came down to see what was going on, Zoe had been released and the men were twiddling their thumbs innocently by the time anyone laid authoritative eyes upon her.

Nevertheless it was clear that the staff at least - Derek, Carl and Eric, and sometimes Dave and Liam, standing in from the night shift - knew very well what was going on, because she sometimes caught sight of them, standing at the back of the crowd watching - their cocks stiff.

At other times however, they would choose to take a different line, and either report her to Madame, who would come down full of what seemed to be genuine anger, or take it upon themselves to punish her for breaking the 'no fucking' rule. On these occasions, she would be put over one of the doormen's knees as they sat by the pool, and spanked extensively, sometimes with a shoe or a belt; or else she would be handcuffed or tied up with rope in the sauna again - in various positions, kneeling or lying across the hot benches, with usually her bottom and often her pussy exposed to anyone who might care to pay them some attention with the dreaded branches.

Zoe felt she could stand almost anything - to a certain extent she had got used to the pain of punishment on her bottom and tits - but each time the tips of the birch twigs caught her on her sensitive pussy lips, she thought she could never survive such pain!

Somehow, though, it never went too far. Somehow, the men by their presence managed to control each other's excesses, and though sometimes it seemed she was completely abandoned in her torment, it did eventually end, and she did manage to get some respite, and remember that this was all brought about by her passionate devotion to her Master - who she longed to see again soon.

With all the fingers and cocks and sometimes even tongues that were constantly paying attention to her private parts, Zoe could hardly help spending a lot of her time aroused. And this led to a constant craving for orgasm.

In fact, she managed to come two or three times a day - and maybe once or twice at night - and this was the one positive thing in her present existence. Her sexual enjoyment went a little way towards counteracting the degree of pain she was suffering from her regular punishments and frequent rough handling.

This state of affairs wasn't to last, however.

One afternoon, as she was lying on the floor in a corner of the steam room with a cock in her mouth, several fingers up her pussy, and quivering at the point of imminent orgasm, the dreaded Madame once again walked in on the action. Apparently, Zoe was to learn later, she had one of the customers to thank for this, who had been sent to spy on her!

Madame turned purple with fury. "Right, that's enough!" she stormed. "How dare you be thrashing around pleasing yourself, instead of spending all your energies serving and attending to our clients!"

Zoe knew that the clients wanted to arouse her and watch her come - and suspected that Madame knew they did too - but there was no point complaining.

"Get up, you slut! From now on I'm going to keep you chained up in one of the cubicles, with your hands behind your back, so you won't be able to indulge yourself. Slaves exist to provide pleasure, not take it! You've obviously been having too much fun down here!"

And so Zoe was marched away from her escapist cocoon of warmth, pain and pleasure, and pushed into the end cubicle in which she usually spent - or at least started - the night.

Carl was summoned, and with a drill had soon firmly embedded a large metal hook in the middle of the far wall. Madame then produced from her office some lockable, leather wrist cuffs and a length of heavy black chain. Within half an hour, Zoe had lost the use of her hands, and been chained to the wall of a bare little room - her prison within a prison.

"Kneel down," Madame demanded, and Zoe obeyed. The chain was long enough for this but not, as she would later discover, quite long enough to allow her to lie down comfortably along the couch. From tonight on, Zoe was to spend her nights lying across the floor at the end of the cubicle, or slumped uncomfortably in the corner of the couch, trying to find a bearable position to sleep in.

And of course she could no longer use her fingers to secretly pleasure herself!

Madame was still standing over her, and Zoe could tell that she was in store for another lecture. Madame was waiting, however, for the girls to join her, which they soon did - crowding into the room and some sitting down along the couch, waiting to hear what Madame had to say.

Zoe had been pleased that she had largely avoided coming into too much contact with the girls, who tended to be so unpleasant towards her. She didn't look forward, therefore, to finding out how the girls were now to be more closely involved in her continued slavery!

"Girls," said Madame. "This is the pleasure slave who, it seems, can't be trusted not to let your potential customers spend themselves up her sluttish cunt."

There was a murmur from the gathered prostitutes.

"So, as you can see, I've chained her up, as befits her position, and I suggest she be put to use helping you get through the punters as quickly as possible. How about if you use this room in rotation - we'll charge the customers more for it - and let the slave suck the guys hard, so they're nice and ready for you? And if any of them wanted to get a little rough, you could simply point them in her direction."

The girls discussed it amongst themselves. "Sounds okay," one said to Madame. "As long as we don't have to talk to her or touch her."

"Yeah, make sure she keeps out of our way!"

"Of course," said Madame. "Zoe will kneel quietly in the corner, with her eyes to the floor, and merely make her mouth available when required. I will instruct her to show you the greatest respect, and never speak unless spoken to."

There was a little more whispering. "Madame, we have another suggestion."

"Go on."

"Well, so many men come quicker when their back passage is explored - perhaps she could lick their arseholes while they fuck us?"

"Perfect!" said Madame, noting how the colour rushed to Zoe's face at this new idea. "I'm amazed I didn't think of it myself! She can crawl onto the end of the bench, or stand and lean over. Yes, what a fitting place for a slave's face to be - buried in the depths of a client's bum, using her tongue to please him round his arsehole, and on his balls! Zoe, you know what you have to do. I expect you to do it diligently and without complaint. And until further notice!"

One long day passed, and then another, and Zoe was indeed mainly engaged in the occupation Madame had so heartlessly prescribed.

A girl would bring a client into Zoe's cubicle. She would explain that if he wanted to be sucked, the slave would do it. Then, when the man was ready to fuck and climbed on top of the prostitute, he would be asked whether he'd like the slave to attend to him from behind while he did so.

Most of the men who were brought into the cubicle did, and so Zoe's poor tongue muscles were strained as she licked and probed endlessly - humiliated and uncomfortable, but with never a thought of complaint. As she couldn't use her hands, which remained permanently cuffed behind her, to help - that is, to help part buttock cheeks, for example - she spent much of the time feeling she was going to suffocate. Sometimes she would come up for air, gasping, only to have the client or the girl shout,

"Keep licking, you lazy little bitch!"

She longed for the occasional drinks of water brought to her. Food didn't matter so much - she had rather been put off it!

She also spent much of her time needing to go to the toilet. It seemed she was often forgotten, and once or twice when she had dared to speak up and tell one of the girls that she was bursting, nothing had happened. They had left her deliberately in prolonged misery.

In general, the girls continued to look down on Zoe dreadfully, and treated her with complete disdain.

Sometimes, between customers, they would come and torment her - pulling her hair and slapping her face. Using her, it seemed, to vent some of their own frustration and anger.

At nights, and even during the afternoons and evenings - whenever any of the men found the door to her cubicle open and her alone within it - Zoe would still find herself getting fucked, and this continued to get her into trouble.

Once, for example, a huge big muscular guy came and hoisted her onto her feet, pressed her forwards over the bench, and fucked her from the back, so long and so noisily that his thumping and grunting and the rattling of her chains could be heard down the other end of the corridor - and drew the attention of one of the girls, who soon came running with Madame in tow.

"Look what she's doing! Look!" the girl squealed. "She shouldn't be doing that, should she, Madame?"

"Certainly not," fumed the heartless proprietress, and said politely to the man, who had just finished, "If you wouldn't mind stepping aside, sir, I have to punish this incorrigible slut yet again."

Madame took a little switch from where she had been carrying it in her belt, and, holding Zoe down firmly with one hand, started to bring it down heavily and repeatedly on Zoe's fleshy buttocks.

"Slut! Slut! Slut!" Madame said as the switch fell and fell. "When - will - you - learn - you - little - tart!"

Zoe positively howled with the pain and the injustice of it. Her chains rattled as she struggled and shook with frustration. The girl who had reported her stood by, watching and giggling, and virtually jumping up and down with righteous glee.

"That's it! Give it to her," she mouthed, under her breath. "More, more, yes!"

Eventually, Madame strutted from the room with an expression of disgust, but a little later, she returned with a small sign which she hung around Zoe's neck with another chain. It said, 'Please do not fuck the Sauna Slave without an appointment.'

Zoe's face flushed with humiliation as she read it.

"Since you're so keen to get shafted, you great slag, I've given Mad Melvin and Weird Winston a ring - a few hours alone with the two of them might just put you off sex for a while! Oh, and from now on," Madame whispered in Zoe's ear. "Whenever anyone enters this room, they are to find you not only kneeling and with head bowed, but with your mouth wide open and your tongue sticking out - to indicate your function! Maybe, eventually, we'll teach you to behave!"

Despite being chained up in the cubicle all afternoon, all evening and all night - with perhaps the occasional release to visit the toilet or get some meagre refreshment - Zoe was freed from her bare prison in the mornings, in order that she might continue to fulfil her function of cleaner.

Usually, her hands were freed, or sometimes chained together in front of her, but on this one particular occasion, they were kept shackled together tightly behind her back.

Derek, who tormented her daily as she performed her chores, had a particularly mischievous expression on his face today, and yanked her roughly downstairs to the steam room, where stood a large soapy bucket and nothing else.

"Madame has decided that this floor needs some extra attention," said Derek. "You will wash it with your hair."

Now this was not the first time that Zoe had been instructed to use her lovely thick blonde tresses as a floor mop - she had been forced to clean the showers and the toilet floor in that manner just the other day. It had been unpleasant and difficult, and grossly humiliating, especially as Derek had stayed to watch her. Her heart sank at the thought of doing it again, but she reminded herself, as she often did, that every such unpleasant task was designed to test her devotion to her Master - and she was determined to pass that test.

"Well, what are you waiting for?" Derek demanded.

She indicated her arms, held together behind her. "You haven't released me," she whispered.

"I'm not going to! Madame's special instructions." His smirk was particularly infuriating.

Zoe felt the blood rush to her face. This was too much!

"How can I do it with my hands tied behind me? It's not possible."

"Difficult maybe, but not impossible. Just dunk your head in, and smear your hair around on the floor. We'll hose the suds down later."

Zoe began to shake. "I can't do it, I can't!"

"Start now, or I'll go and get Madame."

"I don't believe she said it! I don't believe you!"

Derek stared into her flushed face, then abruptly turned on his heel and disappeared.

Zoe sat down on the tiled bench, looking at the ominous bucket of soapy water, and feeling broken.

She had tried - she had tried so hard to do all that had been asked of her without complaint. But surely they were asking the impossible - surely they were!

She jumped up when Derek returned, with Madame right behind him. There was no doubt that he had enjoyed the opportunity of grassing on Zoe to authority.

"Good morning, my dear. What's this all about?"

Zoe dropped to her knees, pleading.

"Madame! Derek says you suggested it, but it can't be true! He wants me to wash the floor with my hair. I'd do it, I've done it before, but I need my hands - to lean on, and to wring my hair out and move it around. He won't let me free. He says I have to do it with my hands tied behind me, but it can't be possible. Please, Madame!"

Madame gave a big sigh, her cleavage heaving.

"Zoe, don't distress yourself. It is certainly possible, because I have seen it done before - and that with a girl who had considerably shorter hair than you. As to whether I instructed it - I did. You only have a few days left with us, and when your Master asks about the manner in which you have been used, I want to have some nice extreme examples ready to tell him about. Now compose yourself, and prepare to begin. I'm disappointed in you; you should at least have tried, before disgracing yourself by begging in this way!"

But Zoe still couldn't believe it. She knelt mutely, shaking her head.

"Derek, fetch me the birch from next door."

"No, no!" Zoe almost shouted. "Not the birch! Okay, I'll try it!"

"Not just try, but succeed," said Madame coldly. "Derek, carry on - fetch me the birch anyway. The sight of it may inspire her further to obedience."

Now Zoe had done some trying things in her time, but she had never found anything quite so difficult or undignified as washing the floor of that steam room with her hair, and with her hands fixed uselessly behind her.

And there was no escape! She knew she wouldn't be let out of the room until she had finished. She had to face this supreme horror and overcome it.

The positions poor Zoe had to assume! The contortions she had to undergo!

Imagine her, splitting her legs, bending her knees, tipping forwards until most of her long hair was in the water - losing her balance, maybe, and falling into the bucket up to her neck - coming up spluttering, and blinking to try to get the suds out of her eyes.

Imagine her kneeling on the floor and pulling her wet hair around on the grubby tiles, moving her head from side to side and round and round til she was dizzy.

Imagine Derek putting a foot on her bum and pushing her forwards - splat, face down on the wet floor - then insisting she get up quickly and carry on working. She's hardly started - that whole side hasn't been touched, and she's got to get into all the corners and make sure they're spotless!

Imagine her trying to work on her back instead - lying flat on the floor, thrashing and twisting around as she drags her wet hair along the edges of the room. Imagine Madame shouting instructions and deliberately walking over bits already cleaned, just so that Zoe can clean them all over again.

Imagine Zoe thinking, at last, that she's finished, only to be told that, in fact, she has to go over the whole floor again with clean water, and then a third time, with her hair wrung out, to dry it!

Imagine her feelings at being told that she would have to do the same back-breakingly difficult chore regularly from now on - and, as of tomorrow, with her feet as well as her hands shackled together!

And imagine her utter misery at Madame telling her that her efforts would be videoed and shown to her Master, in order to demonstrate to him how good she was at the task, and to support Madame's recommendation that he use her at home in this way - to clean the kitchen and bathroom floors daily!

The day finally came when Zoe, kneeling in her corner and exhausted from a morning of polishing the floor of the showers with her breasts, realised that the man on whose entry into the cubicle she had dropped her eyes and opened her mouth, was her beloved Master Philip.

He was clothed in his customary black leather, and was accompanied by Madame, who closed the cubicle door with an instruction to one of the staff outside that they not be disturbed.

"Aha, here she is, my little plaything! How pretty she looks in those chains!"

The sound of his deep familiar voice was too much for Zoe. At last he had come to take her away from this place, back into his own harsh but loving presence!

She flung herself down onto the floor at his feet, and began to sob with joy and relief.

"She has missed you, I think," said Madame, and looked on as Master Philip crouched down and began to indulgently stroke his slave's head.

"I must have both you and her tell me every detail of what has occurred," he said. "I wonder how the accounts will differ?"

"I have been harsh with her," said Madame, "but I think you will find I have assessed her limits correctly. She is a very special creature, I must say. You are lucky to have found her."

"Such creatures are made not found," Master Philip replied, "though I admit she seems to have the natural tendency. And I will make her even more special, believe me!"

He lifted Zoe up and sat her on the bench on which so much action had taken place. He kissed her, and wiped the tears from her eyes.

"Zoe, you must tell me," he said gently. "Have you or have you not enjoyed being a Sauna Slave? Yes or no?"

Zoe leaned against his strong, familiar form, and wondered what on earth to say. Everything that had happened over the last two weeks flashed through her mind, together with the varied emotions that had accompanied the events.

She felt sure this was a test in itself. What did her Master want to hear? No might mean she was unhappy with her lot and was drifting away from him, while yes would imply things hadn't been strict enough, which was certainly not the case. She felt like she had been driven to the very limits of endurance.

It seemed that no was the proper, role-playing answer - but yes was what was hidden in the depths of her soul.

"Master, I'm sorry," she said, looking up at him. "The answer is yes and no. Or no and yes - the no comes first! I cannot say one or the other."

Her Master hugged her to him. "You have given me the answer I hoped for. This is the way it should be."

Madame looked on with interest and some jealousy at the obvious devotion between slave and Master, and wondered if she should leave them alone. Master Philip had not forgotten her, however.

"Zoe," he said. "Madame has asked for a special favour from you. She could have demanded it, but, being aware of your tendencies, hesitated."

Zoe looked over at Madame, and found the look in her eyes kinder than she had ever seen it before.

"Madame would like you to express your gratitude for the way she has looked after you by – " he flashed a look at Madame " - paying some attention to her quite stupendous breasts."

At a different time, Zoe might have found this instruction more than difficult, but she was so moved by her Master's long awaited return, that it seemed a small thing.

"Of course," she said. "Anything you ask, Master!"

And so, for the first time in her life, Zoe found herself kissing, sucking and licking at a pair of huge droopy female breasts. Not just any breasts, but those of the very woman who had whipped and caned her so mercilessly, and caused her so much hardship and distress. Yet such was her state of mind that she was not at all reluctant, but fell on those big soft mounds of flesh, when they were lifted free for her, with genuine enthusiasm and pleasure.

What happened next was a greater shock to Zoe, but she also took it in her stride. Her Master's presence did indeed inspire her to be more and more special!

Master Philip, who had been watching Zoe suck on Madame's big nipples, suddenly whipped a stiff cock out of his trousers, and made a meaningful approach, not to Zoe, but to Madame!

"Do you mind?" he asked the big woman politely, while already hoisting her tight skirt up in anticipation of a favourable reply.

Zoe stepped back as her Master took up position in front of Madame and with one well aimed thrust, impaled her still standing bulk on his shaft. Madame sighed and moaned and seemed to be mounting very quickly to orgasm.

Master Philip gave Zoe a glassy-eyed, sidelong look. "I thought you were supposed to perform a certain service on men fucking in here?"

Hesitating for just a moment with the surprise of what she was witnessing, Zoe fell to her knees again and began to kiss her Master's leather-clad bottom. Her hands were still held behind her, as usual, so she used her teeth to pull at his belt until his firm and quite beautiful buttocks were exposed.

This time she performed her often hated task with rapture, though her feelings were very mixed when he and Madame seemed to reach a simultaneous, mutually satisfying climax.

Worse still, when her Master had withdrawn from taking his pleasure in that big, hot snatch, he pointed his wilting, sticky cock in Zoe's direction, and told her to lick it clean!

When Zoe complied, she knew she was lost. If she would do this, she would do anything.

Madame put away her tits and made to pull down her skirt, but Master Philip stopped her.

"One more service, Zoe." He pointed. "Lick my spunk from the thighs of the woman I have just fucked."

It seemed her humiliation was never to end, but she did as she was told, and would long remember the feel of moving her tongue over the full, sticky thighs of her tormentress, with that hot feminine smell wafting down on her from above.

"Excellent!" said Master Philip, zipping up his fly and returning from his own erotic high. "I'm very pleased with her progress here. You have just the right touch, Madame."

Zoe was ready to leave now - very ready. She wanted a change of environment. She wanted to be out of chains. To sleep in a bed, to wear clothes, to walk outdoors with the wind in her hair.

We can only imagine, therefore, her emotions on her Master's next pronouncement.

"In fact," he said, "since she's getting on so well - and since by her own admission she enjoys it - I think I could leave her here for another week or so, if that's alright with you, Madame. I'm sure a little more floor scrubbing and arse worship won't do her any harm. Bye bye, Zoe dear. Be good!"

Chapter Three

BONDAGE

After her three difficult weeks in the sauna, Master Philip gave Zoe a week off from being a slave.

During this time he kissed her and made love to her and told her he loved her so much, that she was more than ever emotionally bound to him, and more ready than ever to prove herself by submitting to whatever testing experience he might choose to put her through next.

The next experience in fact began with her introduction to a very tanned, very fit man, perhaps a little younger than her Master, who one day appeared on the doorstep with a suitcase.

"This is Bret," she was told. "He used to be my personal fitness trainer, but he's moved into a more specialist field. He's a bondage expert."

Bret shook both their hands. "Hi!" he said. "I've been looking forward to this! I've got piles more equipment in the car - shall I bring it in now?"

Master Philip helped him carry two more cases and several mysterious boxes into the hallway, and Zoe was sent to fix drinks. The men chatted like old friends, as they collapsed into the soft seats in the main room.

"Nice place you've got here," said Bret.

"Thanks," said Master Philip. "The service usually isn't bad either. Hurry up, Zoe! And don't forget the ice."

As Zoe served Master Philip and his guest drinks, she once again found her obedience being tested in front of a stranger. This time, she threw herself into her role with some enthusiasm and excitement.

Although she had survived the sauna, and done her Master's wish in serving a woman, being in a men-only environment was still her preference, especially with her much-adored Master present.

Bret seemed such a big hulk of a man. He radiated fitness and masculinity, and she wondered what precisely her relationship with him was to be. She was soon enlightened.

"What do you think of her?" Master Philip was asking, as Zoe preened and stretched herself before the two men, according to her Master's orders.

"Very nice," said Bret, tipping his head to one side as he watched Zoe move. "Promising. Looks quite supple."

"Yes, I've kept her well exercised. The bondage side of things has always interested me, though, and I don't think I've experimented with it sufficiently. I'd like to see what her body can take. Really see her stretched and bent into the most extreme positions. Take some unbelievable photos to show my friends, that sort of thing!"

Bret nodded. "I know just what you mean. Don't worry - I'm sure you'll be impressed. I've got lots of ideas! May I try something?"

"Of course, she's all yours."

Bret stood up and advanced towards Zoe, at present standing on tiptoe in the middle of the room with her arms stretched up above her head. He paced around her, bending to feel up and down her legs as if she were a racehorse, and lifting her tits up for inspection as if they were something he'd picked up on a market stall.

Then he pushed her on the shoulder and said, "Lie down."

Zoe lay face down on the floor, arms still out above her, and found her wrists being taken from behind and lifted up and back. At the same time, a foot pressed itself into the small of her back, causing her whole upper body to arch painfully backwards.

Bret knew exactly what he was doing, and bent and stretched her body it seemed almost to breaking point. He pulled on her arms, moving them around behind her, testing the present limits of her shoulder and arm joints. Even Master Philip worried for a moment when he saw the extremity of the positions Bret achieved, and the look of silent agony on Zoe's face, but Bret seemed in control, and satisfied.

"Not bad at all," the trainer muttered almost to himself, "but we can get her much further back than this. Wait til I've finished with her - it's all a matter of working on those muscles and joints. I could turn her into a contortionist if you wanted."

He let Zoe's painfully wrenched arms fall back to the floor, and turned her over with his foot. Then he grabbed her lower legs and bent them back over her torso. She gasped as he once again stretched her poor muscles to their limit. The thought of being under the control of this man for the indefinite future began to be more frightening than she'd anticipated.

Still he pushed on her legs and stretched them apart, until her thigh muscles screamed for relief. She longed to voice a complaint, but glancing over at her Master, caught his warning glance.

Her calves were now almost touching her shoulders, and Bret was kneeling between her legs. Suddenly he seemed distracted by her pussy, and, letting her free, stood up.

"We'll have to have a word about the rules," he said, fumbling for his drink. "It can be a tempting occupation, this."

"Good heavens, man," said Master Philip. "Of course you'll be allowed to fuck her, if that's what you mean. I wouldn't expect you to stay under the same roof and work with her every day, and not be able to make the most of it!"

Bret regained his cool. "Thanks. I hoped it would be like that, but some clients get funny about, you know, being the only one."

Master Philip shook his head. "Anything you like. I give you carte blanche. I'll tell you what - why don't we have her sleep with you tonight, so you can really get to know her before you start working together?"

Bret nodded his thanks, and settled further into the sofa, looking at Zoe sprawled naked on the floor, and beginning to feel much more at home. This assignment was going to be fun!

Bret immediately took over from Master Philip as the man to whom Zoe had to submit daily. He was always polite and businesslike, but expected her to give of herself to the utmost, in every possible way.

Each day became a stringent routine of training, exercise and bondage. Zoe felt like she was at some strict military college all of her own. She was constantly forced to give her attention to this amazingly overbearing man who barked orders at her and often seemed to be asking the impossible.

Two whole rooms and the secluded garden were all put to use for Zoe's new exercise routine.

In the garden, she was made to trot round and round her trainer on the end of a rope, her arms pulled punishingly tightly up behind her shoulder blades, and a horsewhip encouraging her to raise her legs like a pony at every step. This was to develop the thigh muscles which, she was warned, would be suffering more than ever before.

Also, she was made to march endlessly up and down the lawn, using a slow, Russian-style step - lifting her legs high and straight every time. Often she was naked, but Bret had brought a special rubber body suit with him which was lined with a thin sheet of lead, and made every movement and exercise ten times more difficult. This began to be used regularly.

In the rooms upstairs, she would be forced to do press-ups - hundreds and hundreds of them - usually with a heavy rucksack on her back, and often with a whip or strap being laid regularly over her naked or rubber-covered buttocks. This was for the arm muscles, of course, and it was true - she could feel herself getting stronger.

Much of her training involved stretching exercises. For example, with her legs forcibly kept straight by the application of iron bars, and her ankles shackled closely together, she would be forced to repeatedly touch her toes. Bret would stand beside her with a cane, and give her a stroke across her buttocks each time she successfully reached her toes.

"Hold it!" he would shout, while she strained floorwards. "Good. And again!"

At first it had seemed so difficult, but with practice she could somehow bend more and more at the waist, and after a few days he had her resting her palms on the floor - even with high heeled shoes on!

What would normally happen was that after several dozen similar exercises, Bret would catch hold of Zoe's wrists and bind her in position at maximum stretch. She therefore knew, for example, that the toe touching would be followed by an hour or two bent double with her wrists chained firmly to her ankles or the floor.

He also worked tirelessly on stretching her legs apart. Zoe would never have thought she was supple enough to do the splits, but after a week or so of horrendous - but carefully monitored and never overdone - exercises, she found herself regularly sitting split-legged on the floor or on a bar, like the most accomplished ballerina or gymnast.

Bret particularly liked her to do the splits standing up, and she spent many hours standing on one leg in front of him - the other pointing skywards. He often strapped a leg to her upper body and left her balancing like that - very aware of how blatantly the position exposed her sex to his view.

He really enjoyed fucking her while she was stretched out like this;

he would take her standing up at the end of a prolonged leg stretching session. Bret had a thing about a woman's legs stretched out absolutely as wide as they would go, therefore symbolising her availability and exaggerating her pussy's welcome to any man about to fuck her. He planned to incorporate this position frequently into Zoe's bondage experiences!

Another thing he would do was put Zoe in suspension - again to stretch her. An hour or two hanging by her wrists with a weight dangling from her ankles wasn't particularly pleasant, but it did wonders for being able to get into astonishing bondage positions, and thus giving pleasure to her Master!

Towards evening, Bret would prepare Zoe for her Master's return from work, by putting her in some sort of stringent and erotic bondage. When Master Philip came home, the men would usually eat together and then inspect and discuss the way Zoe was presented. Often, they would fuck her together, while she was tied up, and frequently they would whip her.

Sometimes, though, much to Zoe's annoyance, Master Philip would announce that he had to go out again, and would leave her to an evening of frustration and boredom as Bret sat and watched telly or made phone calls on business of his own.

The bondage positions Zoe became familiar with were many and varied - Bret was nothing if not creative! They could of course be described in detail, but it might be best to leave something to the reader's imagination! Mix the following ingredients and see what you come up with!

Hoods, gags, blindfolds, handcuffs, shackles, rope, chains, corsets, boots, rubber suits, leather straps, nipple-clamps, dildos, stocks, wall-bars, punishment stools, whipping frames, a hoist, a crate, a cage, a sack, a saddle, a model aeroplane (wouldn't you like to know!) - and last but not least, a struggling, straining, panting, moaning, naked, luscious, very willing, near orgasmic Zoe!

A lot of photos got taken of Zoe in bondage, and these ended up plastered over the walls of what became the main bondage room, or dungeon. Their presence gave the men who were occasionally invited to partake of Zoe's charms something to look at, while they waited their turn to spank and fuck her!

A little game that Bret came to enjoy was to hide Zoe somewhere in Master Philip's house, for him to find on his return. A particular challenge was to do it in the main lounge where the two men often sat and chatted and drank together.

The first time, Master Philip guessed quite quickly that Zoe was doubled up inside the drinks cabinet, but this was slightly because of Bret's unusual reluctance to accept a second glass of scotch, the fetching of which would have given the game away.

The second time took a little longer, and when it was finally revealed that Zoe was inside the little box on which a table lamp was standing, her Master was extremely impressed. He had considered it, he said, but had genuinely thought it must be far too small to be hiding the whole of his Zoe. He hadn't counted on how advanced Bret's bondage methods had become.

On the third occasion, however, Master Philip was truly flummoxed. "Okay, I give up," he announced. "She can't possibly be anywhere in this room."

Bret grinned and grinned, then pointed to the recently acquired designer beanbag on which Master Philip had been reclining.

"You're sitting on her!" he announced with glee.

Master Philip looked down between his legs with wonder, and then settled himself down more comfortably on his seat.

"Touché!"

One morning, after a relatively conventional hour or so's cavorting in bed with a rarely unbound Zoe, Master Philip lay back with a contented sigh.

"I've really been enjoying this bondage business. Have you?"

Zoe formulated a reply. Sometimes, she was about to say, when it's not too uncomfortable. And when you're around, so I can enjoy the fact that I'm pleasing you.

"Yes or no?!"

Zoe sighed. "Yes, Master."

"Bret seems to be very competent, don't you think?"

"Definitely, Master."

"I suspect he'll be wanting to move on soon, but he's given me some useful pointers. You can expect to be tied up regularly, even when he's gone."

Zoe burrowed up against her Master's warm naked body, and kissed his chest repeatedly by way of reply. She accepted his terms.

"Anyway, what I was going to say," Master Philip continued, "was that it's about time we had you tied up in public. Severely tied up. I want to watch people marvel at you and be jealous of me!"

"How the hell are you going to manage that?" Zoe blurted out rather disrespectfully. "You mean the car parks again?"

"No, no. That riff-raff has its uses, but they wouldn't appreciate it properly. I want a slightly more refined audience." He squeezed Zoe's arm - just slightly too painfully, as was his wont. "We're going to visit some Fetish Clubs!"

There were several Fetish Clubs operating in the city - essentially night clubs, but with strict dress codes of rubber, leather and all else outrageous, and not to be found advertising in any mainstream publication.

Some were quite tame, essentially providing a stage for fashion-conscious but not particularly liberated exhibitionists, but others more than tolerated SM games, and if you went to the right club, at the right venue, on the right date, with the right people there, you could see - and participate in - some quite serious action.

Bondage equipment was often provided, and whipping and caning were common, especially as the night wore on.

Now Zoe had been to one or two such clubs before, enjoying being able to have her tits out on the dance floor, and becoming intrigued by the sorts of little scenes that went on in corners. But she had never been 'properly', as it were, in a slave role, and certainly not in bondage. She had no doubt Master Philip knew what he was doing, though, and genuinely looked forward to their first outing.

To her delight, it transpired that Bret was to go with them.

A pretty special evening started after tea, when Zoe unexpectedly found both men climbing into the shower with her for some extended and wonderfully intimate sex play. She felt fantastic when she got wrapped in towels and carried by Bret into the bedroom, where he threw her on the bed and went down on her while Master Philip stood and looked on indulgently before joining in to make a phenomenal threesome.

Afterwards, with Zoe still tingling from the aftermath of a lovely orgasm, they took her into the bondage room, fetched themselves some drinks, and spent nearly two hours getting her ready to go out, and in the process getting themselves just nicely excited again.

Zoe was dusted with talc and then carefully squeezed into a tight rubber suit with heart-shaped holes in it to allow her breasts and buttocks to bulge out, naked and inviting to the touch.

A tight rubber corset was added over the top of the rubber suit, constricting her waist erotically, and sending her into paroxysms of pleasure as both Bret and Master Philip strained to pull it as tight as possible.

Her arms were fastened behind her - held firmly by a thick leather sleeve that bound them together from top to bottom and made her hands useless by means of stiff mitten gloves.

Black, thigh-length boots got pulled on over her rubber clad legs, and the men joked and laughed as they knelt on the floor together and carefully did up the laces, one leg each.

A little zip between the legs of the catsuit gave access to the wearer's important bits, and Master Philip made sure this was left open during the preparations. Occasionally he would give Zoe's wet pussy a little poke, which kept her nicely on the boil and getting more and more excited about the evening to come.

Next, some cuffs were attached to Zoe's ankles and she was hobbled with an extendable bar. They experimented, and Zoe found to her horror that the thing seemed to have no limit. At three feet plus, it was still stretching her legs painfully apart, and she was very relieved when it got set back to only about a foot again. Even so it was difficult and humiliating to walk with. Very erotic too, though, she had to admit.

Next her lovely hair was squashed and flattened with a rubber hood. This had small holes for her eyes, but covered her ears completely, so from this point on she was already existing in a world of muted sound, making her feel remote and isolated, but strangely secure.

Then a large ball gag was inserted into her mouth, which rather shocked her. She'd expected to be able to communicate during the evening (and drink!) but now she realised she was to be totally dependent on her

Master - without a voice of her own, and therefore without an identity except as his slave.

Some discussion followed between Bret and her Master about whether her attire was now sufficient. It seemed that they decided it wasn't, because she was next wound around with some white rope - entirely for effect, since her arms and legs were already well-restrained - clashing deliberately with the black of her costume.

Then a collar was put around her neck, and two leads clipped on to it - one for each of her male companions to lead her around with!

Finally, a heavy chain was attached at one end to the collar, and at the other to the leg spreader. This forced her to lean her upper body forwards quite severely, resulting in the most embarrassing posture imaginable, with her naked buttock cheeks thrusting out backwards for all to see and play with!

All Zoe's cheeks flushed as she thought of the delightful humiliation of the night ahead!

The men left her standing while they got ready, and it was almost an hour before they returned to their plaything, and announced, "Okay, it's time to go."

"Aren't we going to whip her first?" she just heard Bret ask, as she hobbled out of the room after them.

"No - let's do it there. Don't want to get her marked too early, what with all the whipping she's going to get tonight. Come on, slave!"

In the well-guarded car park of a secret suburban venue, Zoe was pulled from where she had been lying in the back of the car, with a blanket thrown over her, and forced to make her precarious, hobbled way towards the building.

Master Philip and Bret, both clad in tight black leather, gave her a little pat on the bum and a word of encouragement to see her on her way.

A security guard approached the trio. "Sorry, but we're asking people to be discrete until they get inside."

They all regarded Zoe - encased in rubber and rope, tits out, and bent forward at an unnatural angle by the heavy chain.

"Oh, dear!" said Master Philip, but quickly solved the problem by fetching the blanket from the car and throwing it right over Zoe. "Will this do?"

The security guard nodded and grinned, and the two men steered their human tent carefully to the entrance.

"I think we'll leave it on and have a bit of an unveiling," said Master Philip. "I'm sure people will enjoy the shock effect of the image our little lady presents."

And so it was with an even greater sense of isolation that a blinded, deafened sex slave became vaguely aware that she was in the midst of a partying crowd.

People pushed against her, and quite a few had little gropes to try to see what was behind the thick black blanket.

She was directed by her Master's hand on her head, onto what was obviously a dancefloor - the loud throbbing music and flashing strobe lights reached her darkened world.

All of a sudden, the blanket was pulled off her with a flourish, and she found herself standing bang slap in the middle of a huge dance hall, with coloured lights flashing all around it and white mist wafting around theatrically.

Peering through her eyeholes, she could see a huge ring of people standing looking at her - and clapping. Her bondage 'costume' was being applauded!

The people were a pretty kinky looking bunch, though none were dressed as severely as her. The ubiquitous colour was black, and there were plenty of stockings, corsets, and naked and half naked tits on view.

Several of the onlookers were transvestites, some with stupendous wigs, and one or two more unusual costumes caught her eye. One man was dressed in a red 'devil' outfit, and another sprouted angel's wings, for some obscure reason.

Many were smiling, though - it seemed she had made a good impression - and there were some more appreciative nods as Master Philip and Bret each took up one of the leads attached to her dog collar and began to parade her around, like a show animal on display.

Master Philip stooped down and opened the leg spreader to about three feet, and this is how wide it stayed for the whole evening.

Never had Zoe known anything like it before. What a situation to be in! She felt so disorientated, standing on that nightclub dancefloor with the amazing music thumping through her and a hundred bizarre faces peering in her direction. She felt like some sort of strange novelty being offered to people to gawp at, and the feeling was a disturbing one, particularly because there were other women in the crowd. Dolled up, exhibitionistic women, smoking and chatting and staring down their noses at her like she was some sort of zoo exhibit.

Then she was plunged further into humiliation as one particular group of tarty ladies began to laugh and gossip about her, in a generally uncomplimentary manner.

"Look at that fat bum!" they shouted over the music.

"What an utter doormat!"

"It's all very well," shrieked the loudest of them, "but what does she actually DO?"

Several of the other observers - male ones - were quick to respond to this question.

"I should imagine she does a fair bit."

"I bet she sucks cock pretty good! Look how wide her mouth is stretched."

"I bet she gets herself whipped a lot as well, flashing an arse like that around!"

Master Philip had been listening and he enlightened the crowd.

"You're quite right about all those suggested uses, and the last one in particular. My colleague and I have decided to be very generous tonight and let whoever would like to experiment with whipping a naked bottom do so with our slave. Some of you, I see, have your own whips with you, but if anyone should need to borrow one, just let us know. Now what do you think, Bret? Shall we perhaps lead the lady into a slightly quieter corner, and tether her to a rail, or something? Then whoever wants to, can come and lay a few strokes across her bum."

"Good idea," said Bret. "But perhaps you should give a demonstration of how it's done first."

"Oh, of course. I'll do it regularly, throughout the night. Now come on, slave. Time for walkies again."

For all their harsh and formal tone, Master Philip and Bret were exchanging humorous glances and in fact getting close to a schoolboy level of giggling and nudging and winking - but Zoe missed all this because of her restricted hearing and vision.

It happened as Master Philip had decreed. The party raged - people danced and drank and talked and snogged and occasionally spanked each other - but for what seemed like forever Zoe stood in one place on her high heels and in her humiliating posture, and tolerated an onslaught of whip strokes on her bum.

She could tell which were delivered by Master Philip - the twenty hard ones at the beginning! And she even thought that she could recognise Bret's slightly lighter touch. (He'd undoubtedly got more experienced and more interested in whipping since taking on this assignment for Master Philip.) But after that, there was no knowing who was whipping her - or when exactly the strokes would fall, or quite how hard they would be.

She was pretty certain that some of the women had a go, but she tried to shut this out of her mind. All that mattered was standing obediently where she'd been told to stand, and accepting the punishment that her two Masters wanted her to accept.

She concentrated on the idea of being nothing but a plump, prettily proffered, punishable (and pink and painful) posterior - and found this thought hugely arousing!

Over a period of several weeks, Zoe got taken by Master Philip and Bret to several major Fetish Clubs, ranging from small, intimate ones, which only a select few knew existed, to huge high-profile ones that got reviewed in the arty press.

Each time she was decked out in some new and amazing bondage costume, paraded around publicly, and then offered for chastisement throughout the course of the night (except on those occasions when the event was too mainstream to make this possible, in which case anyone who expressed an interest was asked to settle for a discrete grope and maybe a few painful pinches instead).

Zoe enjoyed this period, not because of the punishment - though it did have its effect, and remained always difficult to handle - and not because of the public element of these visits; she wasn't really an exhibitionist and had never been particularly motivated by causing a stir. What she liked most was the fact that she had two men, who she knew to be particularly attractive, concerning themselves with her in such an intense way.

She was a sex toy to them, that was true. But she was something else too - the embodiment of their fantasies, and therefore, though she knew they would never admit it, precious to them.

She knew this by the way, occasionally, she would feel them stroke her, perhaps while they talked about her to someone else. They were proud - proud to be able to say, 'yes, she's our full time sex slave and is spending hours and hours in bondage on a daily basis'.

She knew by the way they both looked at her, and by the way they looked at other people looking at them as a threesome. Zoe drew attention - Zoe made her Masters look special.

She also enjoyed the strict bondage element of these excursions. Though often very restrictive and uncomfortable, Bret's handiwork was also exciting and liberating. To be tied up in public was to only partially be existing in society - only partially be in the real world. To be unable to move your limbs, unable to see properly, unable to walk where you wanted to walk, and yet all the time have the knowledge that your freedom would be restored and that while you were voluntarily incapacitated you would be cared for by someone else, was wonderful - or at least Zoe found it so.

Bret, who truly was an expert, would be able to judge how long Zoe could tolerate certain positions, for example, or at what point she would be desperate to go to the loo, or desperate for a drink. He would feed her sips of orange juice or sometimes beer at moments when she'd felt sure she'd been abandoned. He would lead her to the toilets just in time, go into a cubicle with her (no problem at your average Fetish Club, where all the toilets quickly became unisex!), adjust whatever straps it was necessary to adjust, position her over the bowl, and finally pat her dry with tissue.

This service would always make Zoe cry. She truly understood, now, what it meant to be made to suffer and yet be cared for at the same time.

It had not escaped Master Philip's notice that Bret had become very involved with the concept of Zoe, and that Zoe in turn lavished at least as much submissive adoration on Bret as she did on him.

Since he understood Zoe and her motivations, however, he felt not the least threatened in his position as her ultimate Master, but stood back nobly and let things take their course. The possibility of Zoe being 'stolen' by another Master did occasionally cross his mind, but he was philosophical about it. After all, he was human before he was a Master, and he would never have imposed on Zoe against her will.

It was Bret, in fact, who felt that the time had come for things to change.

"It's been the best period of my life, without a doubt," he said to Master Philip over drinks one night (with Zoe safely tied up in bed), "but I don't want to overstay my welcome. I think I should move out soon, so she can focus her mind back on you again."

Master Philip stared thoughtfully into his whisky, a number of emotions well hidden. "You must come and visit us, though," he said eventually. "Regularly. And perhaps unexpectedly - that could be fun! Why don't we plan some really intricate bondage designs? Really over the top. Give it some thought, see what you can come up with. I'll fund whatever you suggest."

Bret's mind dwelt on this comfortable suggestion, and flitted immediately to some ideas he'd had. Hm - maybe he could do something with that wheelbarrow concept. And the revolving oil drum - yes, that would be something to look forward to!

And yet he would miss living here with Master Philip and Zoe - having access to her on a permanent basis.

"Perhaps I could ask you a favour," said Bret. "Before I leave."

"Of course - ask away."

"Could I have her to myself for, say, a weekend? Take her away somewhere - out of the country, maybe - and indulge myself by keeping her in bondage the whole time? You know you can trust me, mate," Bret added quickly, not unaware of Master Philip's concerns. "She won't come to any harm, and I absolutely promise to bring her back!"

Master Philip looked up at his long term friend appraisingly. So the idea that he might not bring her back had at least crossed the guy's mind! Interesting. But then, he reminded himself, there had been plenty of occasions when Bret had been alone with Zoe and he hadn't kidnapped her yet! Besides, if he never trusted anyone, Zoe wouldn't have any trying sexual adventures!

"Take her where you like," he sighed, "and give her a bondage experience she'll never forget! Now let's drink to it - cheers!"

A few days later, after much thought and planning, Bret took Zoe to Paris, where he kept an apartment - quite the place for a romantic, sex filled weekend.

Now you'd have thought that Zoe would've realised by now that Bret was seriously into bondage. You'd have thought that she wouldn't be surprised when he wedged her into a suitcase and threw her in the boot of his car for the journey to France! But Zoe had yet to understand that Bret, on his own territory and on his own terms, was very, very seriously into bondage indeed.

"My own personal passion," he informed Zoe before turning her into a piece of luggage, "is for bondage over long periods - very much longer, probably, than your doting Master would consider realistic. I like to think in weeks and months rather than days. And I once kept a woman in a steel corset for a year! So on the one hand, you should consider yourself lucky I've only got you for one brief weekend; on the other - be prepared!"

The suitcase, Zoe had to admit, was a difficult experience. Not that she was particularly uncomfortable - for she had got rather used to getting squashed into small spaces recently - but because she felt so vulnerable and worried, either that she'd get discovered at customs and have to suffer the embarrassment of an explanation, or that she'd somehow get forgotten or stolen, and end up stuck in her little prison for ever!

But Bret was always careful, and had deliberately left her ungagged and the case unlocked. He had no intention of leaving her for a moment, however, and spent the journey very acutely aware of the special package he was smuggling - particularly in the groin area!

He hummed to himself as he drove, enjoying the sensation of being responsible for his secret cargo, and marvelling that another human being should so trust him, for Zoe once again had not a stitch of clothing with her, nor a single possession - and definitely not even a centime (Euro rather) in the money department.

He would buy her a designer dress and take her out for a posh meal on their last night, he decided. But not before he had brought his bondage plans to fruition!

When at last Zoe was tipped out from the case onto French soil (well, French carpet), and rubbed and prodded sufficiently to get her body back in working order, she was dispatched to the bathroom to relieve herself and clean up a little, then summoned down to the kitchen where Bret personally fed her soup and bread like she was a baby.

His place was pretty amazing - huge and modern. She supposed there was good money to be made in the Bondage Consultancy business!

The decor was a spartan and sexy red and black, and the walls were rather overly plastered with prints of tied-up women. She got rather a shock when she recognised herself in some of them, and wondered how many people had seen and perhaps admired these pictures, all unknown to her.

"Let me tell you the general plan," Bret said, sipping Cognac. "Tomorrow I've invited a few fellow enthusiasts round so it's going to be a bit of a bondage party. Then in the evening - and probably overnight - I've got something special arranged. On Sunday I've booked a top art photographer, and we're going to get some of the most amazing pictures you can imagine. Something for me to remember you by!"

So Zoe resigned herself to an immobile weekend and one which certainly wouldn't involve seeing any of the sights of the city. In this assumption, however, she was wrong, for Bret had lined up for her what turned out to be one of the most amazing experiences of her life.

When, in future, she thought back to her 'Bondage Break' in Paris, it wasn't so much the long and tiring bondage party she remembered, at which an assortment of people - including, to her surprise and discomfort, several women - had admired and discussed elements of her restraint as well as elements of her body, all entirely in French so she could hardly understand a word, and accompanied by cocktails and French jazz ballads. Nor was it the equally long photoshoot, again conducted in French, during which an elderly and flamboyant photographer had treated her absolutely like an inanimate object and spent considerable amounts of time minutely adjusting intricate lighting, and alternately covering bits of her body with oil or talc.

No, what she remembered was the amazing sightseeing tour which Bret engineered for her, which had so scared and exhilarated and aroused her.

At the end of the day-long party, Zoe was carried by Bret and two other men, down in a private lift to a large garage.

Her bondage at the time involved an enforced 'all fours' position on a little platform to which her ankles and knees were strapped, as far apart as they would go, as well as her wrists and elbows which were positioned straight out in front of her so that she looked a bit like an Egyptian statue of a dog or sphinx, only with her haunches right up in the air, and her large breasts bulging out blatantly in front of her.

Said breasts were wrapped around with pretty chains, which matched those constricting her waist, while her head was held proudly up and in position by a 'bridle', from which leather 'reins' ran down to her waist. The rest of her was naked - most notably her pussy, which was quite clearly and glisteningly displayed to anyone who cared to take in her rear view. In short, she was a provocative and supremely erotic sex object, every recess of her body on show, and the eroticism of her predicament underlined by the fact that she was quite clearly, to the knowledgeable and sympathetic observer at least, in a highly charged state of arousal and enjoyment.

Standing in the middle of the garage was a huge silver limousine, sleek and clean and glistening, which was most notable for one thing - the darkened glass in all its windows. Notwithstanding the frustration such a feature created in other motorists, who peered at the black windscreen for some indication of the driver's intentions in vain, such vehicles were favoured by the elite and criminal classes in most of the world's major cities for the sense of power they gave their occupants - who were able to enjoy privacy within, while retaining a perfect view of the world going by (and the plebs on the streets).

Into the rear of the waiting vehicle Zoe was maneuvered - in the middle, facing backwards, with the platform supporting her fixed into place on a specially designed ledge which replaced the back seat.

Zoe immediately discovered that she had an excellent view out of the back window. And of course it seemed as though people must have an equally good view in. There was Bret now, peering in and waving at her, making gestures to imply he could see her bulging, naked breasts just behind the glass, when of course he couldn't.

He wandered round the sides of the car, checking to see if the glass was truly opaque, she supposed, and then to the front, where he and his two colleagues stood and discussed what an amazing view of Zoe's posterior and pussy could've been had from between the two front seats if the windscreen had been a normal one.

Zoe had gathered that they were going to go out for a drive, but still, when the car pulled out from the garage with Bret at the wheel - his two friends waving them wistfully goodbye - she was amazed by the sense of vulnerability that hit her. She felt so exposed! As they moved slowly through busy streets, the cars and people around her seemed so close. Surely they would see her and cry out in shock and horror, but of course she was entirely hidden, and though some of those passing actually glanced at the dark windows of the limousine with curiosity, no-one had an inkling of the amazing spectacle that existed inside.

Though still tense when pedestrians were nearby, or when she found herself looking straight into the eyes of some unsuspecting motorist behind them in a queue of traffic, Zoe soon relaxed and began to enjoy not only the sensual aspects of the experience - for there was no doubt that this pseudo-exhibitionism was having an effect on her pussy - but also the funny side. What a joke to play on an unsuspecting public! What a tease, to think how astonished the male population of Paris would be if they could only see her!

She imagined what would happen if they were discovered - if a ray of sunlight or a spotlight should penetrate the dark windows and give some lucky cameraman a shot of naked flesh and chains. She could just see the headlines:

'Secret of sex limo exposed!'

'Naked British girl driven in chains round streets of Paris!'

Or perhaps an advert: 'Bondage consultant offers unusual city tours to liberated females.'

A tour of the city she certainly got - a long, detailed and utterly unique one.

They cruised past the Eiffel Tower, tackled the back streets around Sacre Coeur, drove back and forth along the river for the best views of Notre Dame. They also crawled through the main shopping streets, explored some obscure parks, and made a trip out to Versailles - stately but deserted at night.

Several times, Bret deliberately left Zoe in the car alone, during which she suffered the most dreadful agonies of worry, and felt she had never been more pleased to see anyone than when Bret came back again - with a cup of coffee, perhaps, or a postcard, and a hearty laugh at her complaints, accompanied by a reassuring slap on her upthrust bottom.

Once they parked on the street right next to a pavement café, where she could watch for nearly an hour Bret meeting up with some friends - a young couple - and sharing a drink and a chat with them. When at last the encounter came to an end, Zoe observed with horror that there was some gesturing and gesticulating towards the car, and she suddenly had the image of a shocked young man and woman squashed into the back on each side of her, being given a rather unusual lift home.

But no, luckily it was just Bret's little joke at her expense - he in fact knew that the couple lived nearby, though it had definitely been a gamble, and Zoe wondered how he'd have got out of it if they'd accepted.

Maybe it would've introduced them to that circle of bondage enthusiasts which was evidently already so well established in this city of liberated love.

When Zoe had had her fill of all the sights, and Bret had tired of the sight of her impotent nakedness, he drove back to his garage, and there, in silence and privacy, squeezed himself behind her and fucked her so slowly and nicely that they both experienced the most delightful and exquisite raptures, and came together, heaving and squirming and crying out in the darkness.

Yes, this was the moment Zoe would most often remember, once Bret was gone, and she had been sent home to be alone again with Master Philip.

Chapter Four

STRICTLEY HALL

It was some weeks after Paris, and Zoe was enjoying life at home.

Things had been quite calm, that is, there had been the occasional day when she hadn't fucked anyone other than Master Philip.

"Are you ready for another major test?" he asked her one morning, while she hung from a hook in a bondage bag.

"Always," she replied flippantly, and got walloped on her rubber-covered bum with a crop.

"I've got a busy period coming up, and I need to get rid of you for a while. A month or so, I should think."

This shut Zoe up. She didn't want to be parted from her Master again. Certainly not for a month.

"Repeat after me - I will do anything you want me to, Master."

"I will do anything you want me to, Master."

"Even if it means going away from you for a month."

"Even if it means going away from you for a month, Master."

"Or two months."

"Or two months, Master," Zoe groaned.

He walloped her again.

"Even if it was back to the sauna!"

No, not the sauna! The thought of the endless beatings she had endured with the birch twigs, and the endless arseholes she had been forced to lick filled her with dread. But then that was what being tested was all about. It couldn't all be easy!

Quickly, dispelling hesitation, she replied.

"Yes, Master, even if it was back to the sauna."

"You're a good girl," he said, and she got a warm feeling. "It's not the sauna, though. It's something completely different. Something that will require a bit more action and effort from you than just hanging around in bondage all day!"

"What? What is it Master?"

"Silence!" he snapped, swinging her vulnerable body around so he could pay some attention to her tits with the crop. "I'll tell you when I'm ready."

He told her the following morning, after playfully making her eat a breakfast of dry cereal from a dog bowl on the floor.

"Do you remember Adam, who came with us to the porn cinema, and the car park?"

"Yes, Master."

"I believe you liked him."

"Well, yes, Master."

"Hm. It might have been more fun if you didn't, but I suppose one can't have everything. Anyway, he's asked to borrow you. He wants you to go and be his assistant for a while. I presume you can type?"

"A little, Master."

"Well, he wants to use you at work. Apparently he organises conferences and training courses all over the country, and he intends to take you with him to some conference centre out in the wilds. No doubt the delegates are going to play a part in things; I haven't really asked him, but as you know, his interests are similar to mine in these areas." Master Philip sighed. "I've trusted you with Bret, I suppose, so I shall have to trust you with Adam too."

Zoe reflected on the prospect of a change of scenery.

"I expect you to miss me dreadfully, slave!"

"Of course I will, Master!" said slave replied. But her mind was already straying to memories of Adam - trying to remember what particular bits of him looked like.

Rather to her surprise, Zoe found that she was to deliver herself to Adam's establishment in the country, by train.

It was some way away, and as Master Philip had a commitment that day, he didn't even give her a lift to the station, but left her to her own devices with little more that a cursory, "Be good - see you in a month" to send her on her way.

She packed a small bag of smart clothes and phoned for a minicab, to find that the driver was one of the many local men who had been invited to the house in the past, and therefore not only regaled her with memories of the particular event, relating in detail what he'd seen her do and had himself done to her - but insisted that she put a hand down his grubby trousers and massage his willy as he drove!

Who was Zoe - whose life was submission - to object?

On the train, however, she was able to relax alone and was glad that Master Philip hadn't stuck to his threatened instruction that she should stand all the way!

Her carriage was almost empty, as it was midweek, and she enjoyed herself reading, looking out of the window at sunlit fields, and reflecting on Master Philip's trust - that he should yet again let her out of his immediate control, and into the control of another dominant man, and yet be certain that she would return.

It was, of course, another test - forcing her to prove her commitment once more - and also a genuine opportunity to leave if she so chose. Master Philip only wanted her subservience if she wanted it herself, of that there was no doubt.

She amused herself thinking about what she could remember of Adam, and wondering how he and Master Philip had met, and what shared escapades they'd got up to in the past. She also thought about Bret, and how much she'd liked him, and that it was rather nice swapping Masters occasionally for someone new and interesting!

It was a long journey and the taxi ride at the other end much longer than she'd expected. The address she'd been given was simply, Strictley Hall (of all names!), near Little Hetherington, and the driver had to stop twice to ask directions in the village.

When they found it, Zoe was impressed. Huge, beautiful and isolated, she could see why it had been chosen as an exclusive conference location - it certainly represented a complete change of environment for stressed executives.

The only trouble was, it seemed to be deserted. No cars in the little car park or driveway, the front door firmly locked and bolted, and all the windows closed and with their curtains drawn. Unfortunately, Zoe had so much had the impression that the conference centre would be open for business and busy, she'd sent the taxi away without a thought, and was only now - after she'd leant on the doorbell for some ten minutes - feeling stranded and silly.

Yet the message she'd had relayed to her through Master Philip had said she should aim for this time on this day, so she decided to wait a fair while before attempting to walk back to the nearest phone.

Having strolled twice around the building and knocked on all the rear doors, to no avail, she left her bag under a bench and set off to explore the grounds. There were some formal gardens - not spectacular, but well kept - an expanse of water something between a pond and lake, and a huge area of grass that started off as a lawn and became a wild field, disappearing into overgrown hillocks and bits of woodland at the edges.

There was also, to one side of the house, a maze - the largest, tallest one Zoe had ever seen. Eight foot hedges, all neat and forbidding! She'd never liked mazes and steered well clear of this one. She wandered round the little lake, enjoying being outdoors in the countryside on such a pleasant afternoon, but getting a little scared about being alone. There was still no sign of life at the house so she kept walking, aiming to explore the perimeter of the grounds and hoping, even in this secluded place (city habits die hard) that her travel bag would be okay where she'd left it.

About an hour and a half after she'd arrived, and when she was at the furthest point possible from the Hall, she saw a black sports car pull into the long drive and park near the house. A moment later she made out a male figure standing looking in her direction.

It had to be Adam. She waved, and though he didn't wave back, he started walking in her direction. She set off towards him and found herself thinking humorously of Wuthering Heights as they strode towards each other across the massive field.

He was walking with his hands in his pockets and her trepidation increased as she saw his face. It was Adam alright, but he didn't look pleased.

"I've been waiting at the station," he announced, as she stopped in front of him.

"Oh! Sorry."

He gave a little grunt and proceeded to walk all around her, looking her up and down.

"Do you remember when we met?" he asked her.

"Yes, of course. In that pub."

"Where you blatantly revealed quite a lot of your body and even more of your soul."

"Er, yes."

He stopped walking - behind her.

"I've thought a lot about that night. I've thought a lot about you."

Zoe actually felt the hairs on her neck stand up at his somewhat sinister tone.

"I can't believe he's let me have you for a whole month!" he went on. "You can't imagine what I've got in store for you!"

She just didn't know what to expect or what to say. She certainly didn't expect to hear his next instruction - not in broad daylight in the middle of a field!

"Lie down on the ground and show me your arse."

She looked round at him, and then at the scenery all about them. No people or houses in sight, true, but the road over there, and lots of places for people to hide - or innocently step out from on a country walk.

"Here?"

"Yes, here! I'm going to fuck you straight away - I don't want to wait any longer. No-one's going to see."

"They might."

"Not your problem. Now lie down."

From long habit Zoe responded, dropping to her knees, stretching out face down, then, tentatively but without further hesitation, pulling her skirt up off her bottom and slipping down her panties.

"Further," he said, looking down at the lovely naked splodge of her bum against the green grass. "And open your legs wider for me."

She did as she was instructed, and even raised her hips a little, but though she waited, resigned and convinced, the event didn't happen. Instead, Adam was crouching down in front of her and smiling.

"Just testing!" he announced cheerily, and chuckled at her expression. "God, you are a slut! Dropping your knickers like that in broad daylight! Did you really think I was going to fuck you out here?"

Zoe flipped over onto her back and pouted up at him. Adam reached over and brushed her blushing cheek gently with a finger, a touch she found electrifying. She had to admit she was disappointed that he'd chosen not to fuck her – she was ready for it.

Then he was being stern again.

"However, for a highly trained submissive, you hesitated too long and you certainly shouldn't have questioned me. I'll decide where and when we fuck, not you!"

Zoe was thinking how incredibly good looking Adam was, and how excited she felt about being under the power of someone like him, and that she'd better control her emotions because she was on the precipice already of falling madly in love and lust with him.

"Turn over again. And get up on all fours," said the lust-object, standing up, and Zoe jumped-to.

"Now, you're to crawl all the way back to the house on all fours - with your bottom out! And this time I'm not joking! Oh, and I forgot," said Adam, turning back as Zoe struggled to her knees. "Welcome to Strictley Hall!"

A morning or two later, Zoe found herself in one of the lecture rooms of the conference centre, dressed in a smart business suit, and laying out training materials - files and papers - on each student's desk.

Strictley Hall had swung into action - transformed from deserted and dormant stately home to busy place of work by the descent of a dozen or so staff, and the arrival of a veritable horde of resident delegates.

Adam was at the podium, checking the overhead projector. When he saw Zoe had finished - after about five trips from a table by the entrance - setting up the room, he called over to her.

"Very good. Now collect them all up again - there's no course in here today."

Zoe's eyes widened. So why had she been wasting her time?

Then she understood. "Yes Sir," she said meekly, and set about collecting the files up again, her high heels clicking on the wooden flooring.

"Finished, Sir," she said eventually.

"Right. Now lay them out next door, and hurry up - the delegates will be arriving in about twenty minutes!"

The day progressed busily, with Zoe being asked to assist with a number of tasks, such as helping on the registration desk, serving coffee and taking phone messages. This was obviously a real working establishment, but nevertheless, Zoe expected at any minute to be shown into a room full of expectant men and asked to suck cock.

It didn't happen. What happened instead was that Adam would repeatedly instruct her to do meaningless, unnecessary and embarrassing things; apparently, she gathered, merely to express his power over her actions in a conventional environment.

"Zoe, take these plates down to the kitchen - one at a time."

The catering staff thought she was thick, but she couldn't explain.

"Zoe, during the next three lectures, stand by the light switch and do nothing except turn the lights on and off when instructed, smile a lot, and look interested in the lecture content." ('Conceptual Arguments In Support Of Total Quality Management As Related To Interpersonal Stresses On The Shop Floor.') (Three times!)

"Zoe, stand in the broom cupboard holding this sand bucket. I'll hear you if you put it down. No - leave the light off please."

Days passed, and still Zoe kept her clothes on and didn't see a single cock - except Adam's, in the evenings.

She was exhausted, though. Particularly after having had to polish the kitchen floors after the staff had gone home, walk three times round the house in high heels, balancing a book on her head, and do about ten pages of typing which were promptly ripped up and deposited in a dustbin - all in one night!

"You see," said Adam, stroking her forehead one night in bed after he'd fucked her (they were sleeping together in a plush four poster), "I wanted to expose you to subservience without sex. I thoroughly approve of everything your Master's been doing with you, of course, but in a way, this sort of training can go deeper. Being a slut is just part of being a slave. Why do you think so many submissive men do vacuuming and gardening for some professional Mistress, without even expecting to kiss her, never mind screw her? It's something in the soul. And I do think slightly that Philip indulges you with sex - which you obviously enjoy. He's neglected these other ways of training and testing you. I'll have to persuade him to keep you celibate for a while - well, except for the two of us, that is."

Zoe adored Adam's smile. She adored the way he screwed her differently from Philip - usually really roughly from the back, pushing her legs wider open with his knees, and pressing down on her back or neck, pinning her to the bed.

There was a special chemistry. She found him so exciting. He sent shivers through her, sometimes, just with a gentle touch – a brush on her cheek as she walked past during the day. ("Chin up, tits forward," he would whisper.)

And his eyes were so beautiful –

"Zoe, are you listening to me? I'm explaining why I'm working you so hard."

"Mm."

"I'm training the core of your soul! I'm pushing your innermost limits!"

"Uh-huh."

"So prepare yourself for lots more hard work and unusual requests over the next few weeks."

She was pushing gently against his fresh erection.

"Yeah - whatever!"

Strictley Hall is a pretty big building. The conference facility only takes up part of it. There are whole floors of empty rooms, a whole closed up wing.

Adam leads Zoe along a dark and musty corridor, throwing open the doors to forgotten rooms. Some are completely empty; bare and curtainless, with dirty, rain-striped windows. Some have pieces of old furniture in them, covered with faded sheets and dust. One contains mountains of old files and papers from conferences held years ago. Another must once have been used as a photocopying room, and is piled up with broken and obsolete equipment. Several in the oldest wing still contain beds, laid with bedspreads and cushions, but not used for decades.

Zoe peers at the assortment of old pictures on the walls, and the occasional vase or figurine standing on a windowsill or in a recess, and wonders if any of these pieces are worth any serious money. She wonders also whether Adam owns all this, or is he just managing or renting the place? She knows it's not her place to ask, however.

Still they walk.

There are staircases, with grand pillars and banisters. There are bookcases, and fireplaces, and chandeliers, and little doorways that look like they lead to secret passageways.

There are ancient ashes in grates, and stacks of old newspapers in corners, as well as the occasional very faded bunch of dried flowers, and incongruous assortment of rusting metalware, and sprinkling of glass from a broken window. And cobwebs - cobwebs everywhere.

In short, the whole place has been utterly neglected, and is filthy.

At the end of yet another long corridor, Adam opens the door to a particular small room, the contents of which are a little more modern and a lot more tidy than anything they've seen so far.

It's packed full of cleaning materials. There are two vacuum cleaners, three brooms, several buckets, a bouquet of feather dusters, piles of rags and cloths, and a broad shelf holding various brands of disinfectant, furniture polish, window cleaning solution, and the like.

Aha, thinks Zoe. This of course explains the maid's costume.

She's been provided with a very short black skirt, a tiny white apron, a white cap – and nothing else.

Adam looks at her. "What do you think happens now?"

Zoe sighs. "I clean, Sir."

"Correct."

Zoe swallows and looks around her. "But, where do I start?"

Adam indicates a dusty alcove nearby. "How about over there?"

But Zoe still feels overwhelmed.

"How much of it am I supposed to clean?" she asks. "It would take a hundred people a year to do all this!"

"That's not the point, and you know it," Adam replies. "You will do 'some'. You will work hard, and to the best of your ability. You will apply yourself to the task in a logical fashion and achieve results. I will inspect the results, and expect to be impressed."

Zoe takes this in, and indeed resolves to do her best.

"You will sleep in one of the old bedrooms," Adam continues, "and I will have food and drink left for you at the bottom of those stairs, back there. You must not show your face downstairs, and not expect to see me for some time. Is all this understood?"

"Yes, Sir," says Zoe meekly. "Sir, how long will I be left alone here?"

"That's for me to know and you to guess." He steps closer to her. "Zoe, I trust you understand that this is about subservience, and acceptance, and discipline. I've been trying to explain to you that I think you've been spoilt with all the endless sexual attention you get. You need to experience servitude without sex, occasionally. This will make you an even better slave, I'm sure. Much as it will pain me, I don't intend to touch you for – well, at least a few days. And neither will anyone else. I thought of putting a chastity belt on you, but I think there's really no need – no-one will know you're here, or bother you." A twinkle enters Adam's eye. "Unless it's one of the ghosts, that is!"

Zoe's eyes widen momentarily, but luckily she's a young lady too much rooted in reality to be afraid of the supernatural.

"So – any more questions, before I leave you to get on with it?"

Zoe looks from Adam, to the broom cupboard, and back again. She thinks of asking him for a goodbye fuck, but realises this might be a mistake, considering what he's just been saying.

"Um," she begins, "um, am I allowed to, well, give myself pleasure?"

Adam is exasperated. "Is that all you can think about? Well, I suppose if I forbid you, you'll only be aroused and distracted all the time – so okay then, yes. But only once a day, in the evening, after you've done lots and lots of hard work!"

"Thank you, Sir," says Zoe, and expects that he will at least kiss her goodbye, but he pushes her away.

"I said I wouldn't touch you at all, and I mean it! Learn to be a slave on your own!"

Abandoned, Zoe wanders disconsolate through forgotten rooms, and wonders how little work she can get away with.

She sits and stares out through grimy windows at the fields, and curls up for a while on a dusty old chaise-longue.

It's so quiet – no television, no radio, no noise even from the busy conference rooms or the car park, which are right on the other side of the house. She gets a little scared when she hears the odd creak or bang, but realises it's just the old timbers expanding, or a loose tile falling down one of the chimneys.

Eventually, she realises she will indeed have to make a start on the cleaning, mainly as there's absolutely nothing else to do!

She explores once more, and chooses the smallest room, with the most modern looking bed, to make her base and sleeping quarters. She dusts, vacuums and scrubs this room all day. She cleans the windows then throws them open, enjoying the rural view she has selected for herself. She airs the old bedspread over the windowsill and props the door to the room open, to help the fresh air to circulate.

She takes to vacuuming the huge long corridor which leads to her chosen bedroom, because there is at least some element of fun in zooming down the spectacularly long carpet. She starts to hum and sing to herself, suddenly enjoying this strange seclusion.

She finds a working toilet, and cleans this too, and tries running a bath, only to find there is only cold water available. She bathes in this anyway, then goes and seeks out the food and drink which has been left for her in a large hamper. She feasts on cheese and ham sandwiches and a thermos of warm coffee, then nibbles on chocolate.

She wonders if Adam will return tonight, but expects he will not. Her assessment is correct.

She has an orgasm on the still musty bed, but can't sleep. She discovers that though there is clearly electricity, many of the lights have bulbs missing or just don't work. Nevertheless, she dusts and vacuums well into the night, exhausting herself so she will sleep easily.

In the morning she wakes with a jolt and misses immediately the feel of a man beside her, the feel of an erection approaching her.

She lies dreaming of Philip and Adam, and remembers that wonderful day they all once spent together. She remembers her instruction only to wank once a day, however, so leaves herself alone. Of course, he'd never know, but she doesn't want to lie to him.

She's sure he'll visit tonight, so she diligently sets to work clearing out another couple of the rooms which take her fancy. She enjoys polishing an old bookcase, and uncovering a collection of china plates in a cabinet.

The work and solitude and silence have an amazing effect on her. She feels immensely contented – not bored, not frustrated, not even lonely.

She cradles to herself the knowledge that she is here, toiling alone, because two wonderful men wish her to do so.

She thinks about them – Philip and Adam – wondering where they are at this moment, and whether they are thinking of her.

She fantasises about whether Master Philip will perhaps come and pay her a surprise visit. She secretly hopes that Adam will not be able to resist her, and will turn up after all for a lunchtime fuck.

She calls on the hamper again to return crockery and pick up more food and bottles of water, but doesn't encounter anyone, and is glad of it. Alone, she's not bothered by the fact that she's topless, but wouldn't enjoy bumping into any of the kitchen workers - one of whom at least must wonder what on earth is going on (unless Adam has been preparing her food himself).

As the second evening passes, she gets depressed as she realises he isn't coming today, either. All night she finds herself waking, expectant, but he really is leaving her alone.

The next day she throws herself again into scrubbing floors – her back and arms aching already from all her recent exertions – and finds that he turns up when she's least expecting it. When she's on her knees on a stone floor, dripping with sweat, her arms deep in suds, and her head full of memories of cleaning the sauna.

"Hello, slave." He makes her jump.

"Master Adam!" she shrieks with delight, and rushes towards him, but he puts a hand up.

"Keep your distance, I'm only here for a moment."

He asks to see what she's achieved, and she shows him around, fully expecting to hear some gratuitous criticism – which doesn't come.

He merely nods his head, saying, "Good girl, keep at it," and makes to leave.

Only he hesitates briefly, and turns to her.

"Zoe?"

"Yes, Master??"

He seems about to say something more, but changes his mind.

"Nothing."

And then he's gone!

She is stunned. Her emotions are all awash. For his wonderful, familiar, masterful presence to have been here, so briefly – but then to have been immediately withdrawn!

All afternoon, she languishes. Cleaning, still, but preoccupied with the thought of him, with the loss of him. With the need for him.

As he correctly predicted, she finds herself aroused, and longing for a man's touch. She is so, so used to it now – getting lots of sexual attention

– that she can hardly bear the absence of it.

She wonders if she's become a sex addict – so great is her sudden need for stimulation and attention.

But then, eventually, the peacefulness she felt before his surprise visit returns, and she finds comfort again in her work and seclusion.

More rooms get needlessly cleaned.

Unseen and unfondled, Zoe's naked tits bounce and flap about, as she moves around performing her maid's tasks.

In another room of the Hall, Adam tosses and turns in his lonely bed, thinking about her constantly – wondering how long he should leave her at her endless cleaning task, wondering if he's doing the right thing by teaching her restraint, wondering how long he can stop himself from rushing over to the old wing and ravishing her.

Downstairs, students of management do carefully crafted group exercises and games, some of which relate to hierarchies and loyalties in the workplace. How many of them would believe or understand the complex, subtle, fraught, sexual game being played out between two people in separate silent rooms, in the very same building?

On an afternoon when there were no courses happening, Adam led Zoe into the centre of the maze.

Naked, of course. And blindfolded (by means of a leather hood that locked round her neck with a padlock). And hobbled with a short leather strap.

Her hands he left free, so she could feel for corners and gaps in hedges.

"Oh please, Sir," Zoe dared to moan. "Not the maze! I've never been able to do them, and I'll never find my way out like this!"

"I'm sure you will, eventually," Adam replied. "It's just a question of how long it will take you."

Adam stepped up to her and smoothed down the hood, making sure she couldn't see, but could breathe easily. Then he ran his hands firmly all over her body. He hugged her naked flesh in a more possessive than lecherous way, but nevertheless felt his cock stir, as ever, at the wonderful sight and feel of her.

"It's another test, a perfectly straightforward one. Find your way out of one of the country's oldest and most difficult mazes, whilst hobbled and blindfolded. What could be easier?"

Zoe leaned against Adam, not wanting him to leave her.

"Oh please, Sir, let me off this one!" she begged.

"No! Do it for your Master Philip!"

The hood covering Zoe's head made hearing difficult, so she missed the subtle touch of bitterness in Adam's voice.

"See you later," he said, and spanked her on the arse.

With the aid of a little map, Adam made his way out of the maze and back to the Hall, where he set himself up with a drink and a book at a spot where he could see the entrance to the maze. In truth he didn't know how long it would take her, or indeed whether she'd ever succeed – he'd probably have to go in and rescue her after a while. But it probably wouldn't do to have some catering delivery driver witness a naked and bound woman step out from the maze entrance at the wrong moment, so Adam settled down to keep an eye out for Zoe's emergence.

In the centre of the maze, Zoe stood stock still, abandoned and forlorn. It occurred to her to engage her brain for a moment, so she stood facing in the same direction, trying to remember the pattern of how they'd walked to get in. Had there been a long curve to the right, near the end? Wasn't there quite a long straight bit near the beginning?

She tried to feel for any clues – from the direction of the sunlight, or the wind on her skin – but unfortunately it was overcast and still. The only thing that might have helped her was the sound of traffic from the road, but what noise there was, was cut out completely by both her leather hood and the tall thick hedges of the maze itself.

For a moment she felt annoyance and despair, but then found a resolve.

Wouldn't it just show him, if she found her way out quickly! Yes, she would succeed in the task more easily than he'd expected, and he'd be so pleased with her, they'd spend the afternoon having mad passionate sex instead of playing silly games.

She set to her task with a sense of urgency.

First, it has to be said, she checked the mask and her hobbles to see whether either could be removed – in other words, to see if she could cheat. Alas, this had been thought of, and there was no chance of it.

So she turned herself around and set off in the direction she thought they'd come from and which she thought she'd heard Adam leave in – only to come almost immediately up against one of the tall, slightly prickly hedges.

She felt her way around the curve of it until she found a gap and passed through. Yes, it must surely be this way, she thought, but was very soon thwarted again. It was clearly a dead end.

After less than ten minutes, her resolve had evaporated. It was an impossible task! She was utterly and totally confused! The maze was a nightmare of twists and turns and forks! She would be lost for ever!

Then she calmed down again, and decided that her only hope was to be methodical and try to form some sort of mental map of where she'd been and hadn't been. And so with this plan in mind, she set off again, exploring the hedges with her hands, looking for any little clue in the feel of the twigs, or the lie of the land beneath her feet, which might help to guide her.

The hobbles didn't help, as her speed of progress was necessarily slow, but she tried to be patient. For a while she experimented with getting down and crawling on all fours, but this hurt her knees too much to be practical, so she soon took to her feet again.

An hour passed and a struggling Zoe was slowly building up a mental picture of the maze. She had a feel for the exit not being THAT way. And surely THAT whole segment she'd now explored.

This certainly was a test, she was thinking to herself, a test of memory and patience and perseverance – but just at that moment something happened which unfortunately knocked the carefully constructed mental map right out of her mind.

A hand grasped her tit.

Zoe screamed.

A hand covered her mouth.

She fought to get free – and succeeded.

"Adam? Adam, is that you?"

Arms were wrapped around her, her bum was grabbed.

"Please tell me Adam!"

She struggled, and found herself being pushed down onto the grass.

She genuinely wasn't sure. Perhaps some stranger had wandered into the maze and come across her? Or maybe it was just Adam, playing games again.

She pushed at the weight on top of her, tried to feel for his face, but he stopped her.

She began to panic, but then he gave himself away. As he kissed her through the mask, he made a tiny noise – a little involuntary grunt of passion, which she recognised.

She was sure. She relaxed and began to cry at the same moment. "Adam, how can you be so cruel?"

Suddenly, his weight was gone from her, and a moment later, her hood was being removed.

Relieved to feel cool air on her face, and blinking at the light, she looked up to find Adam propped up on one elbow beside her, smoothing her hair with one hand.

"Forgive me," he said. "I shouldn't have scared you – maybe I am too cruel."

And to her amazement, Zoe saw that he too had tears in his eyes!

He leaned over and kissed her, ran a hand over her naked curves.

"Zoe, it's no good, I'm getting quite obsessed with you! I shall have to send you back early – if you stay here a month, well, I don't think I'll be able to let you go at the end of it. And I refuse to be quite such a cad as to abuse Philip's trust."

Zoe was astounded. A long moment passed.

"But he's not there, he's away," she said weakly.

"I'll just have to put you in a hotel then." He drew away from her, angry. "You are every man's dream! How am I supposed to resist you?"

Zoe sat herself up, and pulled his head back round towards her.

"Don't send me away, Master Adam. Let me stay here and be with you."

He turned and kissed her again. "You're enough to drive a man mad! Don't you understand what you are? How am I to handle you submitting so perfectly, so willingly, to me – and yet never really being mine?"

Zoe held him, trying to calm his passionate distress, and searching frantically for the truth of her own feelings.

"Zoe," he shook her. "Tell me now. If you stay with me for a month – will you still go back to him at the end of it?"

Moments passed, and the words refused to leave Zoe's lips. She didn't know whether to say, "Of course," or "I don't know".

Then another thought occurred to her. "Is this a test of my loyalty to him? Are you wearing a microphone or something?" She was half joking really, but in reply Adam began to rip off all his clothes and throw them aside, until he was naked beside her.

But now he was calmer, and took her in his arms. "It's alright, I know what you'll answer. Your loyalty to him is clear, you don't need to prove it to me any further. I guess I'll get over it – anyway, I'll probably have had enough of you after a few more weeks, in any case. I mean, how many times can a man fuck the perfect sex slut?"

He followed this wry comment by thrusting himself up Zoe's pussy and fucking her for what seemed an age.

After they had both come, and lay on the grass together sleepily, Zoe found herself whispering in Adam's ear.

"It's only because – " she began meaningfully.

He waited.

"It's only because – " and her whisper got even quieter, "I happen to have come across him first."

He didn't respond, but she saw his lips twitch in a smile.

Ten minutes later, they had both stood up and Adam had dressed.

Zoe fussed around him, cooing and flirting, feeling now that something had changed between them.

"So come on," she said. "Carry me out of here back to the Hall."

He raised his eyebrows. "Carry you out?"

"Yes!" She threw herself at him, playing with his affections. "Rescue me! Take me out of here, and to bed!"

Adam paused and took the effusive Zoe into his arms. "Who's testing who now?" he demanded playfully. "Think you can wrap me around your little finger now? Oh no, nothing's changed."

Zoe pouted.

They snogged.

He nearly relented – but then remembered his role.

"I'll tell you what, I won't put the blindfold back on – that way you'll find your way out easily, but I won't have let you off completely."

"Oh, please, don't leave me in here again!" Zoe pleaded, but suddenly Adam got serious again.

"Look," he grabbed her by a wrist. "We've determined you're going back to him when the month's up, so the terms of your being here are the same as before. Except that I might be even stricter with you now; now that I know I've no chance of winning your.. winning you over. So behave – like a slave!"

An hour later, when Zoe had eventually found her way out of the dreaded maze, she still hadn't made up her mind whether Adam really had winked at her when he'd left.

To the side of Strictley Hall, near the maze and behind some bushes, is a little sunken garden, rather overgrown, with a small fish pond in it.

There's a woman, standing in the pond. The water comes to just above her knees, and its surface is tangled with reeds and water-lilies.

The woman is naked and standing very still. Her arms are reaching down to cover her pubes, in an attempt to reduce her absolute exposure, but it's an unnecessary posture. No-one is looking at her. She's completely alone.

It's night, and very dark. Only a few lights can be seen through the bushes from the Hall, but one of these is turned off, even as she watches.

The sky is starry, and a full moon is rising. It casts strange shadows which frighten her. Her naked feet are buried in mud. She hates the feel of it, but at least it's warmer than the cold water on her legs. She's been standing still for so long, that it seems the fishes have accepted her as part of their watery world, for she is sure she can feel them occasionally, brushing against her shins with tiny touches.

She resists the urge to look around, though the darkness behind her seems infinitely more scary than the darkness in front. A noise nearby makes her jump, but it's only a frog, slipping into the pool with a gentle plop. Not as bad as the strange grunting and squealing she'd heard earlier, which she'd concluded, by a process of elimination, must be hedgehogs, going about their mysterious business in the night.

How can I be doing this? she thinks. Why do I bear it?

But despite this inevitable questioning, a large part of her is calm and accepting and resigned.

She's doing it because she's been told to - indirectly by a man she loves passionately, directly by one she's currently completely infatuated with.

She's doing it because it's in her nature, because it's actually comforting to understand your place and to know what you have to do. Stand naked in a pool at night - a relatively simple task compared to, say, analysing your self-worth in terms of monetary value in the competitive business world, or trying to decide how you can solve the world's problems and what you, in all your insignificance, can do to make it a better place.

She has nothing to do but shiver and worry about the dark and look back over her day, and wonder at the humiliation she's had to suffer at the receiving end of barbed comments from female conference delegates, and sniggers and mockery from waitresses who think she's the resident lunatic, because of the stupid things they've seen her doing.

And yet - she's aroused. Dreadfully. Her pussy is twitching on its own - crying out for stimulation and orgasm.

Three hours into the night, with maybe three more to go. Tired and cold and scared. A lost soul, a humble servant, tied by an invisible thread to the man currently sitting by a warm fire in the huge building she stands cowering in the shadow of. Her feet deep in mud – and frogs and fish. Her naked skin exposed to the night; her naked subservience exposed to whatever human being might come across it.

Adam told her he wanted to test her without sex, but to Zoe, this is sex. No doubt about it - standing obediently in a fish pond, Zoe is engaged in a sex act. With herself, with the pond, with Adam, with Master Philip, with her past - with the world!

Chapter Five

BARMAID

One Saturday afternoon - back home again - all of a sudden Zoe got dragged out of the house and into town by a Master Philip with a mischievous twinkle in his eye. Some new idea had obviously caught his imagination.

"I've found you a job, my dear. Weekends only - not too strenuous." He threw her a sideways glance. "Ever been a barmaid?"

"Yes," said Zoe, thinking back to the pub she'd worked in for a while some years ago. Her feet had ached and she'd been sick to death of washing glasses, but on the plus side it had taught her mental arithmetic. Nowadays, however, that skill didn't seem to be part of the job - the till did the calculation, at the expense of the customer's time, of course.

"I've come across a guy who runs a pub in the City," Master Philip explained. "Busy with office workers during the week, but so dead at weekends he hasn't been opening. Except now he's going to run it as a members-only club at weekends. We had a interesting little chat about it."

"I can imagine!" Zoe could guess quite readily what her own role in this scheme might be.

"This is it," said Master Philip, pulling up outside a smart establishment decorated with flowers and fresh paint.

"Very pretty," said Zoe. "I think I've been in here once or twice."

The doors were locked, but there were lights on inside and a summons with the door knocker brought a huge stereotype of a bouncer to peer at them suspiciously.

"I think we're expected," said Master Philip, pushing Zoe in past the hulky doorman, who locked the door again behind them.

A handful of men were sitting around at tables, and one of their number detached himself and strode over to greet them with a smile.

"Mr Philip! Glad to see you could make it. Come in, come in. What can I get you to drink?"

"Hello, George. Gin and tonic please - make it two, I think we can allow her one drink before she goes on duty."

George paused to look Zoe over, and the grin on his bearded face got wider and wider as he did so.

"Can't wait to see her with her clothes off, though I say so myself!" And he chuckled happily before bustling over to the bar for their drinks.

Master Philip nodded a hello to the other men, who were looking on with interest, and chose a seat.

Zoe looked around her, imagining that this place might soon become very familiar. There were slightly risqué pictures of partially-clad women dotted around the walls, but in general it had an upmarket atmosphere. Mind you, it looked like an adjacent room was still being reserved for the coarser atmosphere of a Public Bar - rare, these days - so bare floorboards, if not quite sawdust, might well be a feature of her overall public house experience.

They sipped drinks, and Master Philip chatted to the landlord and to some of the other men, and occasionally leaned across to re-adjust bits of Zoe's clothing - tugging her neckline down a little, for example, and pushing up her skirt.

As always, but particularly here, she was expected to be the outrageous slut.

"Time to start carrying round glasses soon, my girl," said Master Philip after a while, "but I thought I'd give a demonstration of what's going to happen if you should ever break one. George, are you watching? I'll be leaving this to you, you know."

He pushed back a table and dragged Zoe over his knee. "Now, let's have your knickers down. Look at that for a view!"

The men gawped as Zoe's bottom was so rapidly and unexpectedly exposed, and gawped some more when Master Philip began one of his long, expert, heaving spankings.

Slap - ouch! Slap - ouch! Slap - ouch!

The pub resounded to the sound-effects of punishment.

Over and over, harder and harder, Master Philip's hand kept falling, and Zoe's bottom wriggled and wriggled as it came to terms with the blows.

"Why don't you have a go, George," Master Philip said presently. "Now you've seen how it's done."

"Oh, I know how it's done," said the landlord, hitching his trousers and his eyebrows, and taking a seat. "Pass her over."

Bottom still naked, Zoe was transferred to George's knee, and an even harder and faster spanking ensued.

"You - just - make - sure - you - work - hard - young - lady!" George punctuated his instruction with slaps. "I - don't - want - to - hear - any - complaints - from - my – customers!"

More of a crowd had gathered (naked bottoms had that effect) and there was a lot of excited fidgeting going on. Eventually someone plucked up the courage to ask if they could have a try. "Of course," said Master Philip. "Move on to the next one, Zoe."

What followed was a spanking marathon the likes of which even Zoe had not experienced before. Everyone wanted a go. Complete beginners were heartily encouraged by the more experienced, and a jovial atmosphere arose, as the sharing of Zoe's bottom brought about an unexpected camaraderie.

So this is being a barmaid! Zoe thought, as she used every mental trick she knew to help her handle the pain.

It might not have been what the average barmaid had to tolerate, but it was certainly what Zoe would have to tolerate - every day, for at least an hour before starting work proper. Her rounded bottom being tossed like a metaphorical beachball from one man to another, her tender skin passing through shades of rose to beetroot, and at the end of it - when everyone interested had had their turn - her skirt being fully raised and tucked in at the waist so that everyone could see, throughout the evening, the evidence of the punishment that had preceded her shift!

"Bye, Zoe," said Master Philip, leaving her still being spanked enthusiastically by one of the customers. "I'll be back to pick you up in a few hours. Mind you do whatever – whatever! – George tells you to."

It was during Zoe's third weekend working as a topless barmaid in George's pub, that she met Tony.

Tony was totally tit obsessed, and when he saw Zoe's big fat naked ones, he quite simply fell in love with them. He was mesmerised from the first instant he laid eyes on them, and from then on could hardly tear his gaze away. He would sit by the bar, his eyes glued to Zoe's chest, his mouth half open in rapture and admiration.

Now Tony was tall and slim, and though cocky and charming, was also quite reckless and rough, and could've given Zoe cause to worry, if his infatuation with her breasts hadn't been accompanied by such good-natured enthusiasm and appreciation.

"Here, Miss, can I just tell you – " was the first thing he ever said to her, "that you've got the most perfect and beautiful pair of boobs on this planet!"

"Thanks," she said. "What are you drinking?"

"Drinking in the sight of those, love!"

She poured him a pint and he carried on ogling. He didn't seem to care about that cliché of a man having to drag his eyes up from a woman's cleavage to look at her face. He just didn't bother, and kept staring down at her chest even as he spoke to her, as though he really couldn't help himself.

As she passed him his drink, he reached forward tentatively with his hand.

"Can I touch?" he whispered.

"Yes," said Zoe, and let him run the fingers of one hand, then two, over her curves, and gently over her nipples.

"Oh, God," he groaned. "How big are they?"

"Er, 38 FF I think," replied Zoe, who hadn't actually bought a bra for some time.

"Mm," Tony cupped her breasts in his hands. "I shall dream about these tonight!"

All evening he watched his beauties flop and bounce about as their owner did her duties as a barmaid, groping them as often as he could, and even starting to annoy some of the other customers with how often his hands were to be found on Zoe's boobs.

"Here, move over!"

"Let someone else have a go, mate."

Later in the night, when Zoe got passed around the customers for yet another prolonged spanking, he ignored her naked bottom, but managed to spend most of the time crouching beside her, cupping and squeezing her tits as they hung down beneath her while she lay over somebody's knee.

At the end of the evening, he watched with regret as a taxi driver came in to pick Zoe up, and kept his eyes glued to her tits as they bounced out of the door.

"What was her name, again?" he asked another drinker, which just showed how preoccupied he'd been, because people had been calling her by her name, frequently, all evening.

The next day, he was back in the pub from the moment the doors opened, sitting on the same stool and following Zoe's tits around, first with his eyes, and then literally – getting up and walking beside her as she collected up glasses, staring at her nipples from close up and touching them whenever he dared.

George was about to ask Zoe if the guy was bothering her, when Tony began to befriend him, complementing the establishment and the service, offering to buy him a drink. George was soon won over, and anyway, he was pretty enamoured of Zoe's tits himself, so they had something in common.

They both began to play with them together, devising some tit games such as Holding A Tall Glass Under Each Tit, Trying To Squeeze Huge Tits Into Pint Glasses, and Guess The Weight Of The Tits.

The latter became a pub-wide game throughout the day: a notepad was found and everyone had a go at guessing the combined weight of Zoe's mammaries – after first weighing them carefully and repeatedly in each hand, of course. (It was only late that night that the game ended with the realisation that George didn't have a suitable scale to weigh them on properly, anyway – so no-one won, though everyone had enjoyed playing.)

After a few more drinks together, Tony plucked up courage to ask George if he could suck on Zoe's nipples – only when she wasn't busy, of course.

"What, here in public?"

"Well, everyone's groping and spanking her in public – I don't see why not."

George considered. "But then everyone would want to suck on them."

"So what? Look at her, she's just standing around idle, right now. Why couldn't I get a little sucking in? Go on, I'm dying to do it."

Now George would've said yes, but on this occasion it so happened that Master Philip was present and had been listening to the exchange from behind his newspaper, so George felt obliged to refer the request.

"Look," he said to Tony, "see that guy there? You'd better check with him."

Tony looked over at Master Philip.

"What, is he the boyfriend?"

"Er, something like that."

"Okay, then."

Now luckily, Tony wasn't the jealous type, and didn't care whether or not Zoe had a partner. He didn't want a relationship with her, after all. He just wanted to play with certain bits of her anatomy, and if that meant asking some other guy for permission, he didn't mind (as long as the guy said yes!)

He stepped up to Master Philip and held out a hand with a smile.

"Hi, I'm Tony. Sorry to bother you, but I really love your girlfriend's tits, and I wondered if I'd be allowed to suck them when she's not busy?"

"It's okay with me," said Master Philip, somewhat amused by the request. "But it's George that's employing her – you'd better check with him."

"It's okay with me," said George, but I guess you'd better check with Zoe.

"It's okay with me," said Zoe when Tony asked her, "but you'd better check with my Master, over there."

Having determined it was okay with everyone, Tony pulled Zoe out from behind the bar and had her stand leaning back against the counter. Then he looked from tit to tit with a gleeful expression, like a starving man about to embark on a banquet, and plunged in!

Master Philip put his paper down and looked over to where Zoe's tits were being squeezed, pulled, kneaded, kissed, licked, sucked and bitten. From the expression on Zoe's face, it seemed she was not objecting to the attention.

Now there's a true tit enthusiast – never seen anyone quite as keen, or quite as easily pleased by a bit of female flesh! Master Philip's expression turned thoughtful as he contemplated inviting this guy Tony home with them, and considered how he might be incorporated into his and Zoe's sex games.

Maybe he could be let loose on Zoe's breasts once the rest of her had been put in tight bondage, or pulled into that new, thick, red, rubber suit?

Maybe he could come along to a gang-bang, and keep playing with Zoe's tits while other men took their turn a bit further down?

Yes, there was scope for creativity there.

Now, there were plenty of other guys in the pub who, when they saw what Tony was being allowed to do with Zoe's melons, clamoured to be allowed to do the same, and in the interests of crowd safety, they were all allowed to have a go.

Tony stepped aside, and watched and waited til the tits came free again and he could get back to his favourite occupation.

Somehow, his jovial manner and obvious enjoyment endeared him to his fellows, and by the end of that weekend, the regulars had accepted him as 'that guy who follows Zoe round sucking at her tits all the time'.

Later in the evening, when George was at last thinking of closing up (he was reluctant to, because Zoe had brought in so much business), and Master Philip came back to pick Zoe up (he'd been out for a meal with some friends), Tony was still to be found worshiping tit – sitting on a low stool behind the bar, letting Zoe's nipples rest and brush upon the platform of his tongue, as she dried glasses and placed them on the surface behind his head.

He was like a man hypnotised – he couldn't tear himself away, and had never been happier.

Master Philip watched for a while, utterly unconcerned by any sort of jealousy. Other men might play with Zoe's tits, but he knew that at the end of the day, those luscious appendages belonged to him – donated by Zoe's devotion.

He was in a mood to put his own stamp on events, however.

"Zoe," he said. "I think those flagrant tits of yours have had a bit too much pleasure today. Maybe we should redress the balance."

His voice took on that pre-punishment growl. "Why don't you put those fat, over-indulged objects on the counter, and I'll see if I can find something to use on them – unfortunately I don't have my riding crop on me this evening!"

George volunteered a plastic ruler from the office. He kept a careful eye on Tony, a little afraid that he might react badly to the precious tits being chastised, but in fact he seemed intrigued, and stayed on his stool, his face at nipple height, waiting to see what Master Philip would do.

Master Philip began to spank Zoe's tits with the ruler. He was an expert, and could get the best out of any implement, so the strokes fell harshly and evenly all over the tops and sides of Zoe's breasts.

All the customers still in the pub gathered round to watch the barmaid having her tits spanked on the counter.

They were amazed by how many strokes she absorbed without complaint. Soon everyone was hypnotised by the seemingly endless noise of the stiff plastic falling on springy flesh.

The tits went red and every cock in the place was stiff as a bone.

Eventually, Master Philip stopped, and some kind-hearted soul fished out some ice cubes from his drink and ran them over Zoe's smarting cleavage, to cool down the burning.

Tony looked from Master Philip's face to Zoe's, stunned and aroused beyond measure by what he'd witnessed, which had certainly been a new experience for him.

"Did that hurt, Zoe?" Master Philip asked, still with the growl.

"Yes, Master," Zoe replied truthfully. It had hurt very much, but she had loved every minute of it.

"Are they sore?"

"Yes, Master."

"Are they tender?"

"Yes, Master."

"Well, perhaps your new breast attendant would like to kiss them better?"

Tony didn't need to be told twice – he leapt at the reddened flesh and kissed it repeatedly, licking up drops of icy water in the process.

And from the depths of his own reverie, he made an utterance that would only surprise him the following day, when he suddenly remembered it.

"Thank you, Master," said Tony.

"Dear Mickie,

Hi, it's Reg, how are you?

You're certain not to believe this, but in any case it's true, and if you want I can take you along to see for yourself.

For the last three weekends in a row I've spent the best of two days in this London pub with a mate of mine, doing nothing but drinking, eating, playing cards and watching the amazing antics that have been going on.

It's not just any old pub, you only get in by invitation, and the drinks are really expensive, but I can't keep away from the place - I don't care what it costs!

They've got this woman there. I don't know where they got her from, I guess she's paid for it, though they say she isn't, that she does what she does because she's hooked on some guy. Don't know whether I believe that - sounds pretty unlikely! Anyway she's an absolute stunner with the most perfect tits you've ever seen and gorgeous hair. Unusual looking, in a way, not like a model or anything, and really intelligent, with a posh sexy voice - not that she says much, though. But it's just outrageous what she has to do, and things seem to be getting more and more out of hand each week!

She's working topless behind the bar, right, just serving drinks like normal, and coming out to clear tables. You're allowed to reach over and have a feel, though - not like other topless places I've been to, where you can't touch - and everyone who comes in makes a beeline for her tits and has a good play while she tries to get them their drinks.

The number of guys in there builds up, and you can see the whole lot of them eyeing her up. She's always the only woman there, so there's nothing else to draw your eye except her lovely boobs bouncing around as she walks.

Then at nine o'clock the fun starts. She climbs up onto the bar and starts doing a striptease. Not really like dancing properly, but walking round posing and shaking things and thrusting herself at people. She takes ages taking off her skirt, and sometimes she's got a top on, though it's been undone to let her tits out, and she does the whole thing so sensually and slowly it drives everyone crazy. And she lets people help her, undoing her zip, pulling her skirt up or down. You should see the number of guys' hands reaching up to give her a hand with that skirt!

And then of course there's her stockings and knickers. Sometimes they get left on til later - what often happens is that she at some point gets dressed again and then does another striptease an hour or so later - but eventually they come off as well, usually with lots of male hands competing to undo her suspenders for her.

So there she is, naked in this pub atmosphere, and it's so weird because it's a pub you can go in during the week and it's all conventional and proper and people would never guess that on Saturday nights there's this naked angel prancing around on the counter, crouching down so her pussy's right over your drink!

George, the guy who owns the place, has got a thing about beer, so he always does this trick where he stands behind her and pours a pint over her shoulder so it runs down her tits and her front, making her all sticky. Then everyone starts flicking beer at her and wiping their hands on her rump, and I'm telling you I'm starting to get a thing about it myself, because every time she walks past there's this mixed smell of woman and beer, and it's bloody gorgeous.

The other night I was right at the front of the action. There she was, having had all this beer and stuff poured all over her, and literally, like, sitting in a puddle - God, it was such a turn on to see a woman like that on the floor in a puddle of beer, I can't get the image of it out of my head - and suddenly my mate pushes me forward, shouting something crude about why doesn't she get a bit more sticky or something!

Well, I've been told I'm shy in the past, but what can you do in a situation like that? I looked up at George and he gave me the nod, so I whipped old faithful out and stuck it in her face. I have to say it was amazing, she was so good! It was like being sucked by a machine, so strong, and lovely long strokes just how I like - though, hey, I shouldn't go on about it too much or I'll make you jealous. So it goes on and on, and I can't take my eyes off what she's doing, except when I look down and see the beer puddle - oh, God - and suddenly I'm plunging right down her throat really madly, like.

And then - wait for it - my mate gets his pint of lager and, just when I'm nearly there and she looks like she's choking on it, he pours it slowly all over her head and my cock! And her face is all wet, and I pull out and gush all over the place, and everyone's standing round leaning closer and having a good look, and some of them have got theirs out, and - bloody hell, Mickie, you've just got to come down here and have a look at this amazing bloody barmaid!

Cheers, Reg."

Chapter Six

ON HOLIDAY

"I have a new challenge for you, Zoe," Master Philip announced one evening, on coming home from a meeting. "How would you like to go on holiday?"

Zoe, who was doing the ironing in a leather body harness, looked over at him skeptically. "That would be nice," she said cautiously. "What's the catch?"

Master Philip went over to her and grasped an exposed buttock with his hand. "Now, now, angel, don't be so cynical. It's a genuine opportunity. A few weeks on one of the smaller Greek islands. Chap I've just been talking to has a villa there."

Zoe put down the iron and turned towards her Master, her eyes lighting up.

"With you?" she asked.

"No, sorry, I think not. I have to wind up this Far East business."

"Oh, Master," Zoe cried. "Not another separation! Not more weeks without you!"

Master Philip sighed in exasperation. "Zoe, Zoe! How many times do I have to tell you, you can't have all my attention?"

Then he relented and kissed her. "Look, I'd have been away anyway. At least you'll get a change of scenery - and maybe some sun."

"Only maybe?"

"Well - I expect you might be busy."

"Ah, we're getting to the catch, I think."

"Yes. But you might not be too unhappy about it. My colleague is letting the villa to his twenty year old stepson and some of the son's college friends. I suggested they might appreciate having you along as a companion."

"Er, how many friends?" asked Zoe.

Master Philip's eyes twinkled. "Only five! You should be able to manage half a dozen young lads without any problem - what with all your experience."

Zoe leant against Master Philip as she took in the news. The tingling in her pussy was giving her a very clear idea of whether or not she could manage six twenty year olds!

"I'll send you a postcard, Master!"

Now Zoe was quite young herself, but because of all the things she'd lived through - all the complex sex games she'd played with older men - she saw herself as mature for her years, and had a rather clear image of what she thought twenty year old lads going on holiday to Greece were going to be like. Inexperienced, she was sure. Unrefined, almost definitely, and probably very straightforward in their sexual needs. Fucks that were over in a few seconds, she confidently predicted, along with an immature aversion to anything 'kinky'.

When she saw them, sprawled across some seats in the airport lounge, she felt her opinion was confirmed. They were just boys! Loud, scruffy boys, fooling about together, and giggling a little when they saw her approach.

Master Philip was with her, and so was the acquaintance who owned the villa, a portly gentleman in an expensive suit, who had been introduced to Zoe as Mr Atherton.

"Ah, Oliver," said Mr Atherton to one of the boys, who was obviously his stepson. "This is the girl I told you about, and this is the gentleman who is so kindly lending her to you. Now you will be sure to look after her, and return her safely in one piece?"

"Of course," said Oliver, a lanky lad in a football shirt, shaking Master Philip's hand, and throwing Zoe only a dismissive glance. "We appreciate it, sir."

Mr Atherton was fumbling with some keys, which he handed to Oliver. "These are for the villa," he said. "And see this little one here? That's for the room I told you about. I'm sure you'll find everything you need in there."

Simultaneously, he, Oliver and Master Philip gave Zoe a funny look, and she suddenly realised that there might be more to this experience than she'd anticipated! Still, too late now. She might as well make the most of it.

Master Philip pecked her on the cheek by way of a goodbye. "Now don't forget," he said in her ear. "You're going along as their slave, so do whatever you're told. I'll be embarrassed if I hear any complaints."

Zoe nodded dutifully. "I'll be good, Master."

The two men left, leaving Zoe alone for the first time with the boys.

"Great!" said one of them, who turned out to be called Duncan. "Better looking than I thought! Can't wait to get into her."

"Yeah, it's bloody good of your dad, Oli, laying on the pussy for free, like that. I'm going to make the most of it, I'll tell you." This was from the biggest of the boys, who sported a severe haircut, and who had his name on a chain round his neck - Mick.

"Turn around, love. Let's have a look at you."

Zoe was quite surprised by the tone of these comments, especially as they were in a relatively public place, but it seemed that the little gang were a bit less innocent than she'd expected.

She turned round somewhat gingerly, then perched on the edge of a free seat, clutching her travel bag for security. She tried being friendly, and asked the names of the other boys, giving them a broad smile.

"We're all Sir to you!" was the response she got, with added snigger. "Don't think we don't know all about you! You're coming along as our servant – "

"And whore."

" - and whore, so don't expect us to speak to you!"

But it seemed that one at least of the boys was more civil – a short lad who came to her defense, and returned her smile.

"Oh, shut up, Miles! They're not always like this, Zoe. They're just getting carried away with the idea of being away from home, and having the novelty of - of someone like you around."

This one's name was Steven, and he introduced the quietest of the six, Jamie, who was staring at Zoe with a look of undisguised fascination.

"Jamie's a virgin," Duncan teased. "Couldn't believe his luck when he heard you were coming."

"I am not!"

"Come on, you are. Why not admit it?"

"If he is, he won't be for long."

"Oh, leave him alone."

And so the conversation deteriorated to more squabbling, and Zoe despaired of being able to have a reasonable conversation over the next few weeks.

Their flight was soon called, and on the plane, Zoe found herself sitting between Oliver and Miles, who spent the whole journey surreptitiously fondling her thighs and giggling madly at the fact she couldn't do anything about it.

When they at last arrived, she was left straggling behind the others with all the hand luggage, and then had to recover all the suitcases from the baggage carousel herself, while the boys disappeared into an airport bar.

They still had a boat transfer to the holiday isle, and Zoe spent it standing by the railings because there was a shortage of seats and none of the boys would give her theirs. But it was only when they had piled out of two taxis and piled into the huge and luxurious private villa, that Zoe got a true feel for what the lads' attitude towards her was to be.

They made her strip off and kneel on the floor in front of them, while Oliver outlined some rules.

"Now my stepdad's told me a lot about how to handle women like you, and personally, I can't wait to try it out, so don't imagine that you're going to have an easy time! We're not really interested in you, you know. We're here to sunbathe and swim and surf, and pick up real women on the beach. You're just going to be useful, to do things for us round the villa, and maybe take the edge off our randiness. Get the picture so far?"

"Yes, sir," said Zoe, her head now pressed down to the floor by Mick's shoe.

"Your duties - as approved by your Master guy, by the way - are to cook our meals, do the washing up, sort out any laundry, make the beds, go shopping, and generally fetch and carry for us, so our holiday is as effort and trouble free as possible. Isn't that right guys?"

A roar of approval went up.

"Like a cross between a tour rep, a cook and a chambermaid," said Duncan.

"And of course – "

"Not forgetting – "

"Most important – "

"Our slut."

"To fuck as and when we want."

"Never to object or complain."
"Always to split your legs on request."
"Starting right now!"
They all lasted a lot longer than a few seconds - and Jamie was definitely not a virgin!

There were only six beds in the villa, which meant that Zoe spent the night on a hard plastic sunbed on the balcony, with only a coarse blanket as bedding. She didn't mind too much, though, because she at least had a bit of privacy, and took some time exploring the outside of the villa by moonlight.
It had a beautiful pool, which she couldn't resist sneaking a little skinny dip in, being careful not to make too much noise, and a garden full of fig trees and oleander bushes, from which there was a wonderful view down across the bay and out to sea. She decided that whatever was to happen was already worth it, just to have experienced this exquisite atmosphere for one night!
It was not going to be an easy holiday, however, as poor, longsuffering Zoe was to find out the following morning.
The six young men woke her mid-morning with loud complaints that their breakfast wasn't ready, and a mixture of demands - for sex and food.
She hurried to the kitchen amid a flurry of urgent groping, only to discover that there was no food in the fridge - not even milk for coffee.
"Right," Oliver decided. "We'll go out and explore, and get an English Breakfast on the beach or something. You find a shop and stock up, then unpack for us, and do something about a meal for the evening."
"But first – "
Three out of six of them seemed to have woken up randy, and she dealt with them on the kitchen floor before the whole gang hurried away, leaving her wondering where on earth the nearest shop was - the villa seemed to be quite isolated. In fact it was some way down the hill towards the nearest village, and she found it quite a trek - especially on the way back, laden down with groceries as she was, and struggling with the fierce Mediterranean heat.
She had just made it back and spent an hour or so tidying the place

up and unpacking the boys' bags, when they all turned up again - on six little motor bikes which they'd immediately hired for the whole holiday. She told them about the distance to the supermarket, and even risked asking if she would be able to borrow one of the bikes to do the shopping occasionally, but the response was predictable.

"Slaves can walk! We need these to get around and have fun on."

They had come back for their swimming things, and announced that they would be spending the afternoon on the beach. Zoe would love to have gone with them, but it was obvious now that this wasn't to be.

"So is she just going to be allowed to laze around here all the time?" Miles asked callously. "Surely we mustn't let her enjoy herself?"

"You're right," said Oliver. "We need to do something to make her uncomfortable. Let's take a look at what's in this secret room!"

Oliver got the key and they all traipsed along to the back of the villa, with Zoe in tow. The door creaked open to reveal a windowless room, lit by just a dim lightbulb, in which had been stowed away racks and racks and piles and piles of kinky clothing and bondage gear.

"Wow!" said Duncan, as they all explored. "Look at all these chains!"

"And this rubber stuff! It reeks!"

"What the hell's this?" Steven asked, holding up a mysterious and forbidding metal object.

"God knows! I think I recognize these, though. They're nipple clamps."

Zoe stood and looked at the contents of the room in horror and resignation. What worried her most was the heat. Wearing rubber was difficult enough in temperate climates, but in this sort of weather, it would be appalling!

Still, it wouldn't exactly be a new experience, she reflected. She was an experienced slave now, and she would simply have to grin and bear it.

Oliver was investigating a contraption set up in one corner of the room. "Right," he said, "we've got weeks to experiment with all the stuff, but for now I think this here cage will do. Slave, come here!"

Zoe crossed over to him, and saw that the cage was tiny. She wouldn't be able to stand up in it, only crouch or sit, and she'd have to get down on all fours to crawl through the tiny door, which sported a huge padlock.

"In you get," she was heartlessly instructed. "We'll be back in a few hours, and then we'll let you out to fix us some food. Come on guys! Down to the beach!" He looked back at her just before turning off the light. "Happy holiday, slave!"

So, the highlight of Zoe's first day in Greece was a four hour stint in a tiny cage in one corner of a hot, stuffy little room in which the smell of rubber and leather was quite overpowering. She was thirsty and needed to go to the toilet, but there was nothing she could do to escape or ease her discomfort, so she passed the time wanking and trying to sleep.

In fact this first experience was representative of what most days of this holiday were going to be like. Over the first week, a pattern was established.

Zoe would wake up early and get up from her sunbed - or whichever corner of the floor she might have been instructed to sleep on the previous evening - and make breakfast for everyone. Then whoever wanted to have sex with her would do so, sometimes taking her alone into one of the rooms for an extended session, sometimes sharing her in the private garden or by the pool. The boys would generally laze around and swim and sunbathe and listen to music, while Zoe would do any chores that needed doing, including walking down to the shop if necessary.

Then she would be put into some kind of bondage for the afternoon while the lads went down to the beach on their mopeds.

At first this bondage was quite light - just hobbles and handcuffs, for example, or a tight corset and nipple clamps together with a rope tying her to the kitchen taps. But as time went on, things became much more adventurous.

The store of equipment yielded some pretty severe rubber body suits and body harnesses, and these got tried on Zoe one by one. Since the lads didn't have a great deal of experience with things like this, the equipment sometimes ended up being put on wrongly or done up too tight, and was therefore even more uncomfortable to wear than had originally been intended.

One complex array of straps Zoe was sure got put on her completely upside down, but she wasn't in a position to do or say anything about it because she'd been gagged the moment she'd started to object.

So when everyone else on the island was having a comfortable siesta, poor Zoe the sex slave found herself struggling and sweating in some awful costume or apparatus, and totally unable to get herself free or even move her tortured limbs. Often she would be tied down firmly to one of the beds with rope, and sometimes completely suspended from a sturdy hook in the bondage room. More often than not she was left with her legs stretched wide open, and she often worried about what would happen if some unsuspecting local visitor came upon her by accident - she would give them a heart attack!

In the early evening, all six of the boys would come in from their day of lazing around by the sea and invariably become extremely randy at the sight of whatever predicament they had left Zoe in, and expend at least a couple of hours fucking her hard and fast, before eventually releasing her to make them some food.

After they'd eaten and showered, they would usually go out again to live it up at the night clubs and bars down at the resort, again leaving Zoe either tied up, or locked in the cage, or at the very least handcuffed to the foot of one of their beds, where she would often stay until the following morning.

Zoe took it all in her stride, thinking often of her Master, and what he would have thought had he seen how thoroughly the youngsters were making use of her, and doing her best, as always, to be dutiful and uncomplaining.

She did regret not having any freedom, however. It would have been nice to see a little of the island, and perhaps just spend one day on the beach herself.

After a few more days had passed, Zoe decided to try to raise this point with the boys, and she had an opportunity when Steven, who remained the kindest in his manner towards her, was fucking her on his own out on the balcony one evening.

"Is the beach nice and sandy, sir?" she asked as he nuzzled her breasts.

"Yeah," he muttered, a little distracted.

"And is the town pretty? I would so like to have a look at it, just once."

Steve carried on with what he was doing, and enjoyed a huge and fulfilling orgasm up Zoe's pussy before answering.

"It's a beautiful place. I guess it's not fair on you, not being able to see anything. I'll have a word with Oli, see what he says."

The following morning, after she'd washed up after breakfast, and scrubbed a pile of dirty pants and hung them out to dry, Oliver instructed her to lie on the hot floor of the sun-drenched patio, by his feet, and listen to what they'd all been discussing.

"I understand," he said, as Zoe kissed his feet, "that you'd like to come out with us and have a look at the island. Is that right?"

"Yes, sir, it would be nice, sir."

"Well, it's an extremely impertinent suggestion!" Oliver was still only learning how to be a master, but he was getting more and more into the role every day. "Aren't you aware that you're here as our sex slave? You're not here to have a holiday yourself! How dare you even think such a thing?"

"I'm sorry, sir," Zoe cringed, while several of the others smirked openly. "Of course I'm only here for your pleasure, sirs."

"However, it's possible that you could make yourself useful if you accompanied us occasionally. You could bring us drinks while we sunbathed, and rub suntan oil on us. And we could take you to one of the secluded beaches there are, apparently, on the other side of the island, and fuck you there. It might be amusing."

Zoe squirmed against the floor, pleased that she seemed to have won a concession.

"What do you think, guys? Shall we let her come?"

There was lots of mock head-shaking and breath-drawing.

"Hm, I don't know, Oli. It's a bit too much of a privilege for her. She should have to pay for it in some way, don't you think?"

"Just what I was thinking. How about giving her a good thrashing before we leave - just to make sure she's nice and uncomfortable when she sits on the bike."

This conclusion had clearly been reached in advance, and the young men were all fired up with the idea of giving Zoe a whipping before taking her out for a spin with them. She was sent to get a whip from the secret room, and then instructed to prostrate her naked self in front of them, bottom up, on the concrete.

Without any apparent concern that one of the villagers might happen past and see or hear what was going on, Oliver proceeded to practise his whip strokes on Zoe's bum. Not all that hard – certainly not as hard as Zoe sometimes received from Master Philip – but painful all the same. She kept still and managed not to cry out, but got a bit disconcerted when the whip was passed in turn to each of the other lads for a go.

When it was Jamie's turn, she noticed a slight hesitation.

"Go on, give it to her," his colleagues urged him on, but still he came and knelt beside her, unable, it seemed, to be quite as heartless as the others.

"Are you sure you're alright?" he asked, looking at her with an expression of concern and confusion. "We don't really want to, you know, hurt you too much."

Zoe appreciated his effort to be kind to her, and felt sorry for him, trying to keep up with the antics of the others all the time, but she could also see from the huge bulge in his shorts that he was madly aroused. In fact when it came to fucking her and tying her up, he'd been almost more enthusiastic than anyone else, but there was obviously some turmoil going on, and she wanted to help him out of it.

"Don't worry, really," she smiled up at him from her lowly position. "I'm used to it. Just go ahead."

When Jamie stood up he glowered round into his friends' eyes as if challenging them to mock him for his concern. Then he whipped Zoe harder and longer than anyone else had, until she was squirming and sobbing despite all her best efforts, and all the other boys were so randy that they had to fuck her there and then.

Zoe stayed on all fours while they took turns behind her, each of them fingering and prodding her newly whipped bum, which now had some very noticeable marks on it.

"Ouch, ouch!" she cried out as they slapped away at her, but they were all so fascinated and turned on that no-one took any notice of her discomfort. They didn't know what it felt like to have such a sore bottom!

"Okay," said Oliver, when they'd all finished. "Time for a bike ride, and you can come with us. But you've only paid half the price. I think you need something else to make you remember that you're not just any old tourist - you're our slave."

He dragged her back inside and selected a short, thick dildo from a storage box they'd recently discovered. "Legs open please!"

The dildo went in easily enough, but it wouldn't stay in. Zoe was instructed to pull some tight jeans on and this did the trick, keeping the monster object deep inside her and out of sight. She felt she could hardly move, and wondered how on earth she was going to do any sort of walking about with that sort of thing up her pussy. There was nothing for it though, she'd just have to try.

As a final touch, the boys tied a couple of bits of rope tightly round the base of Zoe's tits before having her put on a t-shirt and climb onto the back of Oliver's bike. She winced as her bruised bottom hit the seat and the dildo seemed to be pressed even further in, but made an effort to tolerate in silence. At least she was getting away from the villa at last, and would see something of the rest of the island!

They all roared down the hill to the tourist resort and spent some time driving up and down the various shop and restaurant lined streets. Zoe got some looks, not just because she was so strikingly attractive, but because her nipples showed through her top, and her big, braless tits bounced and vibrated up and down as the bike sped along.

For her part, Zoe couldn't help expressing some interest herself in the various groups of hunky Greek men who sprawled around in cafés eyeing up all the female foreign tourists. Sampling the local flesh might have been interesting, but here she was, the plaything of a younger generation!

"Push your tits against my back," Oliver shouted back to her, and she leaned forward, forgetting her momentary excursion into fantasy, and remembering her duty.

They drove along the beach and then carried on up the coast road to some of the more isolated parts of the island. This was another world, dominated by olive groves and insect noise, and liberally splattered with overladen donkeys and little old ladies in black headscarves.

Some of the old ladies looked at her curiously. Why was there just one girl with six boys, they might have been wondering. Could they have even conceived of the sort of group sex and kinky games that went on at the villa? Would they have believed or understood why Zoe had a big piece of rubber thrust into her private places? Or that she had whip marks on her bottom, received voluntarily? Their wrinkled faces gave nothing away.

After a good couple of hours exploring, which Zoe thoroughly enjoyed, they stopped in the middle of nowhere and threw themselves down under the shade of some big olive trees to drink warm but welcome beer. The boys pulled Zoe's top up, and at last took the ropes off her breasts, which was a relief as they'd been digging in quite a bit. They then set about gleefully playing with her squashy female flesh, which for some reason seemed to be more fun in the open air.

Just as Zoe was beginning to relax and enjoy this relatively conventional sexual attention, she suddenly got a start, as she found herself looking into the eyes of two rugged strangers. They had appeared from nowhere and were standing behind a bush staring wide-eyed at the wanton spectacle Zoe's big naked tits provided.

They were young and tanned, but scruffy, and both had rather unruly beards. Zoe assumed they were farmers, out checking on the ripeness of the olives or something, but in fact - as she was to learn from local gossip much later - they were escaped convicts, hiding out in the countryside while their friends on the mainland arranged for a boat to come and pick them up.

The boys had also seen them now, and Oliver grinned mischievously at Zoe before beckoning the two voyeurs over. They came cautiously - shuffling and hesitant, for this was hardly the sort of scene one came across often in a remote olive grove - but Zoe's erect nipples were acting like a magnet.

Steven offered them some beer and tried to make conversation, but they didn't seem to speak any English. By use of the primitive method of counting on fingers, however, they were able to convey what amazed them most about the situation.

Girl - they indicated, pointing - one.

Boy - one, two, three, four, five, six!

Coming as they did from a culture where anything sexual took place in privacy and strictly on a one to one basis, the idea of a woman being shared like this was obviously quite overwhelming.

Oliver, however, was quick to amend their observation.

"No," he said, shaking his head and smiling. "Girl - one. Boy - one, two, three, four, five, six... seven, eight."

Seven and Eight thought about this for about five seconds before getting their cocks out and preparing to make the most of their good fortune.

Zoe, who hadn't been consulted, of course, but who didn't particularly object - she'd recently been lusting after local flesh, after all - thrust her breasts up towards the bemused but enthusiastic rustics, who mauled them and kissed them and rubbed their willies on them with huge pleasure and some nervousness.

"Fuck?" one of them asked, no doubt exhibiting the full range of his English vocabulary, and reaching for the zip on Zoe's jeans, so sure was he already of the answer.

Zoe looked up at Oliver and Steven questioningly, wondering if the presence of the dildo had already been forgotten, but as it happened any problem was avoided for at this point the other Greek ejaculated copiously over Zoe's tits, and his friend was unable to prevent himself doing the same.

This was too much for Zoe's six companions, and one after the other they also deposited their loads on those drenched and sticky mounds.

Never would Zoe forget the incongruous sounds of male panting and sighing accompanied by a midday chorus of cicadas and crickets - an unusual combination for her, though of course that same spot may well have witnessed the antics of rampant holidaymakers before, or even a hedonistic orgy or two in the days of ancient Greece.

She rubbed the dripping male liquid all over her chest before pulling her top down, and enjoyed the fact that several wet patches showed through - patches only she and eight men would know the true cause of, though others might guess.

The two convicts presently excused themselves with smiles, doubtless taking away with them a tale their colleagues would never believe. In years to come, however, they would drink together and reminisce about that amazing day they came across a beautiful English woman accompanied by six young men, who joined them in coming all over the lady's stupendous naked tits!

The gang meanwhile got on their bikes and rode on, down to the coast again, and found a deserted beach which became their base for the rest of the day. The boys swam and slept, and Zoe also was allowed to go swimming - topless, but with her jeans still on, to make sure the dildo stayed where it belonged. She enjoyed herself immensely, not at all objecting to the feel of wet denim across her still sore bottom and down her hot legs.

Steven and Jamie swam with her, forgetting for the moment her role of slave, and splashing and dunking her playfully, til she squealed and laughed like any other young woman on holiday.

At one point, Jamie took her in his arms and kissed her romantically.

"You're so beautiful," he crooned in her ear. "I'd take you away from this lot, but it turns me on so much, the things they make you do."

Unsure how to reply to this exposure of a soul, Zoe merely kissed him romantically back, but they were soon reminded of the non-exclusivity of the relationship by Miles, who charged loudly into the waves, grabbed Zoe, and pushed her head underwater - so that he could have the experience of being sucked off by a mermaid, he announced.

Some time later, Zoe finally collapsed exhausted onto the beach, only to find the rest of the guys in a somewhat cruel and playful mood.

"Now, we wouldn't want those lovely tits to get sunburned, would we?" said Mick.

"And we really think you've been out of bondage long enough," Duncan added.

"So," Oliver delivered the punchline. "We're going to bury you in the sand!"

Zoe was a bit taken aback by this suggestion. She looked around her, especially back up towards the road.

"Here?"

"Yes, here! Why not - there's no-one about?"

"You're not objecting are you?" Duncan chipped in.

Zoe sighed. "No, sir."

"Get to it, then."

"What?"

"Digging the hole, of course."

With nothing but her bare hands to work with, Zoe did the best she could to dig a shallow trench in the soft, warm sand. When at last she thought she'd finished, she was instructed to try lying in it, and of course the unanimous opinion was that it wasn't deep enough yet.

"You're being modest about the size of your boobs, love!"

A little longer on her hands and knees in the trench - her naked tits swinging with her exertions, and the intruder in her pussy causing her more discomfort than ever - and it was declared adequate. Now it was time for her to lie down in the hole, on her back, with just her head left above the level of the sand, and for the boys to have the pleasure of filling it in again - packing the sand tightly around her.

It was a new experience for Zoe, and she immediately found it a turn on. While she could probably have escaped with a little effort, in effect it was a totally restrictive form of bondage, and combined with the exotic location and stimulating company it gave her a positive thrill.

If my Master could see me now, she thought. No doubt she would be telling him all about this adventure in detail on her return.

The boys first amused themselves by sitting and lying on the sand over her body. Next they took turns to lie with their crotches pressing against her face, instructing her to kiss their bits through their swimming trunks. Then, screening each other from the road, and giggling somewhat at the novelty of it, they got their stiffening pricks out and slipped them smoothly into Zoe's mouth, one by one.

So it was that Zoe spent the next couple of hours or so in her own, strange little world - her body held tightly in a cocoon of sand, her face full of cock, and her ears full of the sounds of the sea and her companions' crude and increasingly excited comments.

"See, she is useful - we should bring her out again!"

"Yeah, even on a busy beach, we could put wind breakers up for privacy - have her mouth always available to whichever of us wasn't out swimming."

"What we need is a big plastic bucket to cover her head up in, when we're not using it. What a lark! No one would even know."

"How do you fancy getting your head covered up in a bucket, Zoe?"

"Er, she can't talk right now - her mouth's full."

"Maybe we should dig her tits out and cover them up with buckets as well. Then we could surprise some more natives by suddenly whipping the buckets off the tits and saying, look what we've got!"

"Or shock some birds!"

"Yeah! Tell 'em that's what we'll do to them if they don't behave."

"Have them stripping their bikinis off in a rush to please us!"

"Oo, Jesus, guys - this is beautiful! A beach that sucks you off!"

When all six of the lads had again enjoyed a leisurely orgasm, they tossed a towel over Zoe's head and fell asleep.

What a way to spend a holiday, thought Zoe, before, exhausted, she did the same.

Chapter Seven

MASTURBATE!

"I think we should have a break from all these gang-bangs," Master Philip sighed one morning, after a particularly numerous gathering the previous night. "You've been working so hard at giving pleasure - maybe we'll concentrate on your pleasure for a while."

Zoe wasn't sure she could believe her ears. Was he being serious?

"I want you to masturbate for me."

They were lying side by side and Master Philip propped himself up on one elbow to look at her. "Still 'for me', mind! Offer up your orgasm and all that."

Zoe raised her eyebrows. Master Philip in a frivolous mood! A rare thing.

"Go on then," he urged. "Masturbate!"

"What, now?"

"Yes, why not?"

"Okay - thank you, Master!" Zoe said, and moved her hand into position.

It was difficult to concentrate at first, with him watching, but she soon got caught up in memories of the night before and found herself coming along nicely.

Master Philip knew that she liked to have something in her pussy as she came (otherwise orgasms 'didn't take properly' and 'fizzled out'), and so Zoe was very gratified when he inserted a couple of fingers just exactly at the moment when she felt she needed them.

Her breathing rate rising and her hand working faster told him she was getting close, and one strong image later (a nice, heavy bondage fantasy) she was over the edge and gasping.

Immediately afterwards Master Philip grabbed her wrist with his other hand, to see how her pulse was racing.

"How men can say they don't know if a woman's come I don't know," he said, somewhat pretentiously. "Okay, maybe a slit could be as juicy and sticky as this just before an orgasm, as well as after it. Maybe the rapid breathing can be put on. But can any amount of pseudo-grunting and sighing take the pulse rate up this high? I think not!"

After a little more probing, he wiped his sticky hand on Zoe's thigh. "I mention these things because I want you to know I can tell when you've really come. Especially when you're just lying there, relaxed - your pulse will always tell me."

Zoe was slightly affronted. "But Master, you know I never fake orgasms. I either come or not - I've never seen the point of pretending."

"Ah, but maybe you haven't been tested. You see, I'm going to be telling you to do it more often than you might have before."

Aha, thought Zoe. That catch, again.

"As of today, I want you to come - let me see, we'll start off with ten times a day. How does that sound?"

"It sounds like a lot, Master! They don't always come that easily. And they get more difficult if you try to do several in a row."

"Then you'll be frigging yourself all day in a struggle to achieve your quota! Exactly my intention!" He grinned mischievously. "Honestly! Being instructed to give yourself an excess of pleasure and you're complaining! You don't know what a lucky slave you are!"

What a clever, subtle, difficult test this new turn of events was to be for Zoe.

Of course she enjoyed having orgasms just like the rest of us, and had found those occasions when she wasn't allowed to have them quite trying - like during long periods in bondage, for example, and perhaps when being fucked but nevertheless left in an unassisted, frustrated state of arousal.

But to be forced to have so many? A nice idea in a way, but she only hoped that the pressure to achieve wouldn't pollute her pleasure in the future. In short, she was slightly afraid this excess of self indulgence might put her off the same in the months and years to come.

However, after a little experimentation, she found she could 'manage' her orgasm quota quite well. Trying to have them one immediately after the other was the problem. It did get more and more difficult, requiring increasing effort for a less and less spectacular result. But she found that if she rested in between - at least fifteen minutes, but preferably half an hour - they came easily again.

Still, that was five hours a day at least to be spent focusing on wanking! She found it a bit shattering, and kept dozing off and getting behind schedule.

But this was just the start of Master Philip's plans in the masturbation department. On days when he was home (the number of which he now contrived to increase), Zoe's orgasm quota would be raised to fifteen or even twenty, and she wouldn't be allowed to amuse herself between times around the house, but would be chained to a bed for most of the day, with a special heart rate monitor that Master Philip had had specially designed, clamped to her wrist.

Surrounding her on the bed were a variety of vibrators and dildos which she was instructed to make good use of, and she soon got into a pattern of alternately using her fingers and a vibrator to bring herself off.

The monitor on her wrist recorded full details of her heart rate, and though she secretly thought that she could probably cheat and increase her pulse even in her chained down position (by, say, doing some prolonged arm and leg exercises), she didn't dare put this to the test, in case some difference in the digitally recorded pattern gave her away.

Master Philip would frequently wander in as she lay there, and stand looking down on the picture of sensuality she presented - usually while talking to someone on his mobile phone, or munching on a sandwich, or sipping at coffee.

One morning, he first had her dress in some new sexy red underwear, and then lay the bed she was going to be lying on with black silk sheets.

As Zoe correctly guessed, this turned out to be because he'd invited some business associates over, and after a meeting asked them upstairs to have a look at where his sex slave lay wanking herself all day.

They didn't believe it til they saw it, and they were lucky - they entered the room just as Zoe was going over the edge as a result of a particularly filthy fantasy she'd been using to help her. (The fantasies had to get filthier and filthier as the day went on, although sometimes a really good one would work for several orgasms in a row.)

The men stood looking at her open-mouthed as she lay there, legs thrown wide, thick dildo protruding from wet pussy, face flushed, and body shining slightly with the sweat of her exertions, and were too stunned, on that occasion, to consider asking for some sort of gratification. They certainly took away with them an image they'd never forget, though!

Having people wander in for a look became a regular occurrence, and Zoe was sometimes so absorbed in what she was doing that she hardly noticed that there was some man peering at her from the end of the bed.

At other times, however, the men, with Master Philip's approval, made the most of her wet pussy and put her behind schedule again, though she did her best to keep wanking even while she was otherwise engaged.

One evening, when she'd been at it all day long, and was aiming for number twelve of a particularly difficult quota of twenty orgasms, Master Philip dragged her sweaty form downstairs and had her lie in the middle of the floor while he and some friends enjoyed a little cocktail party.

She was so exhausted she didn't really care what a spectacle she made of herself, lying there jerking her hips in an attempt to get more stimulation from a vibrator, and wasn't too bothered when all the men came and stood over her and began unzipping their flies.

"This is too much!" she heard one of them say.

"What a beauty!" said another.

"That's how I like to see a woman!"

Two or three of the men - including Master Philip - knelt down around her head, and she knew what was coming. She paused at the realisation, but was quickly told, "Don't stop! We're going to let the lady come first."

The close proximity of the men did affect her of course, and looking up at them from her lowly position helped her get to that point of no return. Just as she went over the edge she felt the first splash on her thigh, and a moment later Master Philip was giving her a command that would often feature in her fantasies on subsequent attempts.

A common phrase that took on new meaning in this context:

"Close your eyes and open wide!"

Then an unexpectedly pleasant turn of events happened.

Master Philip decreed that he wanted to increase her daily quota still further but, acknowledging the difficulties, intended to help her. By getting a string of male submissives in to give her some good oral!

And so began one of the most enjoyable periods of Zoe's testing, for having somebody else do all the hard work for you was so much more relaxing, and of course the sensations of oral sex were so wonderful that it really felt like a treat to get so much of it.

Master Philip had actually commissioned some contact of his to come up with compliant and experienced male slaves by liaising with a number of professional mistresses in the city.

They came for three hour stints, paid extra for the privilege of an adventure, and were under strict instructions not to even think of being allowed to fuck the lady they would be servicing. Many and varied though they were - from portly executives to slim young students - they all behaved impeccably and caused no trouble at all. No doubt they had each been warned by their own mistresses not to misbehave.

Thus a queue formed at the foot of Zoe's bed, and each of the men - who had to strip naked before beginning their duties - took his turn at immersing his tongue in her pussy for as long as it took for the desired effect to be achieved.

They were all skilful, though their technique varied, and since nobody had told her not to, Zoe was quick to give them instructions and make complaints when things were less than perfect for her.

Since she had absolutely nothing to do except lie on her back and get expertly licked off, then wait a while before starting all over again, she soon receded into an amazingly relaxed and contented mental world of excess pleasure and deep, complex fantasy. Whole books were played out in her mind as she lay there! Bizarre, kinky stories about worlds of dominant men and profusions of submissive women! All manner of secret corners of her mind were explored, and she discovered that things she'd never thought would turn her on, turned her on!

Still, in this stupor of pleasure, she found Master Philip and his friends coming to have an occasional look at her, and it was clear that the added humiliation on the part of the slaves (to be so contrasted with a category of privileged men) excited them even more, for they made huge efforts to try to hide their frustrated erections. They would have to stand aside while the other men were permitted to fuck Zoe, and then immediately afterwards, commence licking her again. Which meant, of course, that... they were further humiliated!

So many submissive men were being presented to Master Philip for the purpose of pleasuring his slave that he let this phase of Zoe's orgasmic odyssey carry on for some time.

Zoe, who had stopped worrying now about whether the excess of stimulation would cause her orgasmic mechanism to malfunction somehow (it didn't - it worked perfectly every time), was enjoying her new state of existence immensely, and didn't want it to end. How wonderful, to be lying in comfort with a soft, warm tongue working away at your bits, reaching that stage when you think - 'this is so brilliant, I don't want it to end, I want it to go on and on and on' - and knowing that you can in fact have your wish! It will go on and on and on!

Until, that is, your Master decides you've had enough.

He was still keen on pursuing the experiment of enforcing and increasing the number of Zoe's orgasms, and he recognised that the slaves were a valuable tool to this end, but he rather thought that his slave was getting it too easy, and considered it about time that he made things a little less comfortable for her.

Late one morning, he arrived home from a shopping spree with a huge roll of something over his shoulder.

"Right, get up," he told Zoe, who was, as usual, lying on her back getting pleasured. Somewhat reluctantly, she dragged herself to her feet, while the wet-faced male submissive who had been interrupted in his favourite task crawled unbidden into a corner.

"Look what I found in that rubber warehouse down by the docks!" With a flourish, Master Philip threw open the roll onto the bed. It was a thick sheet of black rubber, not smooth, but covered with thick rubber studs, protruding upwards like a sea of hard, black nipples. "They make bags out of this stuff, but I've thought of another use. As of now, you're going to lie on it."

Master Philip almost laughed at how Zoe's face fell.

"But Master, it doesn't look very – "

"What? Comfortable?"

"No, Master."

"Oh, Zoe! I have been spoiling you! You can't even remember what discomfort is!"

"Yes, I can, Master!" Zoe insisted.

"Well, I'm pleased to hear it. You certainly shouldn't be complaining about a few little lumps, anyway. It could be a bed of nails, you know!"

Zoe shuddered and looked down.

"Really! All these men grovelling at your feet - well, at your pussy - has got you too close to Mistress mode. You can see that we've got to redress the balance, can't you?"

Zoe nodded, and though pleased in a way to be put back in her place, noticed how difficult it was to even consider the thought of giving up the constant oral pleasure she had got used to.

This was going to be more of a test than perhaps her Master realised. The temptation was definitely there to take herself away to some quiet corner of the world, with the string of willing tongues in tow, and live on in endless orgasmic bliss!

"I'll do whatever you want, Master!" she wanted to say. "Only don't have these guys stop licking me yet."

But she stopped herself, just in case such a heartfelt request prompted her unpredictable dominator to deliberately take the opposite course of action!

Suddenly, Master Philip was bodily picking her up and throwing her onto the studded sheet. Then he was tucking the sheet firmly into place to make sure it would stay under her, while Zoe herself twitched and squirmed and grumbled as she discovered just how uncomfortable this new surface was.

Next, Master Philip produced two sets of handcuffs and before Zoe realised what was happening, had grabbed each of her arms and shacked her wrists to the corners of the bed. Now she wouldn't be able to push on the heads of the men pleasing her, or experiment with different positions, or use a whip to encourage them, as she'd occasionally started to do.

"Ow, Master!" she complained.

"Be quiet, or I'll have your legs up over your head!"

Now he was pulling a tight belt round her middle, and as always, this had such a direct erotic effect on her that she was soon purring and fawning like a proper slave again. This was curtailed, however, but what next appeared in Master Philip's hand.

"Oh, no!" Zoe cried. "Not nipple clamps, Master. Please not!"

"Silence, or I'll gag you! They're only gentle and you'll soon get used to them."

Zoe submitted meekly to the clamps and was rewarded with a kiss.

"Now. How many orgasms left to achieve today?"

"Seventeen, Master."

"Well, get on with it then. I've got a new batch of tongues coming round in a couple of hours, so there'll be no excuse. See you later, slut."

Zoe couldn't be sure whether he left the room at this point, or stood around quietly a little longer to make the most of the highly stimulating image she presented. She only knew - from the speed of her next orgasm once a warm mouth was once again clamped round her clit - that she was happy, oh, so happy, to be firmly back in her Master's power again.

Weeks passed and still Master Philip kept his poor exhausted slave in a near constant state of sexual arousal, though to be fair, he let her have days off, here and there (to do the housework).

The lickers kept coming (for the pool of submissive men in this world is bottomless) but Zoe also had to do a lot of work herself, and had been forced to experiment with countless arousal options, such as standing up and wanking herself off on the corner of a table, finding new uses for a variety of different sized paintbrushes (gosh, how they tickled!), and allowing herself to be fixed up to an electro-stimulator, which was supposed to trigger spontaneous orgasms, but proved completely ineffective, and was abandoned by Master Philip as being too risky anyway.

And she didn't just have to frig herself in the bedroom, or on the floor of the lounge. Oh, no, she was to please herself all over the place, like in the car, out in the parks, in the ladies toilet of a department store, in the luggage compartment of a train, in the back row of a regular cinema and, of course, while restrained in no end of different bondage positions and costumes.

Here's a final image of a wanking Zoe for readers to dwell on at leisure.

Venue: Back of a black cab parked in the quietest corner of a remote trading estate.

Time of day: About eleven o'clock at night, after the grotty pub she's been under the pool table of all afternoon and evening has closed, and just as the kinky nightclub she's being taken to is getting going.

Orgasm quota: Twenty five down, five to go before midnight.

Attire: Thigh-length boots chained together at the ankles and knees, thick dildo held fast up her pussy by a series of leather straps, sexy purple corset reinforced with whalebone and pulled ultra-tight with narrow black laces, state-of-the-art tit clamps gripping the bases of her breasts and holding them close together, wristcuffs, blindfold, and a few extra chains and straps draped around for effect.

Audience: Mick, Bob and Dave, three taxi drivers she's been entrusted to for the whole day and night, and something like twenty of Mick, Bob and Dave's mates, fighting to push their heads and cocks through the windows of the cab, and spreading the word rapidly on their grapevine of radios and mobile phones.

Amount of spunk on Zoe's naked tits: Lots.

Stickiness of Zoe's fingers: Very.

Stickiness of Zoe's pussy: Exceptional.

Number of men who are going to have heard about this event by the end of the week: Thousands.

Zoe's state of mind: Orgasmic! What else?

Chapter Eight

ALL ABOARD!

There was a long period when Master Philip was too busy to bother much with Zoe, and she lived comfortably in his luxury home, her days largely free, and her nights only occasionally occupied with group sex and whippings.

She suffered considerable withdrawal symptoms from the loss of all that perfect, endless licking from hordes of willing sex slaves, but luckily Master Philip had allowed her to select one or two of those slaves (from amongst those who were not already spoken for) to keep for herself, as it were. And so - though he'd drawn the line at letting them 'live in' - Zoe did at least have a couple of eager pussy lickers who came round to the house regularly and took care of at least some of her needs.

She had a wonderful time, lying round watching television and videos, whilst Stickyface (for so she called the first slave) made her drinks and sandwiches, and Lizardtongue (well, he could get really deep!) curled up happily between her legs.

Sometimes Tony from the bar came round as well (with Master Philip's permission, of course) and spent hours caressing her tits, and devising for himself occupations such as smothering her breasts with various substances like whipped cream and chocolate sauce, and slowly licking it all off until not a trace was left.

Adam telephoned her occasionally, and Bret visited once (long enough to leave her tied up in the cellar for twelve hours, in heavy chains), and she found she missed them both; but she missed Master Philip even more, and began to fear he was neglecting her and had lost interest.

One weekend he came home earlier than expected and stood by the door, watching, as Zoe lay curled up on the sofa, enjoying the ministrations of Tony and the two slaves.

It wasn't until after she'd had two slow orgasms that Zoe opened her eyes and found her Master regarding her.

She made to get up and greet him.

"No, stay where you are – it's lovely to look at you like that."

Stickyface returned to licking the juices from between her legs, and Master Philip came and sat beside her.

"Zoe, you are such a personification of eroticism, so superlatively sexual! I forget how much you are made for sex – I'm letting you down by not keeping you supplied with sufficient men to enjoy you, and to do your extreme sensuality justice. Let me apply my mind to it, and think of another way I can keep you suitably filled up with cock."

Zoe gazed up into his eyes, both scared and gratified by his words.

"Now, move over, lads," Master Philip said to the three men clustered around Zoe, ushering them away with a wave of his hand, before standing up again and undoing his fly. "The Master's home!"

Nothing new happened for a few more weeks, but Zoe could tell that some plan had been formulated, from the way Master Philip looked at her sometimes, and definitely from the way he fucked her.

He was mad with lust again, and would sometimes let a clue slip, in a moment of passion.

"Ooh, yes, you'll soon be working hard at being the slut again."

Or, "Oh, yes, Zoe, what a brainwave – thousands of men, oh yes!"

Zoe chose to ignore this mention of 'thousands', certain that this was clearly fantasy. But she was soon to discover how wrong she was!

This time, Master Philip was thinking big – big numbers.

He'd always loved the idea of his beautiful plaything being utterly swamped and drenched and surrounded by masculinity, but suddenly his desire to see her well-used knew no bounds.

Dozens weren't enough, hundreds weren't enough. He'd been there, done that – seen that. Suddenly he was consumed with the desire to up the ratio.

It was too much of a waste, having a woman like Zoe lying round an empty house only getting fucked occasionally. And she had had it so easy recently, he felt she needed to make up for lost time.

So he had pondered the problem. Where did you get huge numbers of sex-hungry men, all in one place? Ah, yes, the military. Maybe some army barracks, or a boot camp, where Zoe would get some gruelling, heartless physical training, as well as an opportunity to work her way through hundreds of young, sexually frustrated men.

But then he saw a certain film on the telly one night, and the brainwave hit him. After that it had just been a question of finding and carefully approaching the right contact, and making some discreet arrangements.

So the morning came when Zoe was told to say goodbye to her little team of occasional playmates, and make herself ready for an extended journey.

Her preparations were extremely simple – to have a good bath and take all her clothes off. This time she wasn't going to be allowed to take one single item of clothing, or anything else, with her.

A large trunk had been delivered to Master Philip's home and now stood open in the centre of the living room. It was thickly padded, and had been further adapted with the addition of hidden air-holes. Zoe stood looking at it and felt certain she was its intended occupant.

Master Philip led her towards the forbidding piece of luggage, spread a huge silk sheet out loosely over the top of it, and gave her a hand to step into the waiting compartment. She stood on the silk in the trunk, naked and shaking, so resigned to doing whatever her Master wanted that she didn't even ask what he was planning.

He looked at her for a long time, in silence.

"As you can probably guess," he said eventually, "I'm having you delivered somewhere – well, smuggled into somewhere, actually. There's no need to worry, you'll only be in this thing for a couple of hours – some special arrangements have been made."

Master Philip sighed deeply and walked slowly around the spectacle of Zoe standing ready to be wrapped up in her trunk, before stopping and looking into her eyes again.

"Will you obey me without question?"

"Of course, Master."

"Do you trust me?"

"Yes, of course, Master."

"Good." He paused.

"Is there any limit to the number of men you would fuck, to please your Master and yourself?"

This question took Zoe's breath away, and sent the blood rushing to her pussy. She trembled.

"I'm waiting for an answer."

"No, Master," said Zoe. "There is no limit."

"Very well, now listen to me very carefully."

Once more, in a private, intense moment, Master Philip outlined what he would expect of his precious slave, and once more, she listened, astounded, resigned, excited, afraid.

"Oh Zoe, my dear, I've tested you before in situations involving lots of men, and you've never failed me. I've left you in the sauna, I've taken you to the busiest outdoor spots, I've deposited you in the porn cinemas – and always you've handled it all perfectly. Proved your slut's credentials, made yourself utterly available to all comers – and enjoyed it all, I know. But this time.. This time – I plan to immerse you so deep into an experience of pure and constant sex, that you'll hardly remember what the real world is, that you'll forget what it feels like not to have a cock in your pussy or your mouth. You'll find yourself surrounded by an enormous number of men, a bottomless pit of sexual desire and sexual energy. Everyone will want you and everyone will have you. Every day, every night, you will be used to the extreme, the ultimate sexual plaything. It will go on and on, seemingly endless, except that you will know that it will eventually end, and that one day, you will stand before me again, like this – my sweet, special slave – and I will have the pleasure of thinking, of knowing for ever, that huge, massive numbers of men have used you. That you have given yourself so frequently and so willingly, that your devotion to me cannot be in doubt. You will have passed a test like no other, you will have done something that probably no other woman has ever done. Oh, don't think that I am prostituting you – the world may be full of men exploiting women for gain, but you and I know that this is different. All I gain is the pleasure of the knowledge of your use. In fact I lose out by your prolonged absence – no, I'm sorry my darling, I really can't accompany you on this voyage, though I would dearly love to. And you, Zoe, are no whore. You are something both better and worse, a free spirit, the essence of womanhood – every man's fantasy, maybe every woman's fantasy as well. Channelling all that coarse male lust, channelling all that pleasure and desire. Think how full your soul will be, once you have held all those men in your arms, embraced them and their passion! Oh, you will be like no other woman who has ever lived!"

Zoe listened with rapt passion, her pussy positively creaming at this unexpected speech from her Master.

Yes, she thought to herself. That's what I shall be – that's what he has made me; the ultimate woman, used more than any other!

"Ah, but Zoe," said Master Philip, studying her expression. "First you have to do the deed – first you have to pass the test! Now – how many men do you think there are going to be in this place I'm sending you to? A thousand perhaps? Does that seem conceivable?"

Zoe nodded slowly. "Yes, Master."

"But what if I told you it wasn't just one thousand, it was two?"

Zoe's eyes widened.

"Or how about three thousand? Do you believe I could be sending you into the proximity of three thousand men?"

She didn't want to believe it, but didn't doubt what her Master was capable of.

"Yes, Master," she said eventually.

"Well, you'd be wrong."

Master Philip enjoyed the long silence which followed, enjoyed this little game of cat and mouse.

"It's not three thousand. It's not four thousand. Guess how many it is, Zoe?"

She was shaking now, but the state of her pussy gave away her true feelings.

"How many, Zoe?"

"Five thousand?" she ventured.

Master Philip grinned and nodded. "Now that's what I call an appropriate ratio for a slut like you!"

Zoe felt weak at the knees. It was all very well as a concept, a fantasy – but how could she ever cope with the reality of it?

Master Philip let her think about it a little longer, before remembering his own role as the perfect Master, and offering her reassurances.

"Now of course it's not a case of your actually fucking all of them – that might take a few years, and I don't want to be parted from you for that long! And anyway, there may well be a fair proportion of that number who will be otherwise inclined, and will have no interest in your pussy. But the point is, there will be enough – more than enough – for it to seem as though the supply of cock is endless and bottomless. In fact

– look! The only thing I'm sending along with you in the crate is this maxi-pack of tubes of lubricant! Wet as I know your pussy can be – and it does look pretty wet at this moment, I must say – I think even you may need assistance when it comes to dealing with that many men! Mm, I'm only sorry I won't be there to witness your unveiling – how erotic, a delivery of a naked woman in a padded trunk, with nothing else inside it but industrial scale quantities of lube! Rather makes your purpose obvious, doesn't it?" He sighed deeply as he imagined the moment, closing his eyes for a while.

"Anyway, my dear, on a practical note, you can be assured that I have handsomely paid two contacts to look after you. You will be safeguarded from harm – at the slightest sign of your being injured, the whole venture will be aborted immediately, and the men will be warned of this in no uncertain terms. If they hurt you, they'll lose you, so they should all be well motivated to take good care of you. Fuck you mercilessly, of course, but take care of you all the same! A doctor will check you every day – your pussy will be positively pampered. And the doctor and both contacts have been told to respect the following code word, which will mean, should you utter it, that you are opting out of your self-imposed sexual slavery, and wish immediately to be left alone and taken back to civilisation."

"I will not need the code word!" said Zoe suddenly and vehemently. "Like you said, I haven't failed you up until now, and I will not fail you this time, Master!"

"Admirable, Zoe, but I insist on giving it to you all the same. Should you wish to be rescued from this ultimate gang-bang, you will say the following words. 'Goodbye, Master Philip.'"

Zoe took this in. In meant, of course, that if she failed this test, she would never see him again. All or nothing, no third way. She might have protested at the unfairness of this, if it wasn't for her certainty that she would never use this challenging exit phrase anyway.

She would never say goodbye to her Master Philip willingly. Which meant she would never be able to stop fucking his five thousand men!

"Wrap me up and send me off in this trunk quickly, Master," she said, dropping to her knees, "because I want to start proving to you how much of a slut I can be!"

A tear almost rose to Master Philip's eye at this utterance, but he held on tight to his heartless persona.

"Suck this first," he said, and gave Zoe his raging erection to take care of.

She swallowed every last drop of his semen – keeping it with her as a memento – and smiled up at him cheekily as he covered her curled-up body with the silk sheet.

"Au Revoir, Master Philip!"

Zoe was a bit scared, wrapped up in her trunk, and being carried towards an unknown destination and who knew how many weeks or months of full time fucking – but she decided to go with the flow, and meditated on her subservient role, and felt a sense both of wonder and contentment at the straightforwardness of her imminent task.

The powerful image presented by her predicament – a lone, naked woman being transported into the proximity of an enormity of men – aroused her to the core, and in that secret, hidden place, she gave herself orgasm after orgasm at the thought of it.

When eventually the trunk was deposited on some mystery floor, and she heard the sound of male voices, she was spent and sweaty – and sticky. When the lid was lifted off and the silk unwrapped, not only were the watching men flabbergasted at the sight of her, they were immediately assailed and aroused by the sweet smells of perfume and pussy juice – the real scent of a woman.

There were about twenty of them, and they were all in uniform – the uniform of military sailors.

Yes, the film Master Philip had been inspired by was an old movie called 'A Hundred Men and A Girl', in which one woman finds herself alone on a ship full of men – though in those days, any impropriety was hardly even hinted at. Master Philip had updated things. Zoe had been smuggled onto a warship. Now it was 'Five Thousand Men and A Girl'. And no subtle skirting of sexual tensions – this was to be the real thing.

Now Master Philip was well aware of the cliché of sailors often being gay, but common sense – and his navy contacts – told him that this only applied to a proportion of servicemen, and that where such activity did take place, a lot of it was out of necessity rather than choice.

It also seemed that these days there were women serving on ships. However, careful choice and a bit of string-pulling had ensured that – seemingly purely by coincidence – there weren't any on this one.

Only Zoe. All on her own.

The men gaped as Zoe uncurled herself, blinking at the light.

"Bloody hell!"

"She's beautiful!"

"This can't be for real!"

"Does the Captain know about this?"

There were two officers present, whose names were Davenport and Forester, and these were Master Philip's contacts and the men to whose safety and management, as it were, Zoe had been entrusted.

"The answer to that question," said Davenport, "is that yes, the Captain does know, and so do all the officers and a select core of men. He intends to spread the world gradually, see how things go. Initially, she's to be kept down on this level and guarded at all times. As more men are informed, we'll have to draw up some sort of rota."

"That's right," said Forester. "The Captain is prepared to trust everyone with this shared secret, but there's one major rule which mustn't be broken. No sex on duty. We've all got a job to do and a ship to run. Zoe's here for our off-duty recreation only."

At the mention of her name, the men all focused on Zoe again.

"Welcome on board, Miss," said Davenport, clearing his throat. "This is, er, a new situation for us, and I'm not sure it's sunk in yet. Are you certain you're aware of – ? I mean, is it really the case that - ?"

Zoe looked around her at the various bemused and disbelieving expressions, and decided that she may as well help the poor souls out by making things crystal clear from the beginning.

"Thank you for your welcome, sir," she said, kneeling up in the trunk, "and I want you to know I trust you completely. I assure you I'm entirely aware of the situation and perfectly happy with it, in fact I'm very keen to begin."

No-one spoke, so Zoe continued.

"Or, to put it another way – I'm here to be the ultimate free tart and sexual plaything of you all – so does anyone want their cock sucked?"

And so, within ten minutes of her arrival and still kneeling in her padded crate, Zoe embarked upon that occupation she knew so well, and would be doing so much of over the coming months.

The cocksucking continuum had begun.

Zoe found herself sucking and fucking in about equal measure, which was indeed what she was used to.

She sucked and fucked for about three hours – in, over and beside the trunk – following which she was belatedly shown to a toilet and offered some refreshment.

Then she sucked and fucked for another three hours, was shown around the immediate vicinity of the ship briefly and introduced to a lot more men – and then sucked and fucked for a couple of hours more!

She spent her first night with Davenport, and her second with Forester. After that she spent several days and nights in the Captain's quarters, while he made the most of his privileges and got his fill of her in private.

Then she got group fucked in the officers' mess – for about three days, with only short breaks for food, and a continuous stream of new faces, and cocks, to deal with.

Next she found herself entrenched in first one set of sleeping quarters, then another. She didn't really register where exactly she was, she just made herself as comfortable as possible, whatever the surroundings, and got on with the job in hand.

At night she was passed around the bunks, snatching a few hours sleep here and there, as one seaman or another took his turn at spending some of the night with his arms wrapped around her, and his fellows looking on with envy or anticipation.

At one point she got carried to the engine room, at another she fucked and sucked endlessly on a large table in some private dining room.

She had made no effort to count days, but around something like the tenth, Forester came and spoke to her as she sat on someone's lap, eating some sandwiches that had been brought to her.

"Er, I just thought I'd let you know that we're sailing tomorrow – so if you've any doubts about staying, well, today's the day to speak up."

"Hey, don't let her go, sir!" said one of the men. "We're only just getting to know her."

"Yeah," said another, "and she's still got a good few more of us to get to know! Don't give her a chance to run away, sir – not so soon!"

"Now lads," said Forester sternly. "You know the lady's free to go any time. Be gentlemen, now."

The men gathered around her.

"What's it to be, love?"

"Don't desert us, Zoe!"

Zoe didn't hesitate in her reply. She hadn't really even registered that the ship hadn't put out to sea yet – she'd been too busy and preoccupied by her total immersion in sex.

"Thanks for asking," she smiled at Forester. "But I'm staying."

Even Forester stuck around to join in the melee that followed this pronouncement.

So the ship sailed, but it was another two weeks before Zoe even saw the sea – and that was only at night, glimpsed between the shoulders of the four young men who had smuggled her up on deck for a midnight romp.

Gradually, everyone on board came to know of her existence – and purpose – and she was allowed to wander around more freely. Always naked, of course – but never, never alone. Constantly accompanied by a whole gaggle of off-duty sailors.

She became a kind of free currency, like a flask of complimentary wine that was passed around and shared out equally. Except that a flask would run dry, while what she had to offer was bottomless.

Sometimes there were squabbles – naturally, with so many men interested in her, there were disputes for her attention.

"Hey, I was just about to do that!"

"Well, I reckon you've had some already, and I haven't – so stand back."

They usually sorted it out between themselves, but more often than not, Zoe herself just – well, made room for one more.

She spent a week on B Deck, a week on C Deck. A week in the storerooms, a week in an empty corner of the hold. A week in the little corridor behind the computer rooms, a week in the pantry beside the kitchen.

She spent every night somewhere different, with someone different. She saw a lot of bunks and hammocks, heard a lot of snoring.

The cocks kept coming – and coming!

The lubricant that had been delivered with her got used up, and more was flown in by helicopter.

She wasn't allowed to do anything except have sex. Davenport had made this clear from the beginning – instructions from Master Philip.

So, yes, she could sit and eat with the men in the canteen – but only if she carried on kissing and playing with them while she did so, to warm them up for the next session.

Yes, she could watch films in the little cinema when the men did – but only if she was being poked at the same time.

Yes, she could play chess with the jovial cook after dinner – but only if she was sitting on the pastry chef's lap at the time, with his thick cock tucked deep inside her pussy.

She began to spend more time on deck, fucking in the sunshine, the men rubbing suntan lotion into her gradually browning skin.

The fitness instructor saw potential in her, and began to incorporate her into his off-duty exercise routines, in vaguely humorous ways.

She would be told to drape herself over the ship's railings, naked bottom uppermost, while the men jogged round in circles and each gave her a hard spank on the bum as they passed.

She would be stretched out on the floor, with the men taking turns to do press ups on top of her, kissing her every time they dropped down, winking at her as they shared the memory of a recent fuck.

She would be tied up with rope against a pillar, used as a marker around which the men had to run. They might have to place a hoop around one of her breasts, or take an apple from her mouth. They would tweak her nipples or grab at her buttocks as they ran up to her, amused and excited by the novelty she injected into their exercise.

Zoe became a sort of mascot for the men. They enjoyed her, they indulged her. They protected her from each other's excesses, but fucked her so thoroughly and enthusiastically that she indeed felt far more fucked than she'd ever been before.

Master Philip had achieved his objective in turning her existence into one long sex session. She never got a day off – but never wanted one. She began to feel guilty that this wasn't enough of a test – she was enjoying herself far too much!

Sometimes it was difficult, yes – when she perhaps hadn't had much sleep the night before, having been kept awake by some over-enthusiastic long-stayer; when she'd worked her way through maybe twenty men and knew there would be at least twenty more before bed-time.

On occasion she got teased and taken advantage of a bit too much, by otherwise idle lads who had discovered and exploited her submissiveness.

"Right, every time I say 'Zoe'," one would say, "I want you to drop to your knees and kiss my feet."

"And every time I shout 'Oi, you!'," from another, "you're to wiggle your bottom and say, 'More seamen please!'"

"And whenever I enter the room," volunteered a third, smirking, "you should immediately stand on one leg and salute me."

"And when I click my fingers," said number four, "you'll kiss my arse! Now will you remember all that?"

Oh, you can imagine their amusement as they proceeded to test Zoe's memory and reactions, and played around at all issuing her with conflicting instructions at the same time – watching her leap and jump about, struggling to obey them all, making an utter fool of herself. How they laughed – until at last a more sensible senior officer came and rescued her from their silly games.

But generally the men adored her, generally they delighted in her.

Constantly they quizzed her about why she was with them, and doing what she was doing.

"They say it's for the love of some guy – is that true?"

"Yes," she would say, shrugging.

"Lucky sod! He's not forcing you to do it though, is he?"

"No," said Zoe. "I love doing it."

And a second later, she would be doing it again!

At least ten different men fell passionately in love with her.

"Zoe, let me take you away from here."

"Zoe, let me save you from all this."

"Zoe, your Master can't possibly love you more than I do!"

"Zoe, will you marry me?"

"I'm so sorry," Zoe would say, genuinely moved. "But it just can't be like that."

"Oh, Zoe, won't you be mine?"

"But I am yours. I'm everybody's."

One morning, a roll call was taken, with all the men standing to attention up on deck and being subject to inspection.

The Captain (who was feeling reckless about the whole enterprise as he was planning in any case to terminate his military career) walked along the ranks of sailors with his arm around Zoe's naked shoulders and a twinkle in his eye.

"What a naughty, naughty girl you are," he whispered in her ear. "Letting so many of these men up your pussy! Really, it's outrageous!"

He manouvred Zoe towards a vantage point on the upper deck, and reached for an intercom.

"Well done, men," his amplified voice boomed around the ship. "At ease. But one last thing. Just for everyone's amusement and information, can I please have a show of hands – and be honest now, there's nothing to fear. Hands up, all those of you who have, er, become intimately acquainted with our guest, here, Miss Zoe? And I mean intimately acquainted in the fullest possible sense!"

A wave of arms shot skywards, and Zoe blushed deeply.

It was nowhere near all of the men – but it was a very substantial proportion of them.

She looked along the long columns of sailors, hundreds and hundreds of whom were confirming that they had fucked her, and was amazed at her own behaviour, her own achievement.

What a shame Master Philip isn't here to see this, she couldn't help thinking. To witness this staggering spectacle which proved just how busy she had been since she'd come aboard.

But, though Zoe didn't know it, her Master would in fact witness the moment – eventually. Because he hadn't been able to resist the lure of seeing Zoe in action at the extreme, and had secretly arranged for Davenport to discreetly video choice moments - such as this one.

Davenport had also captured, over the past weeks, several hours of action from below decks, particularly when Zoe had been busy with very large groups of men, and so Master Philip was in fact able to keep a remote eye on Zoe's activities and enjoy reviewing the images that were relayed to him regularly, at leisure in private.

So that evening, with Zoe slaving away as the centre of attention at a somewhat rowdy officers' party in the assembly hall, Master Philip would in fact see it all.

See flocks of men rush to surround Zoe, and kiss her roughly, and grab at her naked tits.

See them start to fuck her – first two at a time, working away at each end, then three at a time!

See Zoe squirm and moan beneath the onslaught, coming again and again.

See one officer ride her particularly hard and encourage his fellows to join in, exclaiming loudly; "All aboard, boys!"

See her almost collapse with exhaustion after yet another three to one, but drag herself up again quickly, forcing herself to keep hard at work pleasuring all the lads.

See the spunking start, see her getting drenched in it, see her swallowing gallons of it.

See her scream as yet another orgasm wracked her luscious, sweaty body.

See even more men descend on her to take their pleasure.

And if he could have seen what Zoe was thinking, he would have been pleased, for it went something like this.

"Oh my God, this is so – so difficult, but so wonderful! I don't know how I can carry on sometimes – but there's no choice, the men are here, I'm here, and they want me. I can't ever say no, Master Philip says I'm made for sex, so that's what I'll have to do. Oh dear, here comes another orgasm, oh wow, oh some of these guys are so good, it's so good to get some good licking as well as all this fucking – this is a dream. Oh, if only he could see me now, my dear Master, I know he'd be proud of me. Mind you, if anyone else saw me now, though, they wouldn't believe it! They would wonder what on earth I was thinking, how on earth I could put up with it all. But I know what I'm doing – it's all very simple, it's glaringly clear to me. I'm just being a slave – Being Master Philip's slave!"

Chapter Nine

WOMEN

There came a time when Zoe, lying very alone, deep in a bondage cocoon in her Master's attic, found her mind straying to immensely profound thoughts. And the most profound one of all was - when will all this end?

She felt that she had been put through so much, tested so severely, and forced to endure situations and emotions of increasing difficulty and intensity; yet there was always one more test.

She wondered if there would ever come a day when Master Philip would say - yes, you've passed all my tests. Now - now what? Now you can live a normal life again? Now we will enjoy each other on a different, more equal basis? Now I don't want you any more?

Or would it in fact never end? Was this just his way of keeping her fraught and obedient and striving with all her soul to please him until, perhaps, she decided she'd had enough and moved back into normal existence of her own accord? Maybe she was failing a test by not breaking away from him! It was all so complex.

But the main thing she discovered, in her hours of reflection, was that a new element had been added to the overall proceedings. Fear. Because things had now gone so far that Zoe couldn't help fearing that the next test would be something too difficult, too unreasonable.

So far everything that had been required of her went along roughly with her own inclinations; this she had to admit. But what were her own limits? What would she not do for him?

Maybe all this testing had been designed to find that out, and yet had come nowhere near.

What if he asked her to shave her head, for example, or pierce her lips and her tongue and her nose, or tattoo herself all over with his name? Yes, these things she would probably do. But what if the request was something more horrific - like causing herself some permanent injury? And what if he asked her to hurt him? What if his final test would be ordering her to plunge a knife into his arm? Which would be the right option - to do it or not? To obey him, or to injure him? Or if he asked her to leave him forever, or go into a convent for the rest of her life? Or - the idea of the ultimate test sprang menacingly into her brain - kill herself?

She opened her eyes behind her blindfold. How could she even think such things? Surely Master Philip was eminently sensible, and understood what was and what was not included in this long, drawn out game they were playing?

But what if it was no longer a game?

And so Zoe, from the depths of her own mind, created for herself a hell far greater than anything any man had physically put her through, and lay trembling in terror at the thought of what she might or might not do for love of her Master.

Master Philip, meanwhile, was lying alone in a hotel bed, exploring the limits of his own sexuality by attempting his fourth wank of the evening.

He loved the feel of his own cock in his hand. He loved to control exactly, minutely, just how to encourage his own arousal.

He sometimes thought that, much as he loved fucking and being sucked off, having a private pull was possibly the best way of all to come. Doing it your own way, at your own pace.

He thought of Zoe, as he often did, imagining her in some predicament or other, and then enjoying that gratifying leap in sensation as he reminded himself that it was something Zoe really had done. That these things - these bizarre images - were real memories and experiences, not just fantasies and dreams!

He re-lived some of his favourite moments, which usually involved something like coming upon Zoe in some unusual and novel bondage, which another man (or even she herself) had put her into. Or returning to some crude situation he had left her in, to find a far greater number of randy men than he had anticipated swarming round her.

Like that time recently in the porn cinema, when he'd had to peel away layers of men before he could even see her! Or that night when he'd left her outdoors, draped naked over a wooden style, and asked any men who made use of her to mark her back with an X in felt pen. Not only her back, but her whole bottom, her legs and her arms had been covered when he'd returned! Apparently word had spread for miles, and the men in the area still talked about that night in local pubs.

Yes, there had been good moments! His cock was gratifyingly hard again, and still his thoughts were only of Zoe, and of how she had made all his wildest fantasies come true, and how much he enjoyed and needed and appreciated her.

He had sometimes feared he would push her too far, and hence lose her, but in general, his own arrogance sustained him, along with an unwavering belief that he knew Zoe better than she knew herself - which was very probably true.

Zoe wouldn't have feared for a moment that she couldn't trust him, if she could have read his mind now, and seen the immense desire, protectiveness and commitment that engulfed him whenever he thought of her. As images of her familiar and much used and abused body rushed in procession through his brain and swept him towards ecstasy, he realised there was one thing Zoe would never know. Quite how intense and mind-blowing his orgasms had been since he'd known her - especially these solitary ones - and how his emotions were so deeply caught up in their strange relationship that, as his body shook with yet more pleasure, he was quite as lost to the whole thing as Zoe was.

When he next saw her, he was tender and serious, and sat her down on his lap, where she snuggled comfortably, naked, with no idea what to expect.

Master Philip sighed, and then a long interval passed before he spoke.

"Zoe," he said. "We've been at this a long time now, and I notice you're still with me. I've been thinking about what should happen next."

Zoe tensed, all too aware of her recent fears, but suddenly scared most of all by the possibility that everything might be over. How could she cope in the real world, now that she had become what she had become?

"It's quite obvious," Master Philip continued, "especially from your most recent adventure, that you will absorb uncomplainingly any number of men that I might throw at you. God knows how many thousands you've had already, and I've no doubt you could keep going at the same rate til you were old and grey. Much as I enjoy this numbers game as a continuing test of your slutdom and servitude, it proves nothing in itself. I'm quite clear in my mind now that you would fuck all the men in the world if I told you to - including the basest and most repulsive of them."

Master Philip turned Zoe's head by the chin, so he could search for the truth of this statement in her eyes. She resisted, however, and he let it pass.

"No. There has to be another way into your soul, and when I was lying alone in a hotel room the other night, it suddenly came to me what it was. I know Adam has his own ideas about this sort of thing - we've discussed it, and I heard all about the nasty tests he put you through at that Hall. (What was it - two days before you were finally let out of that wine barrel in the pantry?) I think it was all excellent training, I'm sure, but to my mind these things have to be overtly sexual - that's what it's all about. So what I've been thinking of is something else. We've touched on it, but it's an area I've neglected. I intend to put that right."

Now Zoe's eyes sought her Master's of their own accord, and he was quite stunned and ashamed by what he saw there. He channeled these feelings quickly into anger.

"Zoe! I can't believe that after everything, you can be so scared of me! What do you imagine I'm going to ask you to do? Cut yourself into ribbons? Okay, you've taken a fair amount of punishment in our time together, but you know I would never push things on the pain front. I'm appalled that you don't trust me!"

Zoe winced at his words but felt flooded with relief. Unknown to her Master, this little false alarm had given a boost to her desire to do whatever he wanted. It made what came next just that little bit easier.

"You always have been, and remain, quite free to leave me if you don't want to go along with things. Now what's it to be?"

For reply, Zoe merely cuddled up closer to his engulfing masculinity.

"This is what I plan to do. Introduce other women into your varied sex life, to the extent that you become as adept at pleasing this half of the population as the other."

Zoe felt a sense of fate envelop her. It was as if she had always known that a move in this direction was inevitable. It was what men expected of loose women. And besides, it was debatable whether you could really be a submissive sex slave while refusing to operate within such a significant area of human erotic experience.

Nevertheless, she resisted it, as she always had. For men, and only men, where her true passion.

"Master," Zoe said quietly. "I really, really don't want to lick pussy."

Master Philip grinned. "Well, then at last I've found something that will truly challenge you!"

Zoe swallowed. "But it's asking me to change my sexuality!"

"Not necessarily. You just have to do it - I don't insist you like it."

"I certainly won't like it!"

"I don't know; it's not such a big deal. I'm sure you'll get used to it very quickly. Anyway, I'll make sure you're still kept supplied with plenty of cock."

Zoe was still grimacing, but it was clear she had accepted the idea in principle and was now concerned only with how she would handle the practicalities.

"I've made various plans," Master Philip said, "and told various people about you. You remember Madame from the sauna?"

"Yes!" Zoe looked at him sharply, memories flooding back.

"Well, she has a sister, a slightly younger lady, though with a very similar build - big saggy breasts and thick thighs! I've only met her once because she is apparently a bit shy of company. Her name is Natasha, and she is a lesbian."

Zoe shuddered, her mind still resisting what she knew she would be asked to do.

"She's a bit sex mad," said Master Philip, "but in a private sort of way. She's rich, and she hires lesbian prostitutes to come to her house. The rumour is that she really lets herself go and gets up to all sorts of way out things, though you'd never tell from looking at her - she's so retiring and self-conscious in public. Anyway, Madame's told her about you, and she's very happy to take on the first stage of your lesbian training. After all, she'll be getting your services for free."

Not for a long time had Zoe felt such dread as when she was dropped off at the large, secluded bungalow that was Miss Natasha's residence. She watched forlornly as Master Philip drove away, and contemplated only for a moment trying to run away before the doorbell was answered

- for of course, she had no money and no possessions, as usual on such occasions.

How could she have accepted the attentions of so many strange men, she wondered, and yet be so terrified by the likely demands of one woman?

She tried to steel herself. Maybe it wouldn't be so bad. Maybe another woman would be nicer to her than a lot of those many men had been.

But all Zoe's hopes were soon dashed, and all her worst fears realised, for the reception she got was something less than cordial.

The door was opened by a young slim woman in a maid's uniform, who, no sooner had Zoe stepped through the door, pushed her against a wall with shocking violence and snarled in her face. "Don't think we want you here, you filthy, cocksucking trollop! So just you make sure you do what we tell you, and don't get in our way. Or you won't like what we'll do to you!"

What a welcome! Zoe gazed fearfully into the eyes not just of this woman, but of her two companions who had materialised behind her, and quickly worked out that 'we' must be the lesbian prostitutes, who evidently lived here - or at least spent much of their time attending on their Mistress, as they were all dressed as maids and looked as if they had been interrupted in their domestic duties.

"She's a fat thing! Look at those podgy tits!" One of the other girls prodded her.

"Ugh, don't touch!" said the third. "You don't know where she's been!"

Zoe was utterly shocked and horrified by this unexpected turn of events and felt like she'd been plunged into some nightmare. Never, even in her sometimes harsh school days, had she encountered this sort of open unpleasantness from a group of other women, and she wished she'd been forewarned of the situation, though it might only have given her something more to worry about in advance.

She would really have to put on a brave face. However, just as she was making an effort to frame some friendly and non-confrontational words, a shout - or was it a scream - ripped into the tension of the hallway.

"Girls! Who is it? Is it the slut? Bring her in now!"

Zoe was pushed into a plush lounge and actually knocked over so that she sprawled on the floor.

When she looked up she was met with the sight of Miss Natasha's fat legs in fishnet stockings, tight red dress with one breast actually bulging out so the engorged nipple was exposed, and finally, round flabby face surrounded by a frizz of red hair. With one hand she was feeding herself chocolates from a massive box beside her, while the other hand was up between her legs and out of sight.

My God, thought Zoe. I thought she was supposed to be shy and retiring! She looks like a monster.

"Well," Miss Natasha shrieked. "So this is the sauna slave - I've heard all about you, you disgusting thing!" The chocolate hand strayed onto a bottle of vodka, from which she took a significant swig, while the other hand appeared from where it had been and got wiped on her dress.

"Strip her off, girls! I want to see everything!"

The three maids made a big show of literally ripping all Zoe's clothes off, actually laughing as they did so, and then dragged her legs wide apart so that their Mistress could get a good look at Zoe's private (well, had been once) parts. Natasha leaned forward to have a look, and let her eyes move lewdly all over Zoe's body.

"Yes, quite a pretty thing. But the thought of all those - oh, God - all those filthy, disgusting men who have mauled her and spunked on her and fucked that pussy! Oh, yuk, the thought of it turns my stomach! You'd better get her upstairs, girls, and give her a good scrubbing, or else I won't be able to bear to have her near me. Quick, get it done, then bring her back to me. Oh, and by the way," Natasha turned her fierce eyes on the three girls. "Don't imagine I can't see how jealous and scared you are of this slut because she gives out for free - don't deny it! I know you all too well." She reached out for another chocolate. "But you needn't worry. Whatever use I get out of this spunk-bag while she's here, I'm not going to stop paying you. They'll be plenty to keep all of you occupied!"

The scrubbing was a continuation of the nightmare for Zoe, as the three girls, spitting and swearing amongst themselves about how unpleasant their Mistress could be, proceeded to drag her into a bath of water that was just too hot, and scrub her hide with brushes and loofahs as if she was some animal. They pushed her around, got suds in her face, and were generally deliberately harsh, and when at last they'd finished, she felt sore and raw all over.

When it came to her mouth, they made her brush her teeth three times with double doses of strong toothpaste, discussing as they did so whether any amount of brushing could ever remove all trace of the huge number of penises that must have spent time inside it. As for her poor pussy, they declared themselves stumped as to how they could possibly wash away the last echo of its many excesses, and settled for the doubtless unsatisfactory but nevertheless thorough method of directing an extremely strong jet of hot water straight at it (and its neighbouring orifice) for a good ten minutes.

Her breasts were given an extra good scrubbing with coarse damp flannels, and she was forced to soak her hands and feet in disinfectant.

All this was highly humiliating for Zoe, and in fact had an extra effect which her tormentors couldn't have guessed at, for it was as if all trace not only of her beloved Master, but of her whole male-orientated past was being washed away, ready to be replaced by the awful scents and essences of women.

Having rubbed and beaten her dry with towels, the three witches - for so she now thought of them - began to intrude their fingers between her legs, and between her buttocks, and she was only saved from the losing battle of fighting probing hands off by another screech from downstairs.

"What are you doing? Bring her down here now!"

The sight that met Zoe when she was dragged back downstairs sent her into a fit of panic. Natasha had moved from her chair to a couch and taken her tight dress off. She lay sprawled on the soft cushions, legs wide apart and bottle still in one hand, and gestured for Zoe to come closer.

"Okay, spunk-bag. I guess you're clean enough now for me to get a handful of your sluttish flesh. Let me feel your tits."

Oh, why was it so difficult, with the three witches watching from behind, to lean over and let this awful woman harshly squeeze and play with her breasts? Why could her initiation not have been in more sympathetic and less demanding circumstances? There must be lots of nice, warm, friendly, attractive lesbians in the world, she thought to herself. Why did she have to start with this horrible caricature of an unpleasant one?

But then a slave shouldn't complain about hardships, but should face them squarely.

"Now," said Natasha. "Make love to me."

Zoe stood paralysed, looking down at the huge expanse of female flesh that was Madame's sister, and dreadfully aware of the girls' eyes on her back.

"Come on!" Natasha yelled. "Your Master's told you to, hasn't he? So get down to it!"

Only this reminder, and the tiny stab of arousal that went with it, compelled Zoe to move. She reached out slowly to Natasha's sack-like breasts and began to stroke them.

"More firmly! Climb on top of me and put some spirit into it! I want your tits in my face."

This latter statement was so familiar to Zoe, coming as it usually did from the mouths of men, that suddenly she saw a way forward. All she had to do was imagine this was some particularly unattractive man, and go through the motions - distance herself from the situation.

And so she found herself swinging a leg over Natasha's middle, and settling down so her own pussy was resting on the woman's soft stomach, and her own breasts hung down and brushed those other ones below her.

Yuk!

"I thought you were supposed to be a sex slave?" Natasha taunted. "Now come on, let's see what you can do!"

There was nothing for it but to squirm and wriggle and sigh and move her hips and move her hands, and try her best to give pleasure to the woman she was straddling. Natasha closed her eyes for a while, but soon opened them again with a frown.

"I like the feel of you, but you're pretty hopeless, I must say! Though I suppose I mustn't forget it's your first time with a woman," Natasha gazed up at Zoe. "I despise women who insist on playing exclusively with men. Who do you think you are, that you should be so full of disdain for members of your own sex? What's wrong with touching me, you stuck-up cow? Wait til I'm finished with you - I'll soon break you of your picky habits! Now get off me, and let my girls show you how it's done."

A chastened Zoe was pushed aside, only to have to endure the sight of the three maid-witches descending on their Mistress and fussing round her like flies - touching and stroking her all over with six busy little hands, while their eager-to-please mouths attached themselves, one each to Natasha's nipples, and one to the crack of her pussy.

Natasha settled herself down and threw her arms wide to signal her pleasure. "Oh, yes! Oh, these girls know their stuff. Much better. Mm, lovely!"

Zoe watched, feeling remote and unaroused, but drawn by curiosity to what was going on between Natasha's legs. Fingers were involved, and there was a lot of squelching.

And then the dreaded moment came. "Now, spunk-bag. It's time for your first lesson. Get your face on my bits and start licking."

Zoe couldn't help herself - she fought it. She tried to run away, only to be grabbed by the maids and forced physically into position. She fought and struggled - anything not to have to put her face in that dreaded place!

But it was no use, her head was pushed into it, and her mouth even, was forced open so that her tongue could be rubbed up and down, and her first taste of love juice was mingled with her own frustrated tears.

So this was how Zoe had her lesbian initiation - her face rigidly held in place by each of the maids in turn for nearly an hour, with Natasha shouting instructions about what she should do with her tongue and lips, and Zoe having no choice but to respond and give the wretched woman pleasure.

To her horror, one of the girls began to play with Zoe's pussy, and she couldn't help feeling aroused, even though her predicament was so distasteful.

Maybe they were going to try to wean her onto this business by arousing her every time she was doing - this, she thought with consternation. But she needn't have worried, because it transpired that no-one was particularly bothered about Zoe's pleasure - she was to be on the providing not the receiving end. Natasha was indeed sex mad - she wasn't happy unless she had another woman's face in her crotch for several hours of every day.

There was no particular refinement or variety of technique that was required of Zoe - just perseverance. It took at least half an hour of jaw-straining work to bring Natasha to orgasm, but once was never enough. A yank on the hair or a crude remark always signalled that one was expected to continue, and often a session was only considered over when Natasha had come three or four times.

Poor Zoe had to crouch or kneel or lie in a suitable position for hours and hours, and she found it not only uncomfortable and awkward, but immensely boring too.

The only variety was sometimes being pulled up to pay attention to Natasha's breasts instead, and Zoe had to restrain herself from the impulse of biting down hard on those horrible thick nipples, the feel of which she absolutely hated in her mouth.

She wished she could be spending her time pleasuring her beloved Master, instead of this greedy, lazy woman, who often ate and drank and watched TV, and had phone conversations, while Zoe was at work.

However, since she had nothing to think about except bringing her Mistress off - and as soon as possible, in the hope that the session would end quickly - she was forced to acquire that skill she least wanted; the ability to perform cunnilingus expertly. She went on response, learning by trial and error what Natasha liked, and of course incorporating the movements she herself liked, because naturally she'd been plated enough times herself to understand what did the trick.

Only now did she appreciate what the act looked and felt like from the man's point of view, and in a way it was interesting to be able to do to someone else what you had previously had done to you - and get a result! (Unless of course Natasha was faking it, which seemed unlikely with the amount of oohing and aahing she was doing, and the quantity of smelly, sticky wetness that seeped out of her vagina onto Zoe's face.)

Days went by, and all they held for Zoe was pussy, pussy, tits, pussy, and more pussy. Long periods of crotch licking and breast worship, punctuated by the teasing and tormenting of the live-in witches, who never ceased to hate her, and seemed to enjoy nothing more than, immediately after a two hour session with Natasha, making her lick their pussies and nipples too!

This she couldn't stand, and strongly objected to, but unfortunately there were three of them, which meant two could always hold her down and force her into position. ("What's wrong? Prostitute's pussy not to your liking? And we heard you did everything you were told - or is it only everything you're told by men, you traitorous doormat!") Besides which, Mistress Natasha often sat and looked on during these episodes, occasionally encouraging the girls to give Zoe a slap or a pinch when she flagged.

A few times, Natasha had a party, to which a whole houseful of assorted lesbians was invited, all of whom were encouraged to play with and inspect Zoe as if she was some strange fairground exhibit.

At these parties, she was actually forced to lick as many snatches as possible, and to count them out loud as she went along, so she would spend the whole evening pushing her tongue up one hole after the other, til her resentfully uttered score reached over 30!

Only in the middle of the night, sometimes, when at last she was left alone to sleep, could Zoe relax, away from the presence of other women - and bring herself to much needed orgasm. Although, even here her pleasure was sometimes disrupted by unwelcome images creeping into her fantasies. She tried her best to concentrate on her favourite and familiar groups-of-men scenarios, only to find her mind straying to fat, flabby Natasha, with her endlessly hungry pussy, lying there all pink and quivering while a poor slavegirl toiled unhappily between her legs...

At least in the fantasy Natasha got the crude, harsh fucking she would no doubt have abhorred. Yes, cock after cock after cock spunked up her hateful pussy, as Zoe got her revenge!

At last, though, it was over.

One morning she heard the phone ring, and ten minutes later she'd been thrown out of the door, dressed in the same tatty clothes the three witches had first ripped off her.

Master Philip had sent a driver, who looked at her with mingled desire and disgust, but nevertheless she was immensely pleased to see him, and drank in his dependable masculinity as he drove her through the suburbs, and back home.

She contemplated asking him to oblige her with a quickie, but thought better of it. Master Philip might not be pleased.

At last they arrived at the house, and Zoe rushed in, close to tears, and wanting only to see and touch her Master once again. But far from the emotional reunion she had expected, she found herself confronted with yet another unexpected difficulty, and one which shocked her more than anything else had to date.

From upstairs came the familiar sound of a strap falling on flesh, and coupled with it the yelping and moaning of a woman!

She froze, assuming that her Master had let the house out to some of his friends - but then why send for her now? No, there was his voice, strict and familiar, barking instructions at the object of his punishment!

She rushed up the stairs, and pulled up short at the doorway to the 'dungeon', for there was Master Philip, spectacular in black rubber, tawse in hand - and there, on the frame on which she normally lay, was another woman.

Zoe couldn't tear her eyes away from the scene. The woman was smaller and slimmer than Zoe. Her bottom, which was uppermost, was far less fleshy, and bore on it several red blotches where the leather strap had recently struck her.

Her back was narrow, and, as she was twisting a bit from side to side, you could see that her breasts were small. Her arms, tied up above her head, were so thin they seemed too fragile to be suffering such treatment, and her hair was short and blonde, so she looked boyish, and quite young. Her pussy was clearly visible, with the way her legs had been spread out - a dainty slit, with a tiny thatch of blonde hair above it.

Oh, no! thought Zoe. Not pussy at home as well!

"Master – " she began, and stepped forward, but Master Philip turned on her and raised his voice.

"Zoe, stand where you are and keep quiet! I don't want to hear any more complaints from you! This is Petal, my new slave. I want you to watch how obediently she takes a whipping - with much less whimpering and fussing than I get from you."

His new slave! Zoe felt a rush of jealousy and despair, but then her emotions subsided. After all, she could be back with the hateful Natasha - of the two options, she'd rather be here, even if it meant watching her Master whip another woman, something she'd never witnessed before, although she had always known that he must of course have done it quite frequently, for it was his greatest passion. Still -

"Master?" said the woman on the frame, and it occurred to Zoe that she might well be feeling equally confused and jealous at the arrival of another woman.

"This is the slut I told you about – her name is Zoe. Seems to think she's the only slave in the world, so I'm teaching her a lesson. And I don't want you two fighting - I shall manage to whip both of you frequently enough for your satisfaction."

The blonde girl turned her head and looked up at Zoe, her face tear-stained, but incredibly pretty. Petal, thought Zoe. What a ridiculous, pretentious name! Trying to make herself seem frail and precious.

But when Petal looked into Zoe's eyes and held her gaze, something unexpected happened. The resentment and jealousy Zoe was pouring out towards her wasn't returned. What she saw was a deep openness and understanding and acceptance, and in a flash, a different attitude occurred to her.

Maybe, of all the women in the world, here was one with whom she had something in common. Maybe they could be friends.

But then she remembered the three witches at Natasha's and decided to reserve judgment. And anyway, hopefully Petal was only here for today, to teach her a lesson, as her Master had said. She'd probably never see her again.

Her tormentor was playing round with various implements and had selected a heavy duty cane. Surely he couldn't mean to lay that wicked thing across those tiny buttocks?

Unfortunately, he'd caught Zoe's expression.

"Interesting," he said. "You're being protective. But you must understand that the question of limits in this case is between Petal and myself. I know what she can take; I used a heavier one than this on her last week."

Last week. Oh.

"And by the way, take your clothes off and stand in that corner. I don't want you distracting me."

Zoe obeyed and then stood paralysed as the caning began in front of her. She had seen it often enough before - at clubs and parties - but this was different, it was so intimate, and so close!

Master Philip was such an expert - he did it with such style, she couldn't help admiring him. And Petal - she seemed to absorb the heaviest strokes with hardly a flinch, though she occasionally cried out, and seemed to be groaning constantly.

After five heavy strokes, administered in silence, Master Philip addressed Petal.

"Are you happy I gave you those, Petal?"

"Yes, sir."

"Do you enjoy the pain?"

"Yes, sir."

"Do you want five more?"

No hesitation. "Yes, sir!"

"You see, Zoe, there's a subtle distinction being demonstrated here. You are more of a slave - subservience and obedience are your thing. But this young lady is a real masochist - it's the pain that really turns her on and drives her wild. Watch closely, and I'll show you."

What followed was amazing to watch. He'd done something similar to her enough times, but the response he got in this case was more immediate and phenomenal.

In between laying the cane heavily across Petal's bottom, he used a smooth, round end of it to rub her quite roughly on her slit, and her whole body seemed to quiver and jerk when he did this, and she threw her head back and gasped.

A hard slash, and then some attention with the same implement, so that the lingering pain from the blow mingled immediately with arousal and pleasure. Oh, how Petal came alive! Oh, how she bucked and squirmed and thrust her bottom upwards and wiggled her hips from side to side to get maximum stimulation from the smooth round rod.

"Yes, yes!" she was saying. "Oh, more, Master! Harder!"

And Philip obliged, so that about twenty strokes in total had fallen when at last Petal screamed as her body was racked by pain-induced orgasm.

Wow, thought Zoe, standing in silence, listening to Petal's heavy breathing subside to normal. Some scene!

"Now, Zoe, I want the truth," said Master Philip. "Did watching that turn you on?"

No use denying it to him or to herself. "Yes, Master," she said. "I'm afraid it did."

He nodded to himself in approval.

Though retrospectively predictable, what happened next surprised Zoe yet again. Master Philip, led by the straining arrow of his cock, made straight for Petal's glistening pussy, and thrust accurately into it with practised ease.

Zoe watched, aghast but spellbound, as he began to fuck with huge, slow strokes, his cock coming right out each time - covered in Petal's juices. He looked magnificent, but Zoe was crushed with passionate envy.

Petal lay still and spent, but obviously unobjecting, as Master Philip completed his mastery of her. He came with a silent judder, and turned to give Zoe a cold look.

"See to her," he said. "I'll see you both in the morning."

He left the room and Zoe heard him walk along the corridor and go into the bathroom at the other end of the house.

She was alone with her tied-up rival!

After a long period of hesitation, she wandered over for a closer inspection of Petal's recently caned bottom. It was hard not to see it as an object - something out of one of her own male-dom fantasies - but the sight of Master Philip's spunk trickling down a silken thigh was enough to remind her of the reality of the situation.

So what was she supposed to do? Comfort the wretched girl, or cane her some more?

The latter option suddenly became very tempting. Here was her opportunity to take out all her confusions and resentments on a submissive female bottom! She had to admit the thought of actually doing it herself aroused her, and she picked up the cane that Master Philip had so recently and expertly used and played around with it a little, swishing it through the air.

This brought Petal out of her reverie and looking over her shoulder at Zoe with trepidation.

"Please don't cane me any more, Mistress!" she whispered.

Zoe threw the cane on the floor in anger. "I'm not a Mistress! I'm his slave! And whatever you are is just temporary!"

"I know. He told me."

This cheered Zoe up. As long as there was no question of Petal sticking around, she could probably handle it.

"I'd better untie you. I've had enough of the sight of your arse!"

She undid the restraints hurriedly and Petal stood up, rubbing her damaged bottom.

"Have you got anything to wear?" Zoe demanded, affronted by the sight of Petal's skinny body.

"I'm sorry, I think he's locked my clothes away."

Zoe rummaged around but since this was the 'sex room', all she could find was a rubber sheet. She threw it at Petal.

"Cover yourself up."

Tucking it round herself like a towel, Petal sat down gingerly on a chair - and immediately began to cry. "I'm sorry," she said between sobs. "It's just a reaction - I'll be alright in a minute."

Zoe sat down also, a bit stumped, yet feeling she could understand how the various emotions of SM could easily reduce you to bitter-sweet tears.

"A reaction to what?" she asked.

Petal sighed. "To the caning, to the way he can make me come with it, to the shock of you walking in, to all the things that have happened to bring me to this point in my life."

Zoe stared at her, noticing again how pretty and vulnerable she looked. "So where did he find you? Are you borrowed from someone?"

Petal noticeably coloured. "Er, no. I was advertising actually."

"What do you mean?"

"I'm - I'm a professional submissive."

"You mean he's paying you?!"

"Yes. I was doing so much of it anyway, you see, that I thought I might as well start charging. Thing is, I'm so much in demand, I never have time to spend the money."

Zoe was an emotional mixture of angry that her Master should be paying someone else, jealous of the money Petal must be making, and intrigued and sympathetic towards this slight, tender, weeping girl who had chosen such a difficult life for herself.

"But," she asked. "Surely you enjoy it?"

"Well, you know how it is," Petal replied. "I come a lot, but pain is pain. And," she blushed again. "I'm lonely. I don't have any friends. The only people I relate to are the men. It's always been like that."

Zoe leaned towards the other girl, unable to extinguish her interest. "So how did it come about? I mean, you don't have to tell me – "

"No, I'd like to. I've actually never talked to anyone about it before. Only look - it's a bit cold in here. Shall we just go next door?"

The room next door was one of several spare rooms in the house and had a nice soft double bed and a radiator, which the 'playroom' didn't - it would've spoiled the Gothic effect.

Petal lay face down on the bed - mindful of her throbbing bottom - and still wrapped in rubber, while Zoe climbed under the covers on the other side.

And so Petal, finding herself at last with an opportunity to tell her story to a human being who had some understanding of the lifestyle she was involved in, poured her heart out to Zoe.

Petal came from an affluent family and had a happy early childhood, having been brought up on a farm in a remote part of Gloucestershire with three older sisters. There had been traumas, however. Her parents had died when she was twelve, and while her sisters were already old enough to go away to college and forge a life of their own, she had spent several miserable years in homes, before an old aunt materialised who offered to take her in.

The aunt was strict and intolerant, and Petal, a scrawny teenager with a tomboy look, had seriously rebelled. She neglected her school work, skiving frequently, and spent much of her time hanging out with a gang of young delinquents, mainly along the promenades of the small coastal town she now found herself imprisoned - as she saw it - in.

The gang consisted of a varying number of boys - usually at least eight - and three spunky girls who competed with each other for who could be more outrageous. They swore and spat and drank and wore short skirts and flirted blatantly. Petal was the worst, and in an unspoken way actually became the gang leader, suggesting misdemeanours and insisting on being the most daring.

For a brief period, she called herself 'The Vixen'. She lost her virginity on a cold beach, with the tallest and most aggressive of the gang members, and on subsequent nights worked her way through most of the rest of them. Her reputation was established, and the two other girls dropped out of the group, not prepared to compete at this level.

One night Petal was caught by the Police - on a park bench with three of the boys - and locked up in a cell overnight. The aunt disowned her, and she was placed with foster parents in another town, but she ran away repeatedly to be back with her seaside mates.

Some nights she slept outdoors, and for days she lived on nothing but crisps and fizzy drinks. Then one day several members of the gang were arrested - wrongly, as it happened - and The Vixen decided she'd had enough, and went to ground. She got on a train to London and was lucky - or unlucky, depending how you looked at it - in that she was picked up almost immediately after arriving by a lonely middle aged man who offered her a bed for the night, and later a permanent home, whereupon he promptly began treating her as a sex slave.

Petal didn't see this as a bad thing - she could handle it. He wasn't offensive, and was kind to her in a way. It was just that in return for free accommodation and food, she was expected to be available for fucking and spanking. She enjoyed the fucking, and found she could take the spanking easily - she had a naturally high pain threshold.

All in all, it was a reasonable arrangement, and the comfortable, centrally located flat she found herself living in was an excellent base from which to explore all that the city had to offer. She sat in cafés a lot, and crawled around markets, and tried to decide what to do with her future, but somehow, things took their own course, for she couldn't seem to escape the world of sex.

She got propositioned regularly, just because she was a pretty young woman wandering purposelessly round city streets, and began to say yes - more out of curiosity and boredom than anything.

The first time she was offered money, she was genuinely surprised - she'd been prepared to do it for free. But once that easy money had crossed her palm, there was no going back. She opened a bank account and waited several months while she watched the balance grow. Then she parted company - relatively amicably - with her amorous rescuer, and got the 'little place of her own' she'd begun to hope and plan for. Here she carried on working and soon found herself drawn into a niche market. The sex grapevine was pretty effective, and spanking and corporal punishment enthusiasts passed Petal's number on to their acquaintances at a rate guaranteed to keep her busy and solvent. A year later she was still at it most days of the week - doing okay except for a bottom that was always sore, and an emptiness in her heart which she had only recently acknowledged.

Zoe found that she had put her arms round Petal - the smell of the girl's hair was in her nose, and her body was warm against her own.

It was a new experience - she'd never held a woman close like this before. She felt at once protective and sensual, but most of all the situation was calling out to her own unacknowledged loneliness and need of friendship.

"You poor, poor thing," she said. "You poor, poor girl."

Petal looked up at Zoe. "Why don't we be nice to each other? We might only have one night, and never see each other again. Let's not be enemies."

"We're not!" said Zoe. "I'm sorry if I overreacted. I just hadn't seen - him - for a while and I got jealous."

"You shouldn't be, Zoe! At least you've got one man who loves you as well as whips you. I haven't!"

Petal seemed to snuggle closer to Zoe, and the world went away.

"Zoe," she said, tentatively using the name. "Can I - please you? I mean – " she hurried on " - just genuinely because I'd like to. I think - I think you're so beautiful!"

With all the intimate handling and endless appreciation Zoe received from men, it was nevertheless a long time since anyone had called her beautiful. Cocksucking, spunked-on slaves didn't tend to be subjected to the same terminology as more conventional attractive women.

"Really, Petal! You're the beautiful one. You could be a model!"

Petal smiled. "So – will you let me?"

Oh, why not, thought Zoe. Does it matter either way?

"Okay," she said. "If you want to."

Petal jumped up and pulled the covers from Zoe, the rubber sheet falling off her in the process to reveal her slim, youthful body.

"Oh, my bottom!" she said light-heartedly, rubbing it again. "What a beast that Master of yours is! Though to tell you the truth, I wouldn't have minded if you'd given me a few extra strokes!"

"Be careful what you wish for!" Zoe retorted with mock severity. "I'll put you over my knee in a minute!"

"I'll lick you first."

And then all of a sudden it was happening - Petal went straight for the bulls eye, with as much enthusiasm and energy as Zoe had ever encountered in a man. And wow, did she know what she was doing!

From the start it was perfect. Zoe looked down at Petal with a fair degree of shock and wonder. It helped that she had short hair, like a boy. The feel of long female hair brushing on her body at Natasha's had made her cringe. But Petal was small and neat, and in a way not feminine. Except of course in every cell and every chromosome and every molecule!

"Oh, Zoe!" she said, breaking off intermittently. "You're like my queen, my duchess! You're a lady and I'm a lady's maid. I'd love to be your slave - we'd be so good together!"

Zoe was quite taken with this vision, and noticed that Petal was fingering herself.

"It's so different to please a woman for a change, not some horrible, grubby, smelly man! Oh, God, Zoe! I could fall in love with you!"

What? thought Zoe. I couldn't have heard that! But then she was distracted because Petal swung round and began to lick her from above instead of from below. Zoe now had an amazing view of Petal's cane-striped bottom just a foot or so from her face, and also in this private vista was Petal's snatch, with her fingers working away busily at her clit.

Down below, Petal was tonguing Zoe's pussy with deep strokes, and suddenly Zoe felt the moment of no return approaching - far sooner than she might have expected.

Oh, no! she thought. I'm being brought off by a woman, for the first time! But then she was over the brink and grabbing automatically at Petal's bum - kneading it and squeezing it, her eyes and head full of submissive female imagery, and not caring one jot whether she was hurting that tender bottom or not.

Amazingly, Petal kept going, and just as Zoe was about to tell her to stop, that there was no point, her arousal blossomed again, and she felt that her pussy had not yet had enough pleasure. Her mind totally clear, she lay there, accepting what was happening, prepared to accept more attention if someone was prepared to give it.

The second orgasm was weaker but longer, and the feel of Petal's tongue was so perfect, she felt she never wanted it to stop.

Petal kissed Zoe's thighs and worked her way gently up until she was nuzzling at her breasts. She really seemed to be enjoying herself.

Zoe stroked her head. "Thank you," she said, looking into Petal's smiling eyes. Then the impulse hit. "Come on, let me do the same for you."

"You don't have to," said Petal. "I understand if you don't like it."

"Well, I've been doing it endlessly over the last few days – I may as well do it again for someone I like!"

"So you like me, then?" said Petal.

"Yes," said Zoe firmly, and pushed Petal over onto her back.

How strange, to make love to a woman the way a man must make love to a woman. Looking down at her, down into her eyes. Squeezing and kissing her breasts from above, slipping a hand round her waist and pulling her hips up towards you.

Zoe devoured Petal. She guzzled her. She feasted on her. Something was happening - some vestigial male hormone was driving her to behave like a man, and enjoy having the woman beneath her.

Maybe it was true that everyone was bisexual, to a greater or lesser extent. All she knew was that, despite a lifetime's resistance to the idea, at this moment she couldn't escape the fact that she was having a wonderful time. More than that - she was being engulfed by new emotions, overwhelmed by desire and passion! When she made Petal come, her own earth moved, and Petal's screams of pleasure were utter music to her ears.

After a lot more playful exploration and lots and lots and lots of kissing - another new and thrilling pleasure for Zoe - the two young women lay entwined on the bed and stared into each other's eyes.

"Oh, God!"

"Yes!"

"Wow!"

"Exactly."

"I want to be with you."

"Good. So do I."

"We can share being slaves together."

"Yes. It'll be great."

"He'll probably want us to compete against each other."

"See who can be more obedient."

"Yes. And who can take more pain."

"We'll survive."

"I expect so."

"We can console each other."

"Kiss things better."

"Lick things better!"

They giggled.

"I think I – "

"What? Say it."

"Well. I think – "

"Me too."

"Really?"

"Yeah. All of a sudden."

They kissed again.

"This one moment has changed my life. Nothing can ever take that away."

They reflected.

"I hope he lets you stay now," said Zoe.

"I'm sure he will," said Petal. "He's trying to make you jealous, remember."

Outside the door, Master Philip stood listening quietly, a half smile on his face.

When Zoe woke, Petal was gone.

For a moment, she really, really thought she'd dreamed what had happened - it seemed so unlikely in a way - but no, it had all been real. She could still smell Petal's sweet smell on the sheets.

Master Philip, she realised with a jolt, was sitting at the foot of the bed looking at her.

"Where's - the girl?" she asked.

"Well, I know how you object to other women, so I thought I'd get rid of her. What's wrong? I thought you'd be pleased. Or don't tell me we've broken through a few barriers after all?"

Zoe sat dazed, staring at him numbly. She was thinking of the things Petal had said, and considering the possibility - with a huge sense of coldness - that the whole thing had been a test. After all, the girl had been getting paid, she'd said so herself. Maybe her brief had been to get silly old Zoe to fall in love with her, and admit it.

"Ended up liking her, did you?" Master Philip threw into her turmoil. "Now careful, or I'll be the one that's jealous!"

Zoe tried to formulate a coherent question that would tell her what she wanted to know.

"Did she – ? Was it – ?"

"No, actually I didn't set you up, if that's what you're asking. Your little friend was as distressed at being packed off home as you seem to be. Oh, no!" Master Philip was reacting to the relieved expression on Zoe's face, though he still didn't seem genuinely sympathetic. "Don't tell me I've nipped a love affair in the bud! Oh, well, I suppose if you're really good, I might let you see her again, but right now I want you to meet someone else, so put your thick rubber catsuit on, there's a good girl, and come downstairs."

Zoe allowed herself only a few moments of emotional recovery time before crawling out of bed. She would dwell on her recent discoveries and losses later. Now she had to see who this newcomer was.

Please let it be a man, she thought, as she struggled into tight rubber. I couldn't cope with another woman now, not after Petal.

But of course, it was a woman. A tall, elegant, graceful, haughty, beautifully dressed one, standing poised by the fireplace like something out of a stage play. Long painted fingernails and an old-fashioned piled-up hairstyle made her look a bit like Cruella de Ville, and this impression was compounded by the way she looked down her relatively large nose at Zoe.

"Aaaah!" her voice cascaded mockingly. "The slave! How interesting."

Zoe looked her up and down as offensively as she could manage. This was the sort of woman she hated most - polished, self-assured, superior. So different to poor, dear Petal...

"Now Zoe," Master Philip, who unfortunately had caught Zoe's look, said warningly. "This is Vivienne, who I've been spending a lot of time with lately. We have work colleagues in common, but have discovered that we share certain other tastes, which I'm sure you can guess at. We've become rather close, and I expect you to show her the respect she deserves, as one of my most special friends."

Zoe was still dwelling on the reference to work colleagues with the resentful realisation that there remained huge areas of her Master's life she knew nothing about.

Now, so soon after being confronted with competition in the form of a second slave, it seemed she was to be subjected to a live-in Mistress, for standing ominously on the floor next to Vivienne was a very large suitcase.

"Ooh, she's still so fiery," Vivienne said, walking round Zoe for a better look. "I though you said she was trained?"

"She has a sticking point when it comes to ladies. Though you wouldn't know it from the way she was carrying on with that Petal girl."

"Really? I've had that one - a good tongue, but a bit weepy."

Zoe bridled.

"Never mind," Vivienne ran a fingernail across the tight rubber stretched over Zoe's buttocks. "I'll tame her for you if you'll let me use a crop on her."

"Of course," Master Philip walked up to Vivienne and put an arm around her. "What's mine is yours, I've told you."

Please let this be a dream, thought Zoe as she watched them kiss. At least I had Master Philip to myself - at least the bottom line had been just me and him.

"Why don't you go up to the bedroom and wait for me," Philip said to Vivienne. "Zoe will bring your case up in a minute. We'll play some games with her - I've got a new whip you can try - and then celebrate your arrival in bed while Zoe cooks us a late breakfast. I'm sure we'll all get on famously."

He patted Vivienne on the bottom familiarly. "Just let me have a couple of minutes alone with Zoe, first. To make sure she's in the right mood."

Vivienne gave Zoe a final lecherous and condescending look. "I can't wait to get my hands on her. Don't be too long."

She left the room, and for a long moment Zoe stood like a statue, staring at the floor, while Master Philip in turn looked levelly at her. Then he went over and took her in his arms, and kissed her in the most wonderful possible way he had ever kissed her.

"Zoe," he said quietly, stroking her hair fondly, the way he had so often before. "I told you once before, a long time ago, what you meant to me, and what I would expect of you. Now listen to me carefully while I tell you again - you are the only woman in my life, the only one I have ever had such an intense, spectacular bond with." He kissed away her confused tears. "Now the testing has at last come to an end with a choice. Your choice, which you are entirely free to make for yourself. These are your options. You can go and change and get your things, and call a cab and book into a hotel - and never return to this house, or to me, again." He held her head in his hands. "Or, you can marry me. I'll send Vivienne away, and we'll fly out somewhere exotic, and come back as husband and wife."

Zoe's jaw dropped at the unexpectedness of this proposal. She could hardly believe it. It felt like the most significant and beautiful moment of her life. Now she could never doubt how much she meant to her dear, dear Philip!

But Master Philip hadn't finished yet.

"Or," he said, pulling her even closer to him. "I shall marry Vivienne, and you will be our slave. Thereby ensuring for me a lifetime of pleasure and every man's dream - an assertive, impressive, token wife to show off to people at social functions, and a beautiful, obedient sex slave waiting tied up in the bedroom at home. But my love, I will go along with whatever you choose."

Pictures swam into Zoe's mind of the years ahead, and the horrors of being a slave to Vivienne - to Master Philip's wife!

Who knew what humiliations and trials would be in store for her if she chose that option? She would probably have to serve them breakfast in bed every day, and - and wash Vivienne's underwear by hand, and get chained to the bed while they made love, and probably even lick the bitch out afterwards!

She looked up at her Master. "This is the final test, isn't it?"

He stepped away from her. "Well, that depends on what you choose. Now, see that case of hers? If you're staying as my slave, I want you to carry it up the stairs to the bedroom. If you come up without it, I'll understand what you've decided, and you'll have the pleasure of watching me send Vivienne packing." Master Philip laughed. "See what power I've given you? You choose my wife for me!"

He headed for the door. "Come up soon, either way."

Zoe sat down on a chair.

Then she paced.

Then she sat down again.

She thought hard for a long moment.

And then even harder for a moment more.

She looked at the suitcase.

She looked through the suitcase.

She decided.

Printed in the United Kingdom
by Lightning Source UK Ltd.
107126UKS00001B/259-336

9 781905 290338